TEMPTATION AND TRIDENTS

A DEATHLESS LOVE NOVEL

ZORA FOX

WELCOME TO THE EIGHT REALMS

A land of gods and goddesses—a savage, beautiful collection of islands in the Corae Sea. The stories here are violent, with explicit sexual content not intended for anyone under 18. These books about deathless love feature dark, often twisted romances. Enter at your own risk.

ZENIA

Ruled by Thenios, God-King of lightning

APHRISO

Ruled by Cytherea, goddess of pleasure

ERISET

Contested land, ruled by Ares and Bellona, god and goddess of war

MENOS

Ruled by Scira, goddess of wisdom

NALIA

Ruled by Basileus, god of the ocean

HYPERION

Ruled by Lox, god of the sun

KANTHAROS

Ruled by Vesta, goddess of hearth and home

FAR REALM

Ruled by Hades, god of the dead

Content warnings for this story of deathless love: explicit sex, bondage, orgies, reference to primal play, murder, references to off-page sexual assault, abusive parents, BDSM-style scenes, blood, strong violence, strong language

I

MARI

Sweat dripped into my eyes. *Not now.* I was about to beat my record. And I needed to break my record today.

Gritting my teeth, I hauled myself higher on the mast. From up here, the wind shook more violently, dark sails pressed against my body, and I had fewer handholds, not like the easy rigging lower down. It felt like climbing the trees that bordered the swamplands of my childhood. Except, this time, I hovered above cold waves in tight, leather-fronted pants, a leather vest mended in nine colors of thread, and a blue sash tied around my waist where I could stow knives, tools, and provisions. One of the knife hilts dug into my side where it met the hard length of the pole.

"You're slowing down, sweetheart," Zete called from the deck below.

I didn't look down at him, but the gray flutter of wings told me he was seconds away from flying up here. I wanted to yell back, but that would only waste air. *I'm not done yet.*

But it wasn't lack of air that was slowing me down. It

wasn't even the sweat in my eyes from the relentless sunshine. It was this extra weight I felt like I was carrying ever since last week when Calix scoffed in my face.

"You know what?" he'd said. "You're a cold bitch, Mari. I'm done."

I didn't beg for him to stay, not after he'd said that. I debated prying off his fingernails for speaking that way to me, but his accusation hollowed me out. All I could do was leave. Looking back, I hated myself for not saying more, doing more. It was the doubt, the stupid doubt that was I worth defending at all. Maybe he was right. He never said it, but I knew I made him feel shitty about himself because I never orgasmed in bed. It wasn't that I didn't enjoy it, I just...

I huffed, reaching the top of the mast and eyeing the next obstacle. Of all the parts of the course I'd laid out for myself, this was the most dangerous. A carefully calculated jump from the highest horizonal yard to the next mast down. There was no way to make the leap straight across. I'd have to angle to reach the ratlines and then scurry back up. If I missed the lines and fell, I'd crash to the hard deck below.

Being a demi-goddess wouldn't stop me from breaking bones. Hell, I could splatter on the deck. Unlike a full goddess, I couldn't crawl back to myself piece by piece. The Divine had given me a minor power. I could only adjust my appearance—a bend in my nose, freckles there, new eye color and shape—but I couldn't cover up an arm bending at the wrong angle. It wasn't a pretty idea.

Plus, Captain Terion would be furious.

From the corner of my eye, I could see my shipmates pausing to watch me. Zete looked small despite his beard and wings next to massive Ajax. They both gave me hell sometimes, but I knew Ajax at least wouldn't enjoy watching me get hurt.

I had to stop thinking about Calix. His stupid words threw me off. The sea felt choppy enough up here without more distractions.

"Going to fall this time?" Zete cried from below.

"I've got this!" I snapped back, balancing myself on the tiny waving platform amid the sails, preparing to spring. One jump and then—

I wobbled and the world turned. My arms flailed out, the mast tilted away from me, and the deck rose up too fast. My feet floated in air. Scrabbling madly, I finally touched something, grasped at rigging, and jarred to a stop. The rest of my body yanked on the arm I'd managed to tangle in the ropes. A cry ripped from my lips. The dead weight felt like five times the mass of my body, but then I bounced up, and the world stilled.

"Get down," Ajax ordered at the same time Zete laughed.

I pressed my face into the squares of rope, squeezing my eyes shut. Pain lanced through my arm and shoulder. I'd failed, and I really, really hadn't wanted to fail today.

As if Calix's words had knocked me down, they swirled again and again through my thoughts. *A cold bitch.*

I pictured Calix above me, pumping in. It felt like a slightly painful massage. Not bad. Pretty nice, actually. Yes, I wished I felt more, but for whatever reason I almost never felt that lustful attraction toward anyone, even the people I slept with. I tried—I really did—but something was always missing for me. Too many factors had to be in place for me to get really turned on, and no single person fit them all.

One reason why I'd never belong.

I swallowed hard and squeezed the ropes in shaking fists. Normally, I wasn't this shaken up by stupid comments. The crew ribbed me all the time. Why did Calix's words need to feel like a knife to the ribs? I had to get myself together. Maybe stab something.

I had a place here on the *Lusca*, a bed and meals, shipmates who mostly tolerated me, even if they made it clear I was at the bottom of the pecking order.

A few days ago, I got more proof of that when I'd woken up and all my clothes were wet. Humidity on the sea meant they'd take forever to dry. Redley, another sailor, spat when I accused him of doing it, which was as good as a confession.

Despite assholes like him, I wanted to stay. I could use my shapeshifting ability to earn treasure and fame. I hoped, anyway. Serving on Captain Terion's crew was more than I ever thought I'd accomplish when I lived in Nalia.

Sure, there was danger, especially because of what happened with King Basileus before my time, but life was always dangerous.

With a deep breath, I relaxed and slowly made my way down.

"Well, at least you're not jelly I need to scrape off the deck," said Zete. He rarely did that kind of work anyway.

Ajax offered his huge arm. Even though he was first mate, I didn't take it. "Think you need Klep?" he asked, apparently unbothered by my slight.

I shook my head, easing my weight to the planking. I'd had injuries like this a million times. No needed to call the medic. Still, my joints twinged as I released my hold on the rope. "No. I'm fine."

"Your shoulder looks off," Ajax grunted. "That was a hard fall."

Zete squinted at me, lines spidering through his brown skin. "I thought you were supposed to be good at that."

"I'll be fine. I'll do it faster next time." I webbed my power along my shoulder, but it remained a little wonky. At least the bruises wouldn't show now.

Ajax cocked his jaw.

"You're no good to the captain if you break everything," Zete pointed out.

"I'm well aware." My stare finally made him back off. I knew I was being snappy, but I couldn't help it. This week had been a shitshow.

"Mari, you're not even dressed! We dock in half an hour."

I whirled to see Terion swaggering across the planking toward me. He must have come from the lower decks. Instead of wearing his usual captain's jacket and fingerless gloves, he looked... noble. No scarf covering his short black hair, though he still wore his boots. He looked clean and impressive, worthy of all the looks he received in pirate-friendly ports. One glance at his impeccable, shimmering blue suit brought a memory slamming back.

Dio's party tonight. The two of us had been planning to go for a month.

How Terion managed to snag an invitation was beyond me. It wasn't normal to invite known pirates to parties where wealthy and powerful people let down their guard. Dio's parties were legendary centers for wine and gambling and sex —any pleasure money could buy.

Which was why we were going to rob him.

"How did you do that to your face?" I asked, pointing at my own cheek in the spot where Terion's scales were missing on his face. Instead, there was just smooth dark skin—no royal signature left over from his father. Normally, he had a swath of blue-green scales over one cheekbone. Did he find someone else with the ability to change appearances? The idea made me squirm. I'd never been able to change other people's features, only my own.

"You think they'd let me in if they knew who I was?" He laughed. "Come on in, Captain Asterion," he mimicked. "Want a tour of the vaults?"

"Please," I said. No one used his full name like that. He was just Terion or the captain, even to worshippers in his suna. "I said *how* not *why*."

"Ah." He held up a finger. "Forget that. You get ready. I dropped off the dress hours ago. What have you been doing?"

"Obstacles," Zete cut in.

"Again?" Terion's expression became stern.

"She was trying to beat her time."

"Almost did," I muttered, stopping myself from rubbing at my injured shoulder.

Terion grunted. "Never mind. I like that in a subordinate. Always getting better." His eyes twinkled roguishly at me. It was the look he always got before a mission. Even with so much on the line, he couldn't deny the call of adventure, just like me.

I burned to ask what he'd been doing that kept him away from the upper deck for so long, but I already had a few guesses. Adventure wasn't the only thing that made Terion smirk like that.

I scanned the horizon. No visible land yet—I would have noticed it from the top of the mast—but time was running out to get ready. Normally, this kind of assignment got my blood racing. I wasn't good at many things, but I was good at sneaking into places unnoticed and relieving people of their property. That was the reason Terion brought me on board to begin with.

"Put on the dress, Mari," he said. His gaze took in my short wind-swept hair and dirty bare feet. "Half an hour. I want you looking like a girl I'd have on my arm."

My face hardened. The things he said sometimes... "You wish you were so lucky."

"I want Dio thinking that."

Something twinged inside me. We'd discussed the possibility of me having to distract Dio, but I hoped to the ocean gods I wouldn't have to. Everybody rubbed me the wrong way today.

Women at the party would fall all over Terion. Honestly, I didn't blame them. It was easy to forget his effect on people when we were on the sea, just shipmates. Captain Terion was tall, confident, and muscular with buttery skin and dark, intense eyes. His tone could switch from flirtatious to commanding in a second. The allure of being the most famous Nalian pirate didn't hurt either. Royal, too. Pity I couldn't just leave him to it.

Right now, being one of the abandoned princes was hurting him, but most didn't know he was estranged from his father King Basileus. Well, estranged was a kind way of putting it. Endangered was much more accurate.

Hence, the party.

If I had to play the part of the sexy date for very long, the hypocrisy of it would scratch under my skin and distract me.

I might be the girl on Terion's arm at the party, but that

was just a ruse. No one wanted to be the man on *my* arm. At least not after they learned I was broken. It was almost like my throbbing shoulder was a sign. *Pull yourself together, Mari. Stop moping about that bastard.* I moved my arm gingerly back and forth.

"Ever think you'd go to one of Dio's parties?" Zete asked, bumping shoulders with me.

My shoulder shrieked at the contact, but I only shot Zete a glare. He gazed innocently back. I sighed. "We threw lots of those back home."

Terion chuckled. I grew up in the swamps. No one threw lavish parties there. The closest we got was drinking home-made spirits and hoping no one would burn the house down when they got too drunk. And I wasn't even invited to that. I snuck in sometimes, though.

"This will be the one," Terion said, a familiar glint in his eye. He thought we'd succeed in every mission, seemingly forgetting every failure.

Terion was a lot of things—a feared sailor, a cocky pain in the ass—but I wanted this to go right for him. For us.

"It will be," I agreed, with a grim smile.

If we pulled off this heist, I'd lift the shadow of Terion's debt and prove my place. I'd stop feeling inferior. Maybe I'd belong at last. The captain, at least, had a little faith in me.

He cocked a dark eyebrow. His suit gleamed in the sunlight. "That's a look I like."

"Good. It's a look that's going to get your father off your back."

His lips curved. "Even better. Suddenly I can't wait for this party."

2

TERION

I looked damn good. It was too bad I usually couldn't do my own reconnaissance. The scales I inherited from Basileus made me too recognizable. When I wore my customary captain's coat, head scarf, and fingerless leather gloves, most people could recognize me from a distance too. New colors, a new silhouette, a new name, and smooth skin should be enough to mask my identity. Until yesterday, I wore a short beard. This clean-shaven look, though, I planned to keep.

"Stop fidgeting. I have to touch this up." Rhode dabbed at my cheekbone with the makeup. Over her shoulder, I could see myself a full-length brass mirror. I usually liked darker tones—blood reds and deep greens were my favorites—but this bright blue suit was doing good things for me.

"Where'd you find this?" I asked, touching the fabric. "I like it."

She squinted at my skin before tapping the clay in the little pot again. "Nobody's business."

"I'm the captain. Everything on the *Lusca* is my business."

"Don't pull that with me." She smeared my face again.

It was true. I couldn't lord my position over her like I could with others. We'd known each other too long, and she had our father's telltale scales as well. But, unlike me, she didn't matter to him. We were just products of two one-night stands. The only reason Basileus knew I existed was the cursed debt I owed him.

Dozens of his offspring sprouted up around the Eight Realms. Lost princes. But I was Terion, Captain of the *Lusca*, feared pirate.

"You're smiling," she declared. "You're making lines in your skin."

I met her scowl and returned to a neutral expression. "People like my smile."

"People..." She jabbed hard at my face. "Think of what's at stake."

That sobered me up. Rhode didn't know how much danger my debt put us in. No one did. We'd faced fierce waves, huge sea creatures, and ships full of blade-bristling enemies, and they still didn't understand the extent of my father's vendetta. He'd see me and everyone I cared about at the bottom of the ocean. After six months of relative calm, I'd grown too complacent, chasing other fun. Gods were fickle, but they also held grudges. Lanan's unexpected death a few weeks ago was proof Basileus hadn't forgotten about making me suffer.

I straightened my spine, dismissing those thoughts before they could build into a hurricane behind my ribs.

With experts on my crew like Rhode and Ajax, we got a hell of a lot done. Add my beautiful *Lucsa* to that, and it should have been easy to get enough payment to get Basileus to finally leave us alone, but for some godsforsaken reason, everything had gone wrong.

I gripped Rhode's wrist and brought it down. "My face was fine an hour ago."

"But then you were in the sun and touching it," she said, glaring at me. "Couldn't help showing off."

I released her, peeking again at the mirror. "I won't touch it anymore."

"Nobody *else* can touch it either." She fixed me with a green-eyed look that reminded me of sirens. I'd only seen them once, and honestly, they were some of the only beings that scared me. Rhode shared similarities—aquatic abilities, beauty, ferocity—but she didn't have their taste for flesh. She preferred to lure sailors off boats.

"If we're in the dark, they won't see the scales."

She sighed and rolled her eyes. "Okay, it's not my business what you do, but we both know you're not doing that. You have a whole... thing."

It was true. I preferred my sexual encounters tightly controlled. Frequent and hot, but controlled. When I was younger, you could have found me in some random person's bed, but not anymore.

"Fine."

"Ooh!" Her eyes brightened with an idea, and she scurried away. She had a shuffling kind of step when she was on land or on the boat. One of the reasons I needed Mari for more secretive jobs. Emerging from around a door, she had a new pot of something that smelled herby.

I wrinkled my nose. "What's that?"

"It'll help the makeup set."

"You're telling me you didn't think of this before?" I asked.

"I don't put makeup on you every day," she huffed, putting one hand on her hips before smearing the glossy stuff over my cheekbone. My scales were only visible on the left side, not even rising to create a different texture on the skin. One look confirmed no trace of them left. As much as I hated the connection they created to my father, I liked the iridescent streak across my face. Now that spot just looked sweaty and shimmering. Rhode's face always glittered with something along her eyes and cheekbones. Sometimes the glitter even streaked her thick green locks. It looked better on her. At least I had the suit.

"Thank you, Rhode," I said, readjusting the jacket across my shoulders. The sleeves were a little tight, and only one button on the front of the jacket would close over my torso, so I left it open.

"Mari's waiting," she said, cleaning up the cluster of powder and potion jars. "Friendly winds."

"And gold on shore," I called, heading out to the main deck. The captain's quarters sat on an upper part of the deck, so I got a fine view of the ship as I stepped out. The *Lusca* lay dark and sleek before me, subtly scaled like some fearsome sea beast or like my own face but in black instead of green. Its sails were black. I'd made so many adjustments over the years that no craft was exactly like her. Some of the ropes and bolts couldn't be found anymore, so I took care to restore them every few months. The blessing and curse of being a demi-god. We were always cobbling together human-made things from different generations. The chaotic blend I'd created on the ship woke up my blood. It meant adventure and it meant home.

And hopefully, after this party, it meant a hell of a lot of money.

Dio's small island off the shore of Hyperion lay just ahead, a thin line on the horizon. Mari wasn't on the deck waiting, as Rhode had thought. I wasn't surprised. Mari had looked wild and sweaty after her acrobatics earlier. It was that bright, tightly wound version of Mari I liked, but something had been off with her.

I couldn't have *off* today. Things needed to go right. Before we entered the party for our heist, I needed to get to the bottom of her weird mood.

With Hyperion in the distance and a few minutes to spare, I hailed Ajax, my first mate.

"Aye. No need to whistle like a dog," he grumbled.

"You wouldn't hear me otherwise," I replied cheerily. I only whistled because he hated it so much.

As Ajax topped the steps, it struck me again how enormous he was. He had muscles I'd never seen on any other man, deathless or mortal. He was a woodsman by trade (probably made of tree trunks too) but chose sailing instead. He didn't talk about the reason. My theory was simple. Despite being raised in Hyperion himself, he had a Nalian soul. He was born for the sea.

"I need you to stop in Hyperion after you drop us off. Pick up the usual supplies. Drop off Shyama at the port. She thanks you for the ride."

"Couldn't last the entire voyage, Captain?" His irritation turned into an evil smirk.

"*She* couldn't," I corrected. "Not after what she let me do. But don't joke. She has family over there, same as you, so tell her to get ready after we're safely away."

Ajax gave a curt nod of acknowledgment.

Shyama was a nice girl—well, honestly, a bad, bad girl, the way I liked—but our interaction left me feeling suspiciously hollow. It should have been good. It *was* good. Her Hyperion skin, golden like Ajax's, still showed my marks. She'd agreed to all my terms. She'd stayed in the room I kept for such purposes without a peep of complaint. Her back was very flexible. It was good.

No reason to feel so empty. I didn't want relationships. Just controlled sessions in the room downstairs. Did the high of a fling really wear off this fast? The idea left me feeling gloomy, and I had no time to be gloomy. I was the feared Captain Asterion, damn it, and I had a job to do.

"Are you serious?" Mari's voice rose above the waves as she emerged from the door to the companionway leading down to the lower decks.

I blinked twice. I'd seen Mari dressed as a woman, a man, a sailor, soldier, mother, but never like this. She was a shapeshifter—*my* shapeshifter—but I honestly didn't know this was a shape she could take.

The golden dress poured over her body. Thin straps like laces crisscrossed her bare hips, cinching in at the waist. Panels of flowing fabric fell between her legs. At her chest, the neckline formed a deep V with faux golden chains looping across her collarbone. Something glittering pinned her dark cropped hair on one side of her head, and a gold cuff imprisoned her wrist.

"This is a lot," she said, approaching. She'd changed the shape and color of her eyes and nose, adjusted the color of her skin to something with different undertones. Too bad her ability wouldn't work on me too.

The way her hips moved as she walked had me clearing my throat before I could answer. "Perfect for this party."

"Why do you get layers while I get the world's thinnest dress?"

I waved away her irritation. Damn, the way her breasts ended in little points brought my mind back to the room I let no one see. The fabric was thin. I could see everything. *Everyone* could see everything. "I knew you could pull it off," I said casually, even though something like jealousy surged through my gut.

Jealousy? For what? I snuck a closer glance at her as if the secret were a dagger hidden on her person, but all I managed to look at was the bare skin of her hips and the hard tips of her breasts. Maybe I should have chosen something less revealing. She didn't need me ogling her all night. On the other hand, it was the perfect sleight of hand to have our marks staring at her body instead of the treasure we'd be commandeering.

"It'll be hard to run," she said. Her face said she'd definitely caught me looking. Was that a flush on her neck?

My disguise worked, then. I knew it looked good. Mari never blushed around the crew. She never even talked about exploits on shore. Suddenly, that had me wondering who'd gotten to touch that body...

"You won't be running," I said smoothly, jogging my mind out of these strange thoughts. *Mari. It's still Mari.* "You're better than that. And it wouldn't be hard to run. Just tie the dress up." I indicated the space between her legs. "I gave you flat shoes."

She scowled. "I'd like to see *you* try to run in this outfit."

"I'm sure you would."

She met my eyes, the challenge draining out of them,

replaced with the excitement I felt in my own chest. She loved missions like this, no matter how much she griped about them. Yes, I'd pushed her with this choice of outfit, but why not? Dio's parties were lavish enough that this gaudiness would make us blend in more than stand out. I liked my choice of target more and more.

I turned back to Ajax. "Get all hands ready to dock." I gave him an extra look to remind him not to forget Shyama in the lower room.

"Yes, Captain."

Seabirds squawked on the horizon. One glance at Mari told me she was ready to put our plan into action. Despite how godsdamned sexy she looked in that dress, we weren't there for a good time. If this worked, I might actually stop having to look over my shoulder every time a new vessel approached or the sea started churning unexpectedly. My crew, and the *Lusca*, would be safe.

Safer, anyway.

We were pirates, after all.

3

TERION

We watched the *Lusca* pull away, floating toward Hyperion. Its iridescent black exterior glittered in the purple and orange sunset. It was beautiful—my ship was always beautiful—but far too conspicuous. Sunsets were a terrible time to stalk or attack another ship. Soon, it would be all but invisible. A hidden shark in the water.

I turned to Mari. "Ready, love?"

"Ready, handsome."

We'd pulled a similar ruse one other time, pretending to be lovers. This time, though, her golden dress threw me off. *That body*, it said. *Isn't it the sexiest thing you've ever seen?*

Mari was member of my crew. She'd never given me the kind of attention other women did. Frankly, I'd never thought much about it. There was a week soon after I drafted her when I thought I was in love with her, but I was less stable then. I fell in love with everyone. That was before renewed attacks by my father proved an obvious truth—relationships were dangerous. Not worth the cost or distraction. And Mari was a relationship person, not a fling person.

Why was I thinking about having a fling with Mari?

My train of thought had the crotch of my suit bulging uncomfortably. This was ridiculous. Plenty of other women would volunteer for a sordid night or three to slake my thirst. The perfect arrangement, with no attachment. Mari was the opposite—my subordinate, on the ship with me every day, and she had never reacted to me like others had, so she was off-limits.

I was Terion. She was Mari. That was the end of it.

"I don't think anyone is totally ready for a Dio party," I said, smiling and extending my arm.

She placed her hand in the crook of my elbow, but the movement wasn't as smooth as it would normally be.

"Shoulder still hurt?"

She shot me a look.

I raised defiant brows. *Yes, I noticed.*

"I'm fine," she said.

I huffed, drawing myself up as we walked. This way, I could loom over her. Her head came up to my mouth. Her dark, shorn hair smelled like coconut. "I know you'll *be* fine, but there's something wrong with you today," I said in an undertone. "I can't have you going in there while your mind is somewhere else."

She sighed and quirked her lips, her gaze sliding away.

Now she had me concerned. "Did something happen on Zenia?" Nothing noteworthy had happened since the last Realm we plundered. At least not that I knew, and I usually had my finger on the pulse of all my crew.

She cleared her throat and tossed her head. "I was seeing someone there and he broke things off. I don't really care about him. It's just disappointing."

How did I not know Mari was seeing somebody? That queasy, envious feeling flopped through my chest again. I seriously should have chosen a different dress. I thought it would be fun for us to be a sexy couple at the party, but now it invited me to imagine what she had done with this mystery person. Had he touched those exposed hips? Had his run his hands over her? Had he spread her legs and pushed himself inside her slick pussy?

I blinked, forcing myself from getting dragged down further into that whirlpool. "What's his name?" The question came out gruff. Commands were my native language, but she was sharing something personal with me. I didn't want to be an ass. Mari didn't show her true self with many others—I knew her well enough to appreciate that. With me, she had a level of comfort that let her push back when I teased her.

"Calix." She pursed her mouth as if the name tasted sour.

"He's an idiot." I squeezed her arm against my side. "If he didn't realize how good he had it with a member of the famed *Lusca* crew... Anyway, it's better not to get involved, with things as they are."

There was something more she wasn't saying.

I would have pried further, but Dio's palace came into view past the sea wall. It was curved and sumptuous, inviting sin. All black and red with low lights spotting the outside. It reminded me of one of those glittering black rocks I liked when I was young. I'd skip them across the ocean waves, impatient for the day when I'd be skimming over the water instead.

This place wasn't as carefree as it seemed, though. As we approached, the slight but unmistakable pressure of magical wards settled over me like a feather-light blanket.

I bent toward her coconut-scented hair. "Where are you keeping...?"

She patted the area between her legs once. Must have been a small knife to fit without the outline showing.

The movement was cursory, just an answer to my question. I would not think about how close that knife was to—

I fished in the pocket of my blue jacket and tugged out our invitation. Pasting on my most charming grin, I approached the front entrance. A humongous nude female stood at one side of the door, checking everyone as they entered. She stood two heads taller than me, blonde, with gray-ish skin and a tempting figure. No weapons. Evidently, she didn't need them.

Interesting choice. The guard looked like a stone statue representing the pleasures within while also making it clear she could rip someone's head off if they didn't pass muster. *Smart. Very smart.*

"We're here!" I declared to Mari, passing the door guard our invitation and the hefty fee that went with it. "Ready to get into some trouble, Selene?" I nuzzled the side of her head playfully.

She giggled, which only made me smile wider. Damn, she was good.

The gray woman scrutinized the paper with its golden ink and red seal, addressed to Selene and Haloc, wealthy and secretive demi-gods with a small province in Menos. It had taken some doing to secure that.

Mari snuggled up against my side as if she couldn't wait for our night of debauchery a moment longer. Since I'd had to keep the blue jacket mostly open, I could feel her entire outline through my shirt. She made it easy to play the part.

I raised friendly, questioning eyebrows at the deathless

female. Was my face too famous, even without the scales? Did she doubt the letter's authenticity? I kept my grin stubbornly in place.

"Your first time?" the guard asked, tilting her head down and meeting my eyes with her unsmiling ones. Red light from above bathed us all in its sensual glow.

"We've wanted to come for years," Mari said, drawing a hand down my chest. My skin warmed.

"Then welcome," the guard finally said, opening the door behind her with one hand. It was large enough even for her to walk through comfortably. "There are marked rooms for particular play. Once you enter, you agree to participate, not just observe. If you prefer something more relaxed, stay in the main area. That's where you can greet our host and refill your plate and glass."

And if you want to find the vaults, you'll need to search all the rooms.

If everything went the way I expected, I could be out of trouble with Basileus before the next sunrise. The prospect only made seeing one of Dio's famous revels more exciting.

Inside, the dim light was smoky without filling the lungs— an illusion, maybe. Dio's parties attracted people from all over the Eight Realms, so there could be a sprite here to create that effect. Music, low and pulsing, emanated from the room straight ahead, through the long, narrow hallway at the entrance. Was this the only way out? I didn't like the idea of a bottleneck when Mari and I needed to get out of there.

She elbowed my side, looking pointedly to something on the wall. I followed her gaze. This hallway had no doors to these supposed marked rooms, but it did have large paintings of couples in every sexual position. The one Mari pointed out showed a long-haired woman lying sideways with her leg over a man's hip while he, on his knees between her legs, drove into her.

"That how you like it?" I teased.

She pursed her mouth into a line. "Look at the others."

It took me a second to understand she didn't mean the sex poses, but the position of the paintings themselves. The one she pointed out was a little lower than the rest, which were all perfectly straight.

I grunted to acknowledge I understood. One possible spot for the vault—check. But why would Dio put it so close to the door? He was known as a wild god, but nobody was that stupid, right?

A burst of laughter greeted us as we stepped forward into the main room. My smile was genuine as I looked up and up. Beside me, Mari did the same. The palace hadn't looked this big on the outside. I couldn't even see where the ceiling ended in this gloom. It was as if the aerialist hoops and ribbons were suspended from the night sky itself, and the performers were clouds and stars incarnate. They wore a variety of shimmering, barely there outfits that accentuated their fluid movements.

I brought my gaze back down to the huge round space, most of it black and sparkling as the outside of the building. It was like some kind of dream terrain, hills and valleys all strategically placed. If we took two steps to the left, we'd reach steps leading to a round, pillow-filled recess in the floor where guests already lounged, drinking wine and (in one case) straddling each other, seconds away from fucking. Moans and murmured talking filled the air, mingling with faint music. So far, only fifty or sixty people filled the room, not counting the aerialists and servants. Judging from the empty spaces on plush benches and walkways still waiting to be filled, the party would get much busier.

And we couldn't forget the people hidden away in those enticing rooms. There could be three times the number we saw kissing and drinking in the main area.

On the far side of the room was the biggest raised platform. The cushy, wine-colored throne on top obviously belonged to Dio. Deathless men and women dressed in scraps of fur or leaves draped themselves over the steps leading to where the host sat sideways, eating grapes out of someone's hand.

I blew out a breath. Well, I wasn't disappointed. Dio's parties really were the best.

When I glanced back at Mari, who held my hand loosely, she was already scanning the circumference of the room. Even all this sexiness and all the servants pouring out wine couldn't distract her from our mission. I shivered with delight that I'd found her before somebody else who could use her skills of spying and sabotage against me.

We strode in further. There were five recesses in the wall besides the one leading through the hallway to the entrance. That had to be where these supposed marked rooms were. Marked with what? I couldn't help the excitement of getting new ideas for activities in my private room aboard the ship.

Passing the worshipful figures on the steps, we approached Dio, who turned his head languorously in our direction. The grape-feeder pivoted away so we could say our piece.

Dio had golden skin and brown curls, the kind of soft musculature the young and privileged always seemed to have, and reckless eyes. That was the best way to put it. They were sleepy but unpredictable at the same time. I wouldn't have been surprised if he'd stood up and kissed me on the mouth. It took a lot to unnerve me, but it felt like Dio was trying.

He reached for Mari's hip right as I said, "Lord Dio, thank you for inviting us."

Mari didn't move away as he caressed the skin accessible through cuts in the gold fabric. Instead, she wiggled a little, like she enjoyed it.

My good nature melted like a candle. Scooping her against my side again, I added, "We've always wanted to come to one of these parties."

"And just think, next month a shipment of very willing people will be here to make it extra special." He looked on the verge of boredom. Meeting someone's eyes on the steps, he broke into laughter and added, "Well, they'd better be willing, with what it cost to find them!"

My skin crawled. If I could get the knife from between Mari's legs and just—

Dio's hand seemed to crawl toward that very spot. I'd be damned before I let this fucking prick finger my date, real or otherwise.

I rotated her nearly out of his grip.

Thankfully—because the temptation to behead this bastard had grown to dangerous levels—Dio let his hand slip from Mari's skin. "Eat, drink!" he declared, gaze darkening as he looked dead into my eyes.

Mari gave flirtatious smirk and a little bow of her head before we turned to head back down the stairs.

Dio reached out again and pulled at the strings over Mari's hips, even though she was obviously with me. With Haloc, technically. Dio locked eyes with me again as he released the golden tie, snapping it against her skin.

Go fuck yourself, Dio, I thought. I'd fileted people who'd done less. Without even counting his sickening comments about bringing more bodies forcibly to serve at these parties, all my partners agreed before I'd go fondling them like that. It didn't matter that Mari pretended to like it. That only made me angrier, for some reason. She'd done similar things before on missions—briefly distracting someone or gods knew what —but I'd never been there to see it for myself.

I usually acted cheery, keeping my darker, controlling side to battles or that private room on the *Lusca,* but—Divine seas! —I looked forward to hurting our host. He knew how to set my fingers itching toward my blade.

First, treasure. I bared my teeth in something that probably looked more shark-like than happy.

"And remember," Dio drawled, "what happens in the rooms can happen out here too if you like." He drank deeply from the wine a servant handed him. "I like to watch."

Despite myself, my body heated, blood rushing to the head that shouldn't be thinking right now. *I'd love for you to watch us pillage everything you own, you flaccid shrimp.* The thought brought a real smile back to my face. *And then I'll carve out those eyes and gut you like chum.* I laughed. "Ooh," I said, squeezing Mari's hand, "Selene likes to perform."

She winked.

4

MARI

I adjusted the thin straps of my miniscule gold dress, fighting the urge to glare at Terion. Judging from how hard he held his jaw, his motive for making me wear this didn't include touchy-feely gods like Dio. The captain's scowl was going to draw attention in a second.

"Haloc," I cooed, touching his arm, "let's see the rooms." Selene, I decided, would have a sexy purr to her voice, while still hitting a little higher than my natural register.

Terion released a breath, blinking once and returning his attention to me instead of boring into the crowd of light-skinned demi-gods congregating at the bottom of one of the cushioned pits. "Good. That's—"

A wine bottle dropped to hover between us. I jerked my head up. One of the aerialists had lowered upside-down on his hoop to offer it to us.

"A drink?" he asked, smiling, cheeks not even red from hanging like that.

Terion took the bottle. "Do you have glasses?"

"Do you need them?"

Fair point. This place was luxurious but also broke the rules. No one would mind if we drank straight from the bottle. It's what most of us did on the *Lusca*.

"No," I said sweetly, taking Terion's free hand. "Let's choose a room and we'll drink it there."

"There's little time for that in the forest," said the aerialist cryptically, before whooshing up toward the darkened ceiling again.

"The forest," Terion echoed, arching a brow at me. He'd apparently moved on from his anger with Dio, or, more likely, stuffed it down until he could do something about it. Now, he couldn't have looked more excited if he were a dog wagging its tail.

I headed toward the first alcove alongside the round room. I expected a hallway, as if the whole place were like a wheel with spokes coming out, but it was just a rounded recess with one door. Beside it was a plaque.

Honey Room

Enter if you don't mind getting sticky.

I made a face—no one could see us in here because of the angle of the door.

Terion, who had been fussing with the wax seal on the wine bottle, burst out laughing. "Sticky, eh? You have to try that one, Selene!"

"Hmm, sounds interesting." I refused to break character even if Terion was acting like an ass. "We must try them all, Haloc. You go to the next one, and after I'm done here"—I glanced suspiciously at the plaque again—"I'll skip that one and go to the next. We can see which one is best." There was probably an office or storage area in the back of one of these rooms where Dio kept the exorbitant party fees. We'd gotten ours from a Kantharian nobleman beating a horse. At least that was what Ajax told me. I had my doubts.

A suctioned pop meant Terion had gotten the seal off the wine bottle. "Have a little wine first," he said with a wink. "It is a party."

I knew how much both of us could drink before our judgments started to cloud, and splitting a bottle of wine was the limit I'd allow myself while I was on a mission.

Terion took the first swig, exposing his dark, muscular neck, and then handed it to me. The lip of the bottle felt wet, but the wine was delicious. I took another drink.

He snatched the bottle back from me. A few drops fell on the floor and a couple more splashed on my dress.

"Hey!" Red bled through the gold on my left breast (of course it had to be there) and near the bottom of the front skirt panel.

"All ready for the Honey Room," he said with no hint of apology. If anything, he looked viciously amused.

A golden-skinned woman sauntered into the alcove, cutting off anything else he was going to say. She gave Terion a lingering, appreciative look. This woman looked like his type too. It wasn't just a look he went for, but an attitude. Of course, her massive chest didn't hurt.

After an uncharacteristically quick once-over, Terion turned back to me. "Meet you after all the rooms. Then we can celebrate." His voice took on a dark, seductive note that actually made me shiver. He gave me a quick kiss on the cheek.

It wasn't hard to smile after him. *Damn his charm.* The worst thing was he knew how charming he could be.

No time to think about that physical reaction, which swirled up layers of frustration and pride that I could feel a shiver like that at all. It felt good to go breathless for a second, even if it was only because of Terion's practiced charisma.

The golden-skinned woman didn't watch Terion go, but walked straight past me through the door.

Nothing for it.

With one last check to make sure the bruises on my arm couldn't be seen underneath my perfect disguise, I followed her in. The room was... beautiful. Magical, even. The gnarled trunks of enchanted trees spread their branches across the entire ceiling, which was lower than the main room's. Everything glowed green and sparkly. And dripping down from the branches like slow rain were drops of honey.

I swallowed a chuckle of surprise. I'd expected something less magical and more crass. Not to say there wasn't plenty of sex happening in this room. Almost everyone was gathered in the center, a tangle of sensuous limbs. A few males, but mostly females licking honey off each other's bodies. It was hypnotic.

The guard outside Dio's palace had said the rooms were for participating, not just watching, so I closed the door behind me. Couldn't look suspicious. I scanned the edges of the room, but there was so much foliage that a door could have been hidden anywhere.

Someone sat on the floor at the far end of the room, wearing about as much as I was, but with her legs crossed. I refused to take off my dress and reveal the knife strapped to the inside of my leg, so she seemed like as good a target as any to head for. Plus, since she was so far away, I could trail my hand along the wall, feeling for any hidden doors, passages, or safes as I made my way to her.

We locked eyes. Hers were big. I couldn't tell the color from here. Not when so much distance separated us, and a mass of bodies sometimes hid her from view. She was pretty, though, with long blonde hair and a peaceful look on her face.

Honey dripped on me from above. The environment was undeniably sexy, even if it was only a distraction to get through to the prize.

What was Terion's room like? Slow and sensual like this one, or crazy and desperate? Whatever environment the second room held, he'd probably have his fun along the way. To keep our cover, I had to do something too.

Even the woman sitting alone had messy hair and swollen lips. It was a good look, actually.

My plan to move seductively as I crossed the room fell a little flat since I was digging through branches, only to find more wall. So many leaves! Maybe the goods weren't here at all. I had to check the whole room to be sure, though.

I made no discoveries by the time I reached the woman. She peered up at me, that peaceful expression locked in place, like she was waiting for me to do something.

Fine.

"You're here all by yourself," I purred, tucking her hair behind her ear as I crouched next to her. "Someone like you should be doted on."

I honestly didn't want to be the one to do it. I had a job to do, and this wasn't it. Besides, the only thing I could think of was to suck her off, which only brought back memories of being called a cold bitch. I clenched my hand at my side.

I had to have a reason for going into this room, one that wasn't connected to treasure. But I was good at getting myself out of sticky situations.

Poor choice of words.

"Stay here," I said with a mischievous smile.

Approaching the main group all grinding and caressing each other—amazingly still upright, most of them—I drew two away from the others. After a few whispered instructions, they began going down on the woman, giving her all their attention. The air smelled like sex and sugar instantly. I kissed the back of the woman's hand, licked the honey off, and headed back out.

Obstacle cleared. But, despite going out the opposite way, feeling the second half of the wall, I didn't find anything to suggest the money was hidden in there.

I allowed myself a relieved exhale when I left and closed the door. There were still moans and laughter in the main room, but I didn't have to participate, even if Dio said he wanted to watch me. I allowed myself a grimace in the alcove before smoothing my features and emerging. All I had to do was swing my hips and look half-drunk for people to believe I was there for the same reason as everyone else. In these marked rooms, on the other hand...

It wasn't like this was any different from a typical mission. I had a goal. There were obstacles. I'd stay in character until the job was done. I'd done it dozens of times. Just not in one of Dio's parties, where Terion might get too distracted fucking someone to be much help.

The looks he got when we entered the party said he'd have no trouble finding partners. I forgot how handsome he was sometimes. To me, he was a captain, almost a friend, not a famous ocean demi-god with glowing skin, hard muscles, and a pulse-stopping smile. *I guess he's all of that.* Right now, though, I wanted him to focus. Would this environment be too distracting? It was his debt we were trying to pay off. He should do half the work to get it.

On land, I'd actually seen women begging to come aboard. Terion's whispered reputation talked about his expertise in chains and whips and ruthless but effective domination.

Weird things to hear about a friend, but I didn't doubt it. His default mood was optimistically confident. Vain, even, but a good captain to his sailors. For that, I was lucky. Taken in a different direction, that self-assurance could easily manifest in darker, more intense ways. I'd seen hints of it when I got drunk with him after losing a sailor to Basileus' rage or when he stood on deck, soaking wet and grinning after a bad storm.

One room was off limits to everybody but him—a locked room below deck. Rumors rumbled through the crew about what lay behind that door, but we respected Terion too much to push his boundaries.

What he did in his off hours was nobody's business but his. I'd be lying if I said I wasn't curious, though.

I passed in front of Dio's gaze again as I strode back into the main room, skipping the next hallway. I squinted into the alcove but couldn't make out what that plaque said.

I let my gaze wander over the guests, the aerialists, the walls... So many places a treasure could be hiding.

Time for the third door.

Feral Room

Prey or predator. Run.

❧ 5 ❧

MARI

I flexed my toes in the flat shoes. They weren't made for running, like my regular boots. The best outfits had function—lots of pockets, coverage, and grip. This outfit literally had the opposite. The only thing going for it, besides sex appeal, was that I would be hard to catch. I'd slide out of people's grip like an eel in this slippery, silky dress. My fingers itched to hold the dagger.

Run. I inwardly scoffed at Terion's advice to simply tie up the dress. But I didn't have much of a choice. I reached down and tied the silky gold panels together, trying to keep the knife hidden between my thighs while still giving myself room to move. The inherent danger of the Feral Room would make it a decent place to hide a trove of money.

And I could only discover it if I ran around this gods-damned room. What if I was caught? I'd fake excitement. There was no other way.

With a deep breath, I settled myself. Fearing anything at this party was ridiculous. I'd done more dangerous jobs before.

I could outrun or outmaneuver most people. It was the sexual component of this mission that had me on edge.

Fucking Calix.

The longer I stood in front of that door, the more a savage kind of excitement wormed its way into my belly. I could run. I could catch. I could win.

I might have failed to beat my record on the ship's obstacle course earlier, but I could win here. Hell, I could steal this money myself without any help from Terion.

I stepped inside the Feral Room.

My check didn't matter because it was dark. Chaotic. Shadowy forms rushed past, but my eyes couldn't fully adjust. The main party area out there was dim and red, but this was like the darkness of a ship's hold before any lanterns were lit.

Someone screamed. A growl echoed from nearby. Rushing feet. A splash.

This was going to be tougher than I thought. I needed time to acclimate to the darkness. I saw only a few ways to buy time. The most appealing was to run.

Arms reached out of the murk toward me. I slid away in time and started sprinting. Stupid slippery shoes. The captain was right about the skirt, though. My mostly bare legs had room to move.

Hazy shapes started to form. Tree trunks and faintly glistening water running between them like a stream. Males, females, demi-gods with half-animal features.

This was a hunt, nothing like the beautiful calm of the Honey Room. Here, creatures lurked in a dark forest, ready to grab, to take. This room was much bigger than the last, with plenty of room to run. With darkness and shapes in the way, seeing the full size of it was difficult.

A woman shrieked in my ear. I skipped backward, landing one foot in stream water, as a large male pinned her to a tree. Their sounds followed me as I tried to find the edges of the room. Why had I moved away from the wall to begin with? There had to be a door, a lock, *something* to keep all that money. The darkness and disorientation here made this the perfect space. It also made it the hardest to search.

Fingers brushed my arm. I yanked it away with a pleased little squeal.

Go go go! I couldn't afford to get caught here and waste time.

I picked up my pace and hid around a large tree at the far end of the room. The bark felt real. How had Dio pulled that off? Was it another illusion? Had he found someone deathless to grow real trees for this party?

My bare ankle scraped something metal. Was that…?

I spun and crouched down, blindly feeling the spot at the base of the trunk. Yes, it was a hinge! No knob or lever, but definitely a hinge. I knocked on the wood. Although the middle of the trunks had felt solid, the base had a slightly hollower quality. My lips curled in a smile.

I had to test my theory. Quickly, I jumped behind the next tree, crouched, checked. Another hinge. Could I pry it open? I tried feeling for edges, any place I could fit my short fingernails. Bark flaked off, but no obvious way to open the little chamber. Did trees in all the rooms have these openings? I'd have to—

A tall male crashed into me. Desperate annoyance more than anything else surged up in my gut. I was so close to figuring this out, but now I had to pause and interact with this person who smelled like spicy sweat.

I inhaled to shift my emotions to something that wouldn't be a liability. Strong hands gripped my upper arms and hauled me to my feet. A low growl emanated from his chest. I was hoping I wouldn't have to do this. I *shouldn't* be doing this, not with the dagger strapped between my legs.

Just like others did around me, I tugged lightly against my captor, but he had no give. It was like he was made of rock. Maybe he was related to the gray woman outside. This male— definitely deathless—stood tall and immovable. I was tall too, but not half as bulky. His face, hazy in the murk, held no amusement, not even the glow of victory for catching me.

Alarm blinked through my body.

"Oh no," I whimpered, forcing a smile into the protest. "What will you make me do?" I writhed against him, feeling for weapons. Something told me this wasn't somebody with a fucked-up fantasy—he'd seen what I was doing and came here to stop it. If he found my weapon...

My back scratched against the tree as he held me in place. I reached as far as I could, pretending to push him back as I ran my fingers over his chest, his hip, anywhere he might keep a blade or rope or whatever Dio gave his enforcers. One flick and I could disarm him. But he was doing the same with me, one hand moving to my neck to pin me against the trunk while his other hand frisked my body. Unless he stuck his hand up my tied skirt, he'd find nothing, but I couldn't take the chance. It wasn't like there were many places to hide something in this damned dress.

"Dress off," came his gruff command, finally tugging at the fabric.

Shit.

I giggled, but the sound came out dry. "How can I convince

you to leave me alone?" I grabbed at the fabric between his legs. My attempt at seduction wouldn't win any awards, but it was all I could come up with as his breath blew hot and angry against my face, and my odds of finding Terion's money got smaller with every passing moment.

My attacker grunted. I smiled. Maybe this was working. If I could distract him for a few more seconds, maybe I could scoot to the edge of the trunk and bolt for the door. I could claim it was all in the spirit of the Feral Room.

He pawed at my dress.

Nope, that's staying on. I shoved my hand down his pants. "Please let me go," I moaned, joining the chorus of others who panted or screamed in other parts of the room.

"What were you doing?" he gritted out.

So my hunch was right. "Hiding from big, bad males like you."

"Looked like you were—"

An animalistic growl cut off whatever he was about to say as someone else barreled into him. I lost my grip on his length. This new shape I recognized. Relief, immediately chased by concern, flooded my system.

"Mine," Terion declared, grabbing me roughly and pressing us together. His outfit was drenched. "There you are. I caught you, finally."

Pretty convincing show. His raspy voice and insistent body were just like some desperate lover.

I squealed, playing along. "Haloc!"

He groaned. "Selene."

The bulky guard regained his stance and glared. He reached for me again, but Terion caught his wrist and shoved him away. "She's mine. I take her."

For a moment, I waited, holding my breath. Would the guard call him out? Fight him?

"Find someone else," Terion ordered, using his most intimidating captain voice. "I get Selene." Water dripped onto my skin. What happened to him?

A dim glint in the guard's eye told me he was sizing up Terion, glancing up and down, before backing off. But he didn't go far.

Terion ground his entire weight against me so hard I could feel the muscles under his outfit. He still wore everything he came in with, including the jacket, so he must not have gotten too carried away in the other rooms. Which begged the question...

"Why are you here?" I breathed into his ear. "The guard's still watching."

"Trees."

I nodded against his neck. "Other rooms too?"

"Ah, yes," he growled, loud enough for others to hear.

I tapped the base of the trunk with my foot. I didn't have to explain. We both understood. Make this look like... something else, while we tried to get the little door open. This room was dark enough to hide what we were doing if we were careful.

"Down," he snarled, pushing on my shoulders.

I slid to my knees. The metal hinge pressed against the back of my hip. I let out a cry as if Terion were doing more than just crouching in front of me. "Fingernails don't work," I whispered. One glance above Terion's shoulder showed the guard, pointedly immobile, still staring at us.

Move on! Nothing to see here. If he just walked away, we could investigate in peace.

I spread my knees, a clear message for Terion to reach in and grab the dagger. It was the easiest ploy. I refused to think about how sexual this was. My captain's damp hands untying the silky panels of my skirt, feeling for the strap on my inner thigh... His fingers didn't wander. He was all business, but the warm pads of his fingers against my sensitive skin made me slick anyway. *It's fine. It's fine. Nothing embarrassing about that. I need to sell what we're doing.*

His hand almost reached the knife. I bucked my hips, tapping the little sheath against his palm.

A rumble vibrated through his chest and into mine. He wasn't kissing me, wasn't stroking me, but the hot contact of his hard, wet body against mine and his hand easing the knife out of its sheath between my legs had me gasping. I grabbed his wrist, partly to avoid him accidentally reaching further and finding out how wet I was and partly to guide his hand to the metal hinge in the trunk. As he reached past me, wrist against my exposed hip as he pried the edges of the hinge, I rolled my body. He growled, thrusting down, but neither of us had lined up the parts we needed to really get friction. I was bucking against his leg and he was thrusting into my lower belly. From the guard's perspective, though, this should look like breathless sex. I let out little screams to fit the theme and cover any noise his knife might make against the bark. Considering our position, Terion didn't touch me more than he had to.

If he moved lower, rubbed the spot between my legs, could I break like I'd wanted to with Calix?

The memory of my ex doused the heat flaring up in my body. What was I thinking? Terion and I had a job, that was all. If he knew how turned on I was, he'd laugh at me back aboard the *Lusca*. That ego of his would expand even more.

But it was natural, right? When a handsome person thrust against you and you could feel the muscles and the wine-scented breath rising up from where he gasped against your neck...

"Almost there," he panted.

I blinked before I realized he meant the knife. The door. The money on the other side of the door.

I cried out, moving my hips to the side so I didn't block the opening.

Damn it. That guard was still there.

I screamed louder. Pretending wasn't a new thing for me. *Cold bitch, cold bitch, cold bitch.*

My next sound was fueled by spite. *Fuck you, Calix.* I had the wild idea to make Terion come—the famous Captain Asterion—just to prove to myself that I could give pleasure, at least, even if I didn't reach that height myself.

No, no, calm down. Stop being stupid.

Behind my back, near the base of my spine, Terion's hand worked. "Right there!" I cried.

He groaned, and I felt something hard and cool replace the heat of his hand. It had straight edges. The door.

I smiled and gripped him in the world's most strangely intimate hug. But I couldn't help it. We'd done it, and it turned out he felt really good. I wanted to touch him more often.

Now that we knew where Dio hid the money, we had to figure out how to take it and get out of here. Lust clouded my judgment in this room, and I needed to be sharp.

He pressed even closer as he explored inside the opening, his shoulder against mine, his chest against mine.

"Yes?" I panted.

"Oh gods, yes!" he grunted. Something shifted in his movements. Something *real*. Money, relief, *something* had turned him on. This was barely a show anymore. He ground against me, his care from before all but gone. He rubbed my lower belly and then—

My eyes flared as he ground against my throbbing pussy. Once, twice. My head fell back.

It ended almost instantly, my body crying for more. With a gasp and a groan, he sat up, making orgasmic noises. He shoved a fistful of the spoils down the front of his pants. So there was money in there. We were right.

A brief apology shone in his bright eyes. He'd lost control, and he was obviously just as surprised as I was.

My chest shuddered as I tried to compose myself. That was... Well, that was better than Calix. It said something that simulated sex on a mission felt better than real sex with a lover. Maybe I wasn't the whole problem. Maybe Calix wasn't good at sex either.

I quirked my eyebrows to tell Terion it was okay. We stuck to the plan. We knew there might be some uncomfortable moments.

Now, the important thing was to move on and figure out how to steal the rest of the treasure.

When he covertly handed me back the knife, I allowed myself a glance at his crotch, where the first handful of spoils were. The spot bulged. It couldn't be comfortable for him since, just a second before, I'd felt his rock-hard cock stroke me. He couldn't possibly consider putting more treasure down his pants. I cast him a look that said, *Really?*

He raised his eyebrows and shrugged.

❦ *6* ❦

TERION

Mari was a damn good actor. Made me wish I could see her do more missions, don more disguises. It was hypnotic. It was... fucking sexy.

This place was getting to me. There was no other way to justify how I'd lost myself just now. Hopefully she didn't mind too much. Hell, I'd almost...

I sat back further on my heels. Mari's glazed eyes and sweaty collarbone glistening in the darkness as she leaned against the tree suggested she probably enjoyed that. Couldn't have been too bad.

I stood and pulled her to her feet. The bag of coins I'd found in the hollow trunk pressed against my hard cock. I sucked in a breath and adjusted myself.

Mari's eyes flitted to the burly man behind me, the guard, who hadn't run as the plaque outside the room demanded, but watched our whole encounter. We couldn't have men like that following us.

Before I could tap her to get her moving, Mari ran. *Good girl.* She moved slower than I was used to seeing—the ribbony length of her skirt kept wrapping around her legs like tentacles —and I followed. The adrenaline of our find mixed with the scent of sex threatened to disorient me.

Before a moment ago, I'd have said I never lost control, but too much excitement apparently turned me into a horny adolescent. We had to get the rest of the gold and then make it back to the *Lusca* where I could spend quality time in my chamber belowdecks.

The problem was getting the rest of the treasure. It was in gold coins, the standard currency accepted in all Eight Realms. That made sense, even if gold was clunky and hard to carry. Storing it in so many small locations made the job even harder. Mari apparently thought so too, because as soon as I shut the door behind us, she pinned me with a meaningful gaze. "Did you see all the rooms?" she asked sweetly. Her tone didn't match the intensity in her face at all.

"Just that one." I pointed.

"It's a forest too?"

"A pool."

Not only was my beautiful blue suit ruined, but that gold dress was wet and rumpled now too. Pity. At least our escapade made a good story, which would be even better once we unloaded bagsful of treasure on the *Lusca*. My pulse beat a thick but unsteady rhythm. Would Dio's money be enough to dismiss Basileus's threat?

Mari and I headed out into the main area together. She walked as lightly as a Hyperion acrobat. Every line of her body declared how excited she was by our find.

"What's this?" I ran a finger across a thick dot of something next to the drop of red wine on her dress.

Right over her breast, which, right now, was pointed and hard with arousal.

Divine seas, I needed to stop thinking like this.

"Honey."

I laughed. "Seriously? That was literal?"

"It dropped from the trees."

"Sticky," I mused. "Was it as dark as the last room?"

"No. It was much brighter."

"Lots of people to play with?"

Her mouth stretched with a non-committal answer. This party crawled with people. Yes, most of them were distracted by drink or sex, but that didn't mean they wouldn't notice us prying open the bases of all the trees to get at the money inside. The number of people in the main room had tripled since our arrival, and more poured in through the bottleneck hallway. I itched to use the knife in my sleeve.

"Tell me about the room with the pool," Mari said, voice low, running a finger down my chest.

My cock was still hard from our display. It didn't understand she was pretending. "We should go there," I said, voice a little hoarse. "It's all underwater up to your waist. Trees and rocks rise up from the floor, and there are platforms where we could..."

She nuzzled against me.

"More people from the ceiling," I whispered in her ear. Protectiveness reared up in my chest as I smelled her bare skin. "They have a good view of the people in the water, but they won't be able to tell what we're doing if we shield each other."

"And you checked?" she breathed.

The warm air made me shiver. The things I wanted to do

with her. With someone. Not Mari, but Selene, if she were real.

"Hinges," I confirmed, taking her hand and leading her back to that door.

"Wait, Haloc."

I didn't.

"I want to stay here all night," she continued. "How long do these parties last?"

Now I understood. "Two days."

"Do we have that much time?" she asked, rounding her eyes innocently. "Could we stay longer?"

I smirked. My shapeshifter thief. Once everyone left, it would be much easier to crack open the trees and make off with all the gold we wanted. I hated waiting two days, but after years trying to pay off an impossible debt, two days wasn't much.

"Anything for you."

"Would Lord Dio allow it?"

I'll make him. Now my hands had touched the skin of her hips too, and I'd cut out Dio's eyes if he ever touched her again. "I have connections."

She lips stretched in a smile. "Good."

"I still want to show you the Enchanted Pool Room."

"And the Honey Room."

We'd nose around, disappear under the pretense of getting some sleep, and then figure out a way to break in later to loot the place. Perfect.

"We'll do it all," I assured her, opening the door leading to the pool. Waterfalls splashed into blue water, cascading over platforms in a rock face that formed the far wall. In front of it there were floating people supposed to be fairies or sprites or something. You'd have thought I'd know, since I'd been damn near everywhere in the Far Realm. I'd even sighted the Beyond more than once.

Mari's amazement didn't look feigned. But that was the thing. When she was in character, nobody could tell. Her performances were flawless. Yes, full gods could shapeshift entirely into animals and such, but they couldn't die and were therefore a liability. I had no full gods on my ship. No one expected Mari.

I pulled her into the water after me. About half the people in here still had clothes on for some reason, so we didn't stand out too much. I adjusted the bag of gold between my legs again to make sure it didn't fall.

We swished forward, past swimmers and people engaged in other activities—the reports of these sex parties certainly weren't exaggerated—and made it to the nearest large tree.

"Darling," I crooned, sliding my hand down the front of her thigh. She'd have to go under to get a good angle to pry open the door with that knife. I scanned the others, both above and below. Could anyone see if she got this bag of money too? We could make off with a few samples before the big haul.

Mari's face said she was considering the same thing. What could we pretend, that she was giving me head while—?

"I think we should go back and see the rest of the rooms." Her foot passed between my legs, obviously feeling evidence of the hinge for herself. Her dress glittered like sunset gold, making my head swim.

She was right. Waiting was better. I was getting ahead of myself, distracted by seeing her roll her hips against me. Normally, that wasn't even the kind of sex I liked, but something about this place, that dress, hidden gold... It all knocked me off balance.

I smiled at her. Thank the Divine she said something. But she shouldn't have had to.

"Let's go," I agreed, taking charge. No more sexy thoughts. No more wine.

Just pirating.

This room was humid compared to the others. That, plus the warm water, made my power simmer. It wasn't the most impressive ability—to touch people and direct water over their skin—but the conditions were perfect here to do it without any effort.

"Come play with us," cried a woman, tugging the sleeve of my jacket. Light brown hair formed a big circle around her shoulders as her nude body caught up with her hand.

I cast her a grin. "Selene and I are heading out if you want to join."

Mari stiffened next to me.

"I like it here," the woman declared. Mari and I hadn't stopped walking, but everyone's movements were sluggish in this water. "You don't want to stay?" The woman cupped my cheek and planted a kiss on my lips.

"Not tonight. Tomorrow?" To punctuate my answer, I touched my mouth to Mari's temple.

The woman sighed and returned to a group of others. I might have invited her to the *Lusca* if I'd found her at a port, but that would be a terrible idea now.

"Ooh!" I looked up to see a dark-skinned woman standing in the doorway, eyes big with surprise and delight as she stared at me. "Captain Asterion? Are you Captain Asterion?"

The room quieted as others turned to look at me.

Mari cursed under her breath.

"The one who sailed to the Far Realm?" someone else added.

I moved faster, hand in hand with Mari. This was very bad. "No. But I hear he's very handsome, so thank you."

"You are him!" the woman by the door shouted, pointing at my face.

My face. Had the makeup...?

Well, shit.

A large, square demi-god appeared out of the air in front of me, on the first step peeking above the waterline. I tried stepping through the air to disappear back onto the *Lusca*, but no luck. Wards. Dio must have given him permission to travel like that within the grounds.

"You're not on the guest list," said the square guard. His chest strap held a collection of mismatched weapons. He pulled out a machete that glinted in the watery reflections.

Excitement zinged through my blood. The prospect of a fight eclipsed my lust for treasure.

Mari chuckled, touching a fingertip to my cheek, where everyone could see my scales. "I did too good a job, Haloc. We like to pretend," she added in a stage whisper.

The guard took in the Enchanted Pool Room with its winged aerialists, his mouth set hard in a look that said, *No shit.*

"I promise we'll be good." This from Mari again.

"No," I put in. "We'll be bad. I'm Captain Asterion, remember?"

She giggled as I swished my hands near her waist. I didn't tickle her. I stopped even holding her hand. In seconds, we'd have to run, so she needed both hands to tie up her skirt and retrieve that knife.

The guard rolled his eyes. We had everyone's attention now. I got curious stares from everywhere, the reactions ranging from lust to fear, the two most common expressions I elicited.

"Get out," the guarded demanded.

"But..." Mari's protest died. She hung her head.

We made our way slowly to the steps. The blade in my sleeve wasn't dislodging like it should. I shook my arm lightly. The hell was I going to go without I felt the hilt hit my palm underwater. Closing my fist around the weapon, I tried my best to look non-threatening, like Mari.

I grinned, not managing to look apologetic. "Sorry for the confusion, but there's no need for—"

I launched forward, pushing the woman out of the way, who stood frozen near the top of the steps with the guard. The knife was small, but long enough to drive into the flesh of the square male's neck. Blood spurted into the water, turning it pink. Screams echoed off the walls. I stabbed a few more times, quickly, to make sure he wouldn't follow, and then caught up with Mari, who'd already taken off running.

✦ 7 ✦

MARI

I sprinted for the exit. Someone fell into a sunken pit in the main room as I hurtled past. Half-drunk guests at the party watched us, including Dio on his throne. Scattered screams shot through the air, but most people were drunk enough to think we were part of the entertainment. No one got out of the way fast enough.

If only I could travel through the air... but the place was warded inside and out. Terion and I had discussed that before the mission even began. Our only hope to escape was to make it out of this building by running. Hopefully there would be a spot to travel from the dock to the ship. For now, my only choice was to race for the hallway leading to the main exit.

Damn that bottleneck! If there were other windows, other exterior doors, even a big enough chimney, I might have been able to shimmy through.

Terion, though.

One glance behind showed him blazing in all his blue glory. He was about as subtle as the moon on a cloudless night. He knew how to move, though, jumping between slow-moving couples, spinning out of reach of grabbing hands. A new guard took the place of the square-faced one Terion had stabbed. This time it was a thin, vampire-looking person, probably male, definitely fanged.

I doubted they'd fare any better than the square guard. Terion's dark eyes blazed. Blood glittered on the blade he clutched in the dim light.

No one hangs the captain, I chanted to myself. I'd heard strangers repeat the line when I took to land for other missions. Children sang the full rhyme in morbid little games. They always meant Captain Asterion. *No one hangs the captain.*

Hopefully that meant no one would hang me either.

I vaulted over the corner of the last sunken pit. *Almost there.* But at the end of the hallway was that gray woman. How the devil were we supposed to get past her? All I had was speed.

A cry and a brutal laugh meant Terion had skewered someone else behind me.

I dashed into the hall with the pictures. A grunt escaped me as my flimsy shoe caught on a divot in the ground. I pitched forward, getting caught in the flaps of long gold silk. *Shit!*

A firm hand squeezed my bruised arm and hauled me upright. Terion.

He passed me and I followed. Would he slice the gray woman? Did he need to?

"Terion," I began.

But he was too far away. His long legs catapulted him out into the night. The gray lady didn't even say anything. Maybe she was too stunned. Perfect. If she'd spoken a word, one of us would have finished her, or tried to. Terion was the one with the weapon, leaving me totally exposed out here.

We were running too fast for me to get the blade from between my legs. The tied fabric blocked my access—a major oversight. One of my panting breaths turned into an angry huff.

New guests were arriving, all feathers and little pieces of fabric. I narrowly avoided ramming into a light-skinned man with bones lining his suit jacket. He sent a violent curse after me as I fled.

Footsteps along the path told me we had pursuers, not just an audience.

Terion must have heard them too because he looked back to make sure I was still there. I picked up my pace, but his legs ate up the distance faster than mine could. We headed for the dock.

I cheated a glance back to see how many chased us. Maybe six.

The tails of Terion's blue suit streamed behind him. I watched them, watched his back as he ran, as *we* ran, to safety. His skin all but disappeared, but that damned blue... For that matter, my damned gold! We practically glowed in the dark.

Something swooped above us. Not Zete with his gray wings. It must have been the vampire. Black wings wouldn't show up against a black sky.

My heartbeat kicked up. *It's okay. We'll make it.*

I skimmed the sky again. Vampires couldn't walk through the air at all. That was a demi-god ability. If we could just make it to the dock...

Wards pressed down on me like a light touch.

"Selene!" Terion barked, holding out his hand.

I took it.

Blackness crushed around me, askew, wrong compared to how this type of traveling normally felt. I gripped his hand harder. He'd reached the edge of the warded area, but I was still partially inside it. My bones felt it, especially my injured shoulder. If I let go, would the wards hurl me back at the feet of Dio's guards? They'd kill me, for sure.

A thunk. A sloping pitch. A wheeze as I went down hard on the deck. Something heavy fell on top of me.

My eyes flew open. All I saw was Terion's face above mine, soaking and sprayed with blood, a look of wild frustration on his face. He didn't linger, but for a split second I felt him between my legs again as he'd groaned, reaching for the door in the tree. My face heated. He shoved himself to his feet.

"Full speed to the east!" he roared. "Zete, wind! All hands!"

I pushed myself up just as the ship tipped into a deep turn.

"Watch the boom!" cried Ajax from his place at the helm.

I ducked in time to avoid the swinging equipment. Tying up my minuscule skirt, I scanned to find a job to hurry the ship along.

"Put out the lights, Mari," Terion ordered. "Everything but the lantern in the quarterdeck."

In seconds, the job was done. Zete flew among the black sails, summoning heavy wind to push us forward, and the *Lusca* tore away into the dark.

"FUCK," SAID TERION.

"Fuck," I echoed, holding up my glass and clinking it with his. A lantern swung above the wooden table where we sat, glinting off the amber liquor. We took a long, deep drink.

I'd changed out of that gold sliver of nothing and into something sturdier—my softest pants and a short-sleeved shirt with leather accents I'd added myself. Simply being dry and covered to the collarbone was a relief. The knife I'd stored between my legs lay near my hammock. I had to clean it, but when I went to fetch clean water in the mess, I ran into Terion pouring himself a glass and settled down at the table with him instead.

He didn't seem to mind. We rarely spent time alone like this, but it felt right after what we'd just been through.

Only a skeleton crew remained above deck after Zete touched down. His power was impressive, but only in short bursts. He'd stirred up so much wind helping us escape that he was inevitably passed out in a hammock somewhere.

The sun hadn't risen and we were exhausted, but this wasn't a night for peaceful sleep. Now that we were far enough away from Dio's island to avoid more trouble, it was a night to get drunk.

"You think he'll come after you?" I asked. The dark liquid swirled my mind into something less sharp-edged.

"Dio or Basileus?"

I raised an eyebrow. "Both?"

"Hm." Terion tipped his seat back, peering up at the plank ceiling as if he could see the stars. "Of course they will. With the tides."

His excitement as he sliced our way out of Dio's party had clearly worn off. Now, the expression on his dark face had turned dangerous. His eyes pierced, his movements calculated and reckless at once.

Well, those things were always true, but they flared like sparks when he was angry or disappointed.

Tonight, he was both.

If my ability had been strong enough to cover Terion's blue-green scales, we wouldn't be here. Those guards wouldn't be dead. We'd be sitting on so much treasure we could slide down piles of it.

He poured himself another glass and turned his attention back to me. "We gained nothing," he seethed, voice low and treacherously calm. "That first tree paid for our entry fee." He slammed the bottle down between us.

I flexed uncomfortably. Did he blame me?

"We know where the treasure is now," I tried. "Could you send someone else?" Even as I asked, I heard how ridiculous that idea sounded. Zete couldn't go incognito with those wings, and the *Lucsa* needed him to sail. Ajax was as subtle as a tidal wave. Klep was too nervous. Terion's sister Rhode knew the oceans better than any of us.

I, on the other hand, was expendable and good at slipping into places unnoticed. This time, Terion had simply wanted to come along. And what Terion wanted, Terion got.

He snorted.

"Yeah, you're right," I said.

He stared into the imaginary distance as he took another gulp of his drink. "We've hit Muja and Abru. Didn't get enough. Eriset was too dangerous. Hyperborea doesn't exist. Far Realm?"

Was he actually suggesting that? "You said you almost lost the crew that one time."

He held up a finger. "Almost."

"And Hades would kill you."

He still looked far too contemplative.

"Eviscerate you," I clarified. "And the rest of us. If the sea monsters don't do it first."

"My father has enough sea monsters for us already. I've dealt with the bastards long enough." He heaved a sigh. "We go to the Far Realm after one more try. I'm done waiting for something to work."

"You're not waiting. You're... working."

"Yes, all these godsdamn little jobs that aren't enough and you know it."

I clamped my mouth shut. I'd been in charge of most of those "little jobs." His words shouldn't have hurt.

"Dio was the perfect mark," he went on. "All that money he didn't know what to do with. We could have wiped that fucking smug look off his face. Cut off that hand that touched you. It would have been perfect."

I nodded.

He scrubbed absently at his scales, jaw clenching. Unlike me, he hadn't changed out of his party outfit yet. The damp coat lay flung over the back of his chair. "Months of planning for nothing," he muttered, slinging back another gulp. His throat flexed as he swallowed and poured us both another.

Basileus would keep haunting the *Lusca*, trying to kill Terion. His debt wasn't paid off. And I couldn't help feeling I should have done more. Used my power to somehow cover his damned scales.

I should have stayed, pretended I didn't know him, and then slipped back to gather the loot in the trees. There had to have been another way.

Such a stupid thing caught us. And I'd almost been left behind on the island. If Terion hadn't grabbed me...

I took another long drag. "How much would have been enough?" He'd never put a number on his debt. The crew gossiped about it, and I suspected some of them knew exactly what Terion had done to rack up such a debt with King Basileus, but he'd never told me.

"We much as we could get."

So, no answers today. Too bad, since I was risking my life to help him settle whatever difficulty he had with his father. My gut told me it went beyond gold.

Terion's gaze shot to mine, sharp and glowing with drink. "You deserve at least another bag of coin for letting that eel's ass touch you."

I burst out laughing. "Eel's ass?"

"Shark's anus? Squid's limp dick?" The humor died in his face as he went introspective again, his eyes turning possessive and dangerous. "I'll come back for him."

No question. That was a threat.

I didn't protest. The way Terion looked at me while also seeming to see whatever torture he imagined for Dio written across my face unnerved me. I shifted in my seat. Pleasure chased the unease. It wasn't often that anybody offered to hurt somebody on my behalf. No one else on the crew would have done it, unless they were only looking for an excuse to spill blood.

The captain's hand flexed around the base of his glass. "All that, just for somebody to lay his hands on you. Did anyone else touch you?"

Besides you? His intensity brought back the gasping sensation of him leaning into me, all that wildness pressed against me... "No. I'm fine."

"That's my girl. Always ready."

I paused with my glass halfway to my lips. "Crew comes first," I murmured. It was the mantra that meant all pirates on the *Lusca* stuck together, fought for each other. Terion applied it even to me.

"Crew comes first," he agreed. One of his fingers caressed the tabletop in a gesture of pleased ownership. "You're a good actress."

I tipped my head. No use denying it. That ability was the only distinction I had among the crew. Blending in, changing identities, never being a recognizable part of Captain Asterion's crew in public. Changeable as the sea.

But I suspected he was referring to something else.

"Lots of practice," I said bitterly, then glared at my glass as if it had made me say it. The warm bubble I'd felt a second ago popped, replaced with Calix's irritated face when I'd admitted the truth to him.

Terion's eyebrows rose. "Is that why you left?"

"Calix? He left me." My head swam now and the air felt humid and sticky, but I took another long sip anyway.

"That's no loss. A man who can't pleasure you?" The smirk that cut through the scowl of disappointment declared how much he believed in his own abilities.

I'd never experienced Terion's particular brand of pleasure before, and I didn't know if I'd like it. Honestly, I didn't know what he did with those women. It probably wouldn't matter if those methods were used on me. History said so.

"Chin up, Mari," he said. "You can catch him sleeping the

next time we're in port, show him what you really think." His free hand drifted toward where his sword usually hung on his hip. "Unless you did already?"

This conversation was beginning to depress me even more. "I didn't hurt him."

"He hurt you." Terion rolled up the sleeves of his blue dress suit, revealing muscular forearms branded with a trident tattoo.

"I just..." Thank the Divine I wasn't sloshy drunk, or else I would have gone into detail about my lack of orgasms and about how Calix was probably right. I was cold, broken, unable to follow through. If I was sloshed, I might have commented on Terion's arms and how they were better than what I'd seen on Calix. I might have run a finger along the tattoo marking him as Basileus's unwanted son.

"He hurt you," Terion insisted, this time more slowly. He lowered his head to meet my eyeline. "Fuck him."

My lips curled in a tiny smile. Terion would kill Calix if he met him in the street. The famous Captain Asterion, standing up for me. My smile widened. "I'm glad I don't anymore."

He guffawed. "I could offer him a few lessons. If he didn't need to be gutted like a fish."

"You think you know what I like?" I challenged. Then I heard myself. *Shit.* Did it sound like I was coming onto him? That wasn't what I meant.

He cut me a look. "Of course."

I barked a laugh. "Cocky."

"Experienced."

I rolled my eyes. Somehow, our glasses had filled again. "Okay then. What do I like?" I'd only been half-pretending in the Feral Room as Terion ground against me, reaching for the door that would lead to our money.

"You doubt me?" He arched a brow. "You shouldn't."

My stomach twisted. "You haven't acted very satisfied yourself lately." That blue suit really did look good on him. That smooth skin, those familiar rough hands all lured me to wonder what he kept in that secret room. Was he right? Would it be enough for me? I couldn't help but be skeptical.

Skeptical and curious.

"Don't make the mistake of thinking *they* were unsatisfied," he replied, leaning back. The fabric of his shirt stretched over his broad chest.

I stayed quiet, took another drink.

He tilted his head back to regard me down his nose. "Think you could do better? I choose very eager partners."

I shrugged. Maybe not *me,* but I could guess exactly what he liked. He had started to lose himself in the Feral Room, after all.

He smirked, dark and tempting. "Oh no, darling. But yes, about the room..." He pursed his lips, smile fading. Was Captain Terion about to... apologize?

"It was the only way," I cut in. "Good thinking."

"It was. And you enjoyed it."

I leaned back for another drink, not contradicting him.

"Yes, Captain," he mimicked before angling forward. "That's what you say." His self-assured, controlled attitude came to the forefront again. His captain self. Around anyone other than the crew, he rarely let it go. Even on board, it could snap into place suddenly, and we had better be ready. Commands had to be obeyed immediately.

"Yes, Captain," I obeyed.

His eyes darkened. So vain, but with good reason. With that lush mouth, the planes of his face, and those keen eyes, he looked ready to be painted. Well, painting wouldn't do much good. It wouldn't capture the sense that he could *overtake* you at any moment. Something would change in his expression, in his movement, and neither enemies nor lovers stood a chance.

I cleared my throat, forcing a deep breath, but couldn't take my eyes off him. Could he push me over the brink? I wanted to see him try.

"We can go back to Zenia," he declared, holding up his glass to the light as if it were a jewel.

His abrupt change in topic made my shoulders relax, but I couldn't shake the breathless, heavy sensation that had started to build between us. Drinking made us talk like that, made me think like that, but I didn't stop. Today had been shit. This week had been shit. I didn't want to stop until memories faded permanently from my brain. "What's in Zenia?"

"Lots of marks."

"Aren't those 'little jobs'?"

He met my eyes. "Criticizing me, are you? What the fuck else would you suggest?"

I bit my lip. Terion watched. I stopped. "I dunno," I said.

"Not helpful. How about we kill your land-loving bastard bedmate while we still can?"

Terion never talked like this. He was an optimist—at least, a whole lot more than I was. This failure really affected him.

Guilt twisted my stomach.

"Your scales," I slurred. "I should try to cover them. For the next job."

"You can only shift your own face." He sounded too amused. "That'll be enough to throw off Calix."

"I haven't tried hard. Maybe..." I knew I couldn't do it, but I was on my feet anyway, glass in hand.

Terion stood, catching my wrist in an iron grip. "You always try."

The lift at the end of the sentence sent heat through my veins. I tried but couldn't follow through. Not with this mission that could have been life-changing for the whole crew. Not even with my own pleasure. I wanted someone to count on me and have it pay off, for once.

He let me go and his forearms flexed as he poured us another round.

I blinked, clearing some of the haze.

"I want to try on your face." I lifted my free hand to touch the scales embedded his cheek.

Terion shot back another swig and leaned into my touch. Enough permission for me.

To get the sense of the skin around the iridescence, I softly touched the entire area. His skin felt warm, weathered, but soft and alive. He watched me.

"He got in your head." Terion's voice went soft. Fuzzy around the edges.

"Bad week."

"Can't have that."

I gave him a look. "Too late."

"Because you need a challenge. That bastard wasn't one."

My brows ticked down. "That's what this is. A challenge." I smoothed my thumb over his cheek, willing power into the touch. With my own face and body, I just needed to make small adjustments in order to change. Here, touching Terion, I was guessing and he knew it.

"Is it working?" he asked.

The scales gleamed as clear as ever. I blew out a breath. "Not yet."

"And I didn't mean this kind of challenge, Mari. Your ex —*he* didn't give you a challenge."

"What are you talking about?" The room was sweltering. Did he not feel it? I pushed up my sleeves to match his before touching his face again.

"Sex. You need a challenge. You can't just lie there and take it. Am I right?"

My face went even hotter. "I don't—"

"Without a job, some record to beat, you'll get bored. Unsatisfied. Tell me I'm right."

My heart jogged up to my throat. He wanted to talk about sex while we were standing practically nose to nose? "Yes, Captain," I said, part automatic response and part sarcasm.

His answering expression was liquid and predatory at once.

My mouth went dry.

"I told you I knew better," he said. "I know *you* better. Fucker wasn't listening." He looked away and I could breathe again. But it didn't last. He hooked me with his eyes again a second later.

Why hadn't I moved my hand from his face? My power wasn't working yet. But a tiny voice said it might. If it didn't, I still got to touch him and feel powerful, when the rest of this week I'd felt so worthless.

"And you want praise and someone to obey you," I said in as normal a voice as I could muster.

A muscle jumped in his cheek and his eyes brightened. "Someone thinks she's been paying attention."

I caressed his face too sloppily. "I know you too."

"Prove it."

This was dangerous. Life on Terion's crew was everything to me. I couldn't make a wrong step or show my weakness or... I couldn't remember why I shouldn't do this. The room sparkled and washed against me in waves of heat.

I set down my glass. He set down his. Like a duel. This was a duel to prove something. My vision wavered, then cleared.

"You are the most feared pirate on the ocean," I cooed, letting recklessness take me. I lifted up on my toes to whisper in his ear. "You know everything about this ship. If you wanted to, you could sail to the ends of the earth and I'd sail with you. I've never seen anyone as handsome as you are. When you were on me, I felt your big cock and I wanted more."

Releasing a breath, I slid back, feeling a little shaky. I hadn't noticed his hand snake over my hip, but he held it now, tense over the soft fabric. I dropped off my tiptoes. He didn't let go. "See?"

Terion let out a dark chuckle. His eyes were so dilated, I only saw black. "Hmm." The rumble sounded deep in that broad chest.

I shivered at the sound. Maybe I'd meant those things after all. I'd only wanted to turn him on. Mission accomplished.

"And now, Mari."

I skittered backward as he pressed me back against the wall. The smooth, leather-like texture of the black wall kissed the bare skin of my arm where Terion held it steady. My guts somersaulted.

Terion wasn't even breathing heavily as he pinned my

wrists at my sides, keeping the rest of his body a breath away from mine. Like in the Feral Room. He hadn't touched me more than he had to there either. Except for those few strokes, but that was an accident.

"Escape if you can," he ordered, taking a small step forward.

His grip felt like metal, and that small step brought his thick thighs flush with mine so I couldn't bring my knee up. I could move my head, but his was still too far away. I wouldn't headbutt my captain anyway. All I had left was to writhe, to twist my way out of his grasp. I was strong, but I wasn't Terion strong.

The more I thrashed and squirmed, the closer Terion came, trapping me with his big body. I was moving and he was immovable. I wasn't as coordinated as usual—my breath probably smelled like Terion's, heavy with liquor. All I could do was grind, grind against him. The skin around my wrists chafed against his rough hands. He was all muscle, all heat around me, and I was struggling under his weight, and there, *there!* That felt so good. I rubbed myself against his strong body, secretly (or not so secretly) hoping to strike that place between my legs again that throbbed with pinprick sensitivity. Oh, there! His groin bulged hard and I—

"See?" Terion backed away.

Lost in a haze, I could only blink at him, panting. *See what?*

Then the truth rushed back. My flushed neck blazed even hotter. This was Terion, for gods' sake. My captain. And I'd let myself get carried away, all because of disappointment and drink and how damn good he looked. I was still sopping, still practically in pain I was so turned on. It was hateful because I ached to say "fuck it" and experience what it would be like to take someone like Terion to bed. Another part of me was glad I still worked. Maybe.

Terion cocked a brow. "I know what I'm doing, Mari." His burning expression shifted and he swallowed. "Zenia, then the Far Realm. If you feel swells tonight, we'll need all hands."

Because waves and monsters are coming after us. Right.

He swept up the bottle of liquor from the table, not bothering with the glass. "Good night."

8

TERION

When Ajax presented the conscious half the crew with burgoo the next morning, I scowled at it. My roiling stomach and pounding head wouldn't let me eat. Or forget yesterday.

Halfway into the bottle last night, I hadn't felt a thing. Then suddenly, memory fell away as if it had dropped into the ocean.

"What is this slop?" Zete heckled.

Ajax waved him off with a massive hand, disappearing through a dark doorway. First mates weren't supposed to cook, but Ajax did it more often than not. It helped him think, he said. I didn't need him to think—I needed him to do. But sometimes his food was tastier than local tavern fare or rations, so I let him do it. Today was not one of his good cooking days.

The seven others who sat with me tucked in, sucking up the porridge with noises that turned my guts. This table was the one where Mari and I had sat after escaping last night.

We should have taken the treasure and gutted Dio on the

way out. I'd frankly been having a good time before it all went to hell.

The crew sitting here didn't know it was my own face that outed us. It wasn't Mari. I'd heard a rude comment or two hurled her way throughout the night. She just gave them rude gestures and kept working.

There was no chance Dio wouldn't alert my father. It was only a matter of time. Hard to say whether we'd be safer on land or at sea when the attack arrived.

I'd take my chances at sea.

I pushed the plate of food away, something scratching at my mind as if I'd forgotten it. But what? A place to find new loot to pay my father back?

"Take it," I said to nobody, indicating the gray porridge left in my bowl.

Tromping up the companionway into the light, I tried to run through my liquor-addled thoughts. I squinted as the sun shone its rays directly in my eyes. Gods help any ship that crossed our path today. I'd storm their decks, take everything valuable, and scupper them.

I ran my thumb along the hilt of the cutlass that swung at my hip. Without it, I'd felt off-balance at the party. Freer, maybe. I should have been more focused.

Across the deck—thank the Divine for my black ship or else my eyes would have burned away—Mari repaired rope, running oil over the length of it where it tended to fray. She sat cross-legged, and the breeze fluffed her short hair.

Shit. I remembered.

Something about last night...

She was underneath me in that gold nothing of a dress,

moaning into my ear. My knife pried open the tree trunk behind her hip and inside…

My cock hardened at the memory. But that wasn't all. There was something else.

Sitting over there, she was just my shapeshifter doing chores. Nothing out of the ordinary. Nothing that should make me hard as stone.

You could sail to the ends of the earth and I'd sail with you.

It was coming back. We'd dared each other. Claimed we could satisfy each other better than our last partners. All she'd done was whisper in my ear and I'd reached out as if I had no self-control. But I was usually all control. In that moment, I'd wanted to control her.

And I'd been right to assume she needed a challenge, not some boring, limp-dicked meeting on shore. She responded to me simply pinning her.

How would she respond if I had my way with her in the secret room?

I exhaled. This was stupid. This was what happened when adrenaline had nowhere to go and two competitive people clashed.

Mari's eyes rose to meet mine. Did she remember what had happened? Well, she remembered that room at the party, at least. We'd done good work. Until it all went to shit.

Stuffing down an irritated growl, I let the sea air wash over me as I walked past her up the steps to take over the helm from Rhode. "Captain," Mari acknowledged.

I gripped the dark polished wood. Already, the sound of the waves and the breeze and the scent of salt brine began to lift my spirits. My nausea and headache subsided to the background. Above us, sea birds called to each other, black against wispy clouds. Ahead was possibility.

A sail snapped. Setting my jaw, I flexed my fingers against the helm, releasing a tiny bit of my power. It was limited at best—a distraction, a component of seduction, a way to wash off blood—but it felt good. A film of water slicked from my bare fingertips across the wooden knob, first warm, then frozen. I changed the temperature quickly, seeing if I could freeze the drips before they fell. The wetness stopped before it covered much of the helm. My power worked better on skin than other surfaces. But still.

We'd figure something out in Zenia, a way to get out of this mess. Right where it all started.

"Take a swim," I told Rhode, sensing her mood. She hadn't moved off the platform. "Be back in two notches." We didn't have a loud way of keeping time like the traditional bells, since we needed to sail unnoticed, so Euporia tracked a water clock, making sure it kept time with the sun.

Rhode smiled, her cheeks glittering. "Fish?"

"Of course. If you can get it."

She snorted. "If."

"Bring a net if you like."

She tipped her head to the sun and ran both hands through her green hair. "No need."

"There's the sister I know. Then I insist that you bring enough up for everyone's supper. Ajax gave us that slop again for the morning meal."

Rhode made a face. "He must have been up all night."

"Most of it." *Like all of us.* "We need strength. Get going. Off the side."

Her eyebrows lowered at me.

I met her gaze levelly. "You're wasting time."

She released a breath and shuffled down the short steps. In a flash of movement, she stripped down to her water resistant underthings before diving gracefully over the railing into the sea. A flash of green fins and she was gone.

Gauging our direction from the shadow of the mainsail, I adjusted north by degrees, easing the helm with leather-clad palms. Zenia had treasure. It was God-King Thenios's domain, and he'd have nothing less. People who'd done him personal favors had sprawling estates along the coast. Doubtful any one of them would have enough to pay my debt, but maybe the combination? Mari had shown a dozen times that she could slip in and—

Boom!

I spread my feet and held on as the *Lusca* keeled forward with a deep splash. The bowsprit dipped into the churning ocean. No wave had done that. Something was beneath us.

I ground my teeth. "All hands!" I shouted, spinning the wheel. The sheen of frozen water melted and dripped off as I focused on this threat. No one but my father could churn the entire sea and command its creatures.

Mari jumped to her feet on the deck just below me, abandoning the rope.

And Rhode's in the water...

Crew members poured into the light, running to their stations. We'd all felt the collision.

Come on, Rhode. If this was one of Father's monsters, it was huge. She would see it, even if she'd swum fast and far. I needed her out of the water *now*.

"Lower ladders!" I ordered. Most creatures couldn't use them, but Rhode could. "Batten down the hatches!"

Mari unrolled the ladders. They splashed lightly in the sea as sailors rolled out four crossbows, positioned both starboard and portside, and angled them down at the water.

Just beyond, the endless blue churned as something gigantic moved underneath for another strike, leaving a trail of white froth.

"Full sails! Where're my fire shots?"

One crossbow on each side replaced the bolt with a new launching device. Missiles made of pine resin and pitch, the size of Ajax's fist, attached to the front before getting set ablaze and launched. Euporia's invention that I'd adjusted over the years to make it more deadly.

"Hold steady!" I yelled, raising one hand and still gripping the helm with the other. The sailors manning the crossbows halted. "Mari, go aloft and report!"

She heard and sprang up the ratlines. I'd seen her climb in the middle of storm, so she should be able to handle this movement. With a higher view, she might be able to track my sister and the sea beast better than I could from the upper deck.

A flash of movement tore my eyes away from Mari's spry form. A spiny head half as long as the *Lusca* bobbed above the water before descending again. I couldn't see its teeth. But the sheer bulk and power, its spines and rubbery skin, meant only one thing.

Leviathan. It had to be.

Its serpent-like head and thick tentacles rammed and crushed ships before dragging them down into the deep. Gripping the helm tighter, I ran through the stories I'd heard at pirate-friendly ports. The Leviathan hadn't fed in two months. A silky line of water showed where the creature rushed toward us beneath the surface. At that speed, it would reach us in—

Boom!

The ship pitched wildly to starboard. I clung to the helm, wrestling to hold it steady. The wind floated my dark red captain's coat up to my waist. The crew tumbled like fish in an overturned basket. Mari wrapped her arms in the ropes. I only got impressions of her between waving black sails—legs kicking the air, her body curling, trying to find something solid. Someone else fell with a scream, skidding to the edge, propelling against the rail, clinging to air, and tipping over.

The *Lusca* righted itself, heaving left again. The fallen sailor —he'd been new, picked up in Hyperion—was gone. No chance to save him now. That brought the crew to fifteen.

My pulse churned, deep and fast as the sea. We were all one mistake from ending up in the jaws of the beast too. None of us were fully immortal, and who would even want to be when they could spend eternity in the belly of sea serpent?

"Shoot when you have a clear shot!" I shouted. Rhode could look after herself. She knew the world underwater as well as I knew the world above it.

Tentacles frothed above the surface of the water, snaking up half as high as the main mast. Water crashed onto the deck from the splash as one limb smacked down again. Sea spray drenched my front.

"Fire!" I bellowed, turning the wheel away from the creature.

A sailor holding the crossbow steady shrieked as a slimy suction cup latched onto his leg. The tentacle, thick as a dolphin, curled around his calves. His companion jumped back, leaving the crossbow to get dragged toward the edge too.

I inhaled a sharp breath, itching for my cutlass. "Fire!" I said again.

Someone of the opposite side of the ship turned the crossbow around, preparing to fire across the main deck.

Wood creaked under the weight of the Leviathan's limb as he dragged sailor and crossbow to the edge of the ship.

"Now!" I yelled.

The flaming bolt released, springing over the tarred planking and embedding into the flesh of the creature. A stir. A deep underwater scream of pain.

My guts twisted as I forced myself not to think of Rhode down there. She had to be far from this. She'd see the creature and retreat until it was safe.

Damn Basileus. Damn him to Abaddon.

A crack sounded as the railing snapped under the weight of the tentacle and both crossbow and sailor slipped overboard, gripped by the sucking limb of the Leviathan.

"Shit!" I hissed, my gaze ricocheting from the broken railing to the ropes high above.

The ship tilted like a drunk, back and forth. Mari reached the crow's nest.

"Mari, report!" I shouted above the scramble and spray.

"It's turning due south!" She put up her hand to shield from the sun.

Others heard and readied themselves for another attack from that side.

A small, high grunt keened into a scream of effort. My attention shot to the right, where someone clung to the starboard ladder. No, two people.

"Get her up!" I pointed.

With all this splashing and struggling, Rhode still had a fish tail, unable to shift completely. No wonder she had no focus. She was clutching the sailor who'd tipped over the side first. His limp body weighed more than she did.

Ajax sprang into action to tug them both aboard.

My grin was a ferocious grimace. Nothing to stop me from sending Father's creature to the depths. "Launch fire shots!"

With a sizzle and a hiss, two flaming bolts flew over the water in the direction of the Leviathan.

"Again!"

Two more.

From my vantage point, I had a good view to track the beast now. Its snake-like form writhed only a few ship-lengths away. It was angry.

The waves whipped up by the creature's thrashing rolled the *Lusca* side to side.

"Wind!" I ordered.

Zete flew up to the sails, forcing wind into them.

Our sudden speed made me brace myself. Spray misted my cheeks and the backs of my exposed fingers as I held the wheel steady. "Arm crossbows!" I looked back. "Here it comes!"

Two sailors to a crossbow placed the bolt and cranked the mechanism back to tighten the bowstring.

Klep knelt with Rhode beside the sailor who had fallen overboard. My sister had shifted back into her regular form, finally, naked and dripping except for a short sleeveless underdress. Was that a circular welt on her arm?

The *Lusca* skidded along the waves, but our enemy was faster. If I hadn't needed to grip the wheel so tight, I'd have flipped off the huge serpent in honor of Father. I'd show him what I thought of his tactics.

No one hangs the captain. No one drowns the captain either.

"Fire!"

Crossbow bolts shot into the water. The next thrash was violent. We'd hit center. A coil and a head flung above the waterline, big as whales. The sea shook. Maybe it was screaming underwater.

Good.

"Redouble wind!"

Even with Mari, who clung to the side of the crow's nest, Zete flapped hard among the black sails to keep up with the pace he set. He hated it when I told him to go faster. But if there was ever a time...

The sailor who'd gone overboard vomited water. He was alive after all. Thank the Divine. Klep turned his attention to my sister, wrapping her upper arm in a cloth bandage. If that creature had harmed her, I would chop it into filets and serve it to my crew.

As the doctor finished, Rhode met my eyes as if she could read my thoughts. In the briefest moment, she indicated she would be okay, and then stood unsteadily and limped to help, even injured and sopping wet. Some of the water running off her ran pink.

Twisting around, I looked back. Behind us was a mass of flailing, snake-like limbs. The Leviathan might die. I couldn't be sure, but it wouldn't attack us again today. It wouldn't eat anyone else on my crew. Basileus had not won this round. Despite the horror of what had just happened, a savage laugh escaped my lips. Victory rushed like storm through my veins.

Crew bustling, coattails flying, sea water spraying, we sailed on toward the horizon.

9

MARI

Later that afternoon, Rhode and I rummaged around below deck, righting the cargo that had tipped, rolled, or spilled after the Leviathan's attack. I eyed Rhode's bandage. Even in the dim light, the skin around it looked angry and red. I'd gotten my fair share of injuries, so I knew what infections looked like.

"You should have Klep look at that again."

"It's fine." Her eyes, which usually looked bright green, were glassy.

I bit my lip. Like her brother, Rhode didn't tend to follow advice. I didn't tend to give it, but the way Rhode was sagging in her work and dropping things into the thin layer of brackish water that lapped around our bare toes had me worried.

"Does the captain know?" I asked carefully, setting a barrel of liquor right-side up.

"I'm fine," she snapped. "I'm not the only one who was injured. Most of us lived. That's what matters."

Most of us. Acastus got dragged under by a tentacle. I could still hear his scream. We'd only met in passing. He all but pretended I didn't exist. But part of the reason I volunteered to help down here was to avoid the sight of that broken rail.

I grunted agreement, but couldn't stop my spiraling thoughts. If Terion knew his sister's wound was worse than a scratch, he'd do something drastic. That triumphant smile he'd worn as he steered us away from the churning sea monster—I didn't want to ruin that. The *Lusca* survived the Sea God's monster. Here was a victory to replace the mission that had failed.

But...

Rhode dropped to one knee. "Don't." She held out a hand to stop me from getting closer.

"Rhode," I pleaded. "Maybe you just need medicine."

She closed her full lips. Didn't she wonder what kind of poison infected her wound? She and her brother liked to pretend injuries didn't exist, unless they were the kind that could be avenged bloodily and quickly. After a pause, she said, "If you can get Klep to my room without Terion noticing."

Terion's turn on the watch was ending when he ordered us down here. Maybe he was napping in his cabin. We'd already had a hell of a day. Then again, maybe he'd take double watch. It wouldn't be the first time. I might be able to sneak Klep into Rhode's room. It was worth a try.

A splash told me she'd dropped something else.

"Okay, that's enough," I declared. "The captain needs you strong, not dead, so I'll take over doing this."

"I'll get someone to help if I need it. You need rest. I'll get the doctor for you." I'd done plenty of covert missions, but none aboard the *Lusca* itself. I understood why she didn't want to alert her brother, but right now, Rhode's wellbeing mattered more.

She actually listened to me, turning toward the door. My aching shoulders relaxed. My climb to the crow's nest had re-aggravated my shoulder injury, with the ship bucking wildly on the waves, but mine was a simple ache. Hers was something else, something deeper. Did that monster have poison in its bite?

Rhode's eyes flashed white, the only warning I had before she collapsed backward. I hurtled toward her, trying to catch her, but the ship rolled and she angled too far away.

Shit shit shit!

"I'll get the doctor!" Leaping over barrels and boxes strewn around the hold, I wrenched open the door. A thin pool of water skittered out. In the short hallway was a winged back. "Hey!" I yelled.

The sailor turned. It was a sleepy-looking Zete, his beard and hair wind-blown. His eyes narrowed when he saw me.

"Rhode," I hissed.

"Are you looking for her...?"

"No, she's—"

"What happened?" He picked up his pace to join me at the door.

"Can you get her up?" I asked, pointing backward into the room where Rhode lay face up among the debris. "You're stronger than me. I'm getting Klep. Bring her to our room, but, Zete"—I forced him to meet my eyes—"don't tell anyone about this."

Teeth gritted, Zete nevertheless followed my orders. "You owe me a bottle, sweetheart," he grumbled.

I sprinted down the hall to the steps leading up to the main deck. Even though we'd left the Leviathan behind hours ago, the crew still buzzed with activity, employing security measures, taking inventory of the ship's working parts, navigating, scrubbing. Someone stood in the crow's nest with a spyglass. A ladder leaned sideways across the gaping break in the ship's railing. My stomach coiled.

I ran up to the nearest sailor, Philamon. "Where's Klep?"

"With the captain."

Of course he is. "Is Terion injured?"

Philamon shrugged.

Had anyone else been injured or killed in the short fight for our lives? I glanced around but couldn't tell.

Quickly, I made my way to the stern, to the captain's quarters. The door was right behind the helm.

As much as I wanted to honor Rhode's wishes, she was lying unconscious with a festering wound. I wouldn't pussyfoot around trying to spare her feelings. I was much more interested in her life.

When I knocked, Ajax, who steered, gave me a strict look. He opened his mouth to speak but I yelled over him.

"Captain Terion, is the doctor in there?" Secrecy be damned.

"Doctor?" Ajax asked from behind me. "Mari, what do you think you're doing?"

But Terion's voice answered from the other side of the door. "Come in!"

I obeyed and went inside. In all my time on the *Lusca*, I'd never been in this room. Terion himself invited you in, or you stayed out. The captain's quarters were magnificent. A large bank of windows overlooked the sea from the back of the ship. On the left were shelves and a medley of tables and chairs, looking almost as if they had washed ashore that way. Maps covered the tabletops, and fine netting hung in strips over the shelves, protecting the contents. On that side of the room were oddments and treasures and souvenirs haphazardly piled or displayed like memories. A sculpture of multiple mermaids looked vaguely familiar. There was a shrunken hand in a jar, its nails long and black. Over there, a number of fine knives skewered a wooden statue of Basileus. Pens and poison darts hung from the netting as if placed there. A cup and bottle stood on top of Kantharos on the nearest map.

The other side of the room was totally different. Plain, austere, except for one feature. On the right, inset into the wall and covered by a dark red curtain pulled back by a golden tassel, was a large bed. Beyond the foot of the bed was a door to another room.

"Is that Mari?"

I shook off my curiosity and followed the voice. It came from the adjacent room. "Yes, is the doctor there with you?"

I entered the short, dark paneled hallway and entered... a washroom, where Terion lay naked in a claw-footed bath, his face half shaven. His arms draped along the lip of the tub, strong and veined and tattooed. From one hand dangled a flask of rum. His dark eyes were half-closed in apparent contentment, which I was about to break. His wet skin and rounded muscles brought back memories from last night. Had I really...? Hopefully he didn't remember.

Terion didn't look at me. Klep sat on a stool next to him, holding a blade to his cheek. Steam trailed along the floor.

"Klep," I said calmly, "could you help me with something?"

"Is that why you burst into my quarters?" Terion drawled.

I fisted my hands. "There's something I'd like you to look at."

Now Terion perked up, eyes darting to me at last. He set down the flask. "What?"

Klep lowered the blade. I exhaled. "I think someone might have gotten injured in the fight," I said, watching that lowered blade. "It would be good to take another look."

Terion sat up in the bath, sloshing the water and giving me a view of his entire naked chest. I'd seen it before—we were shipmates—so why did the sight throw me off now? Why did it make me want to see more and *not* see more at the same time?

"You were with Rhode in the cargo hold," he said. "Is she all right?"

I swallowed. "She's fine. Just needs a new bandage."

His fingers tightened on the edge of the tub. "You wouldn't have interrupted for a bandage." He squinted at me, assessing.

"I'll come and take a look," Klep said, stowing the shaving blade and laying a soothing hand on the captain's arm. He didn't look at me, which was typical.

Terion, on the other hand, didn't take his eyes off me. "How bad is it?" he demanded. Froth from his shave still covered part of his face, so how did he manage to look so menacing?

I hesitated.

"How bad?" Terion opened and closed his hand without looking. Klep laid a towel in his open palm before sweeping past me out the door without a word.

"No, no!" I protested, but the captain was already wiping his face and standing up.

Oh...

I'd seen Terion shirtless and knew he was objectively beautiful. We all knew it. Seeing him now—*all* of him—wasn't the same kind of clinical, everyday experience. My core heated, tightened. Memories of him holding me down as we ground against each other bloomed sweat at the hollow of my neck. This man, this demi-god, my captain, had briefly simulated sweltering sex with me. The sex wasn't real, but the contact had been.

I'd felt those biceps, that toned stomach, those thick thighs against mine. But there was more I hadn't touched. Skin. So much skin, dark and weathered and somehow still soft. He had a burst of the same blue-green scales on his chest that he had on his cheekbone. The swell of his pectorals, the cut line above his hip, his long, thick—

Terion's eyes briefly met mine before becoming was all business, knotting the towel around his waist and stepping out of the water. "Where is she?"

Did he even notice how he had knocked the wind out of me? Besides the slight widening of his eyes and movement of his throat, he didn't seem proud or embarrassed. Mine must have been a normal response for him. Gods, I saw why.

He didn't look at me now.

"In her room," I answered honestly.

He stalked past me, leaving me to trail behind. Terion had a fierce concern for all his crew, but he cared most for Rhode. We all knew it. People had their favorites and the captain's was his sister.

Terion and I got along, but I was a tool for him. That was okay. No reason to feel the syrupy glue of envy through my chest. I wasn't injured—his sister was. Still, the moment he pushed me aside to get to the door clogged my throat.

Stop whining and work. I couldn't stand my aunt, the one who'd said that all the time, but she was right. I'd check on

Rhode, see if I could do anything for her, then return to the hold and finish my job. Terion and Klep would see Rhode through this, if anyone could. My heart twisted at the image of her eyes rolling back.

Enough with these selfish thoughts. Dwelling on them wouldn't help Rhode and wouldn't help myself.

But whenever I closed my eyes, Terion's fierce, inaccessible body shone there like a tattoo on the back of my lids.

10

TERION

Salt air clung to my skin as I marched over the main deck. The smooth, tarred surface against the bare soles of my feet began to ground my panic. Rhode was alive. She must be. Mari wouldn't have been that careful with her words if the message was death. Death was blunt, like a punch to the head.

I ran back through the Leviathan attack. My sister had seemed all right once she got out of the water. A little bruised, with a cut or suction mark on her arm. What could have gone wrong in the hours since then?

Was it the curse? Had I not been careful enough?

The bleeding image of Lanan lying dead filled my mind as I jumped the distance down to the darkness belowdecks. Basileus would not take my sister. He would not.

Rhode shared a room with Mari and Euporia. Their door was just beginning to close, a light brown hand gently pulling it shut behind him. I'd caught up with Klep. Grabbing the handle, I yanked the door open, following the doctor inside.

"Rhode! Rhode?" I demanded.

My sister lay slumped in her hammock, one leg draped off the edge, her eyes closed and green hair clumped in wet strands around her face.

Behind me, light brightened. Mari must have brought a lantern. But more light only highlighted how flushed Rhode looked. Blankets balled up around her feet, and her hands made fists as if she braced for something.

"What's wrong with her?" I snapped.

As if answering me, Rhode drew in a rattling breath. My core seized.

Klep finished taking her pulse and added a few more prods and jabs that meant nothing to me. These checks and signals had better tell him exactly what was wrong with my sister, or I'd replace the skinny doctor with a new one at the next port. "It looks like poison," he declared softly. "Octopus toxin, if I had to guess, or something like it."

"Don't guess," I snarled. "Fix her."

"Her limbs are stiffening. This..."

His next words disappeared in the roar of my own pulse beating in my ears, my vision blackening, my lungs forcing sips of air out. *Fuck!* This hadn't happened since Basileus' henchman slit a woman's throat in front of me. We'd just met and had a fuck. I was walking her back to the tavern where she worked when the attacker jumped out of the shadows. I took revenge first, then came a whirlpool of adrenaline so intense I shook in cold sweat fighting for breath in my cabin. Ajax covered for me. We almost missed the vessel we came there to rob. No one else knew what had happened, and they would never know.

I couldn't panic.

I couldn't panic.

I curled my toes against the planking and dug my short fingernails into the faint grooves of my trident tattoo.

"She's..." I said, too breathless.

"Alive," Klep confirmed.

"How long?"

He turned his eyes to me. "Not long."

My hand wandered to where my sword usually hung at my side, but I only wore a towel. If I'd had the blade, I'd have stabbed him through the gullet for those two words.

I drew in impossible air. "What does she need?"

Klep exhaled. Nothing rattled him. "We could try wide-leaf penthesilea."

"Do you have some?"

"We would have to find some but—"

"Where?" I'd be damned before I'd let my sister die. If this plant grew on the northern tip of the Beyond, I'd find a way to get there.

"I don't think—"

"I don't fucking care what you think. Your captain asked you a question."

Rhode drew another painful breath. She still hadn't opened her eyes.

"Zenia's markets might have some," Klep answered.

Perfect. That was the closest Realm anyway and our destination.

"I'll tell Ajax. And Zete."

I spun at the voice. Mari stood behind me. She'd been silent the whole time until now.

"Go," I said.

She sprinted from the room.

Light flickered over the green-blue scales on Rhode's cheek

when I turned back to her. "Do everything you can to keep her alive," I growled. "If she dies, so do you." I could find a new ship's doctor. I couldn't replace Rhode in a thousand lifetimes.

Basileus had gone too far. Again. *Fuck him!*

Nerves in my hands tingled and my vision sparked again. I'd held off the panic for a moment, but it washed back like a riptide. All my tight control hadn't protected her. It hadn't been enough.

I tried to form fists so my hands wouldn't shake, but my body wouldn't obey. I was flying apart.

Had to get back to my cabin. No one could know.

Reputation. Never panicked. Wasn't weak.

Confident. Unbeatable.

I tried to breathe, but the air was thick as water.

Quick as I could, I paced the length of the ship back to the stern. *Just get behind a door, wait for it to pass...*

Captain Asterion was Prince of the Ocean, not a fucking weakling who couldn't protect his crew. Vulnerability like this, when I couldn't think, couldn't see, made us the perfect target.

I climbed the short steps on shaking legs. My unfocused eyes fell on Ajax at the wheel, and Mari beside him. She watched me with concern.

"Leave him be." Ajax.

Another step was all. Over the threshold. I reached back for the door. Closed it. Didn't make it to the bed before I crumpled to the floor, drawing my knees to my chest, holding myself tight so I didn't fly apart. The *Lusca* whispered to me. It didn't say what would happen tomorrow.

II

MARI

Something was wrong with the captain. His eyes looked as glossy as Rhode's had been when she collapsed in the hold.

Octopus toxin, Klep had said. Someone from home had that once. Her limbs locked up, her breathing stalled, she was dizzy and nauseated, and then the healer gave her... something, and it worked. In two days, she got up.

I glanced at the horizon. Zenia was nearly five days away. We'd taken this route often enough that I knew it as well as any. Hell, Calix lived on the coast of Zenia. I wasn't excited to go back, but we needed that plant or medicine Klep had mentioned. Its name didn't sound familiar—it wasn't available in the swamps where I'd grown up. So what had the local healer used?

"What happened?" Ajax rumbled from his post at the helm.

Rhode's condition couldn't be secret anymore, not now that Terion and Klep knew. "Rhode," I answered. "She got scratched or bitten. The toxin is spreading and she's... She needs help. A plant in Zenia."

We both swayed as the ship picked up speed. I'd told Zete we needed him—he wasn't thrilled—and then I'd run to Ajax, telling them both to make for Zenia as fast as possible. The black sails billowed with Zete's wind. He was already tired, so I didn't know how long he could keep up his power. Would he give out before Rhode could get what she needed?

"That explains the captain," Ajax said grimly.

"He's not sick too, is he?"

Ajax closed his mouth.

My pulse spiked. "Do you know what's wrong with him?"

"It's not your affair."

I chewed my lip. Of course it wasn't. Unless I needed information for a mission, the others usually avoided telling me more than they had to. I glanced at the door.

Overhead, a sea bird called.

A memory rattled loose and I gasped. Peering up to squint at the bird, I couldn't get a good look to see what kind it was. If the white wings were black at the joints...

"Zete!" I cried, cupping my hands around my mouth. "Stop!"

He didn't so much as look at me.

"What are you doing?" Ajax demanded. "Captain's orders, you said."

"I need to look at that bird."

"What the devil—"

"The bones. If it's an ocean petrel, we can use the bones to help Rhode. They have a breeding ground where I grew up. Something like this happened to a person I knew, and the bones make—"

"Mari, stop."

A big hand landed on my shoulder, close to my neck. I froze.

"I'm following orders, not you." Ajax, huge and immovable, focused again on the horizon, effectively dismissing me. The flapping of Zete's wings and the slapping of waves against the hull throbbed against my urgent thoughts.

My jaw flexed. Desperation surged through my veins. I briefly considered cajoling Ajax, playing to his pride so he would do what I wanted, but he was far less susceptible than most to that tactic. Playing the camouflaged cuttlefish didn't work on the *Lusca* the way it did everywhere else. Years with the crew had revealed too much of myself.

I unhooked a spyglass from the wall and aimed it at the bird.

Black joints. And there were three of the creatures. In our speed, they became little specks.

With a cry of frustration, I set down the spyglass and dashed down, across, down, and into the ship's mess. Smell guided me to a small barrel of salted fish. I grabbed a handful and ran back on deck. I could still see the birds, but they were far away. Breathing hard, I flung a fish high in the air over the ocean.

"Hey!" someone yelled behind me.

Being reckless with rations earned a strong punishment, but I didn't care. Rhode didn't treat me as an outcast. We were even friendly, and her life was on the line.

The birds swooped closer at the glint of scales and scent of fish. Good. I hadn't been sure the salted kind would work to lure them closer.

I hurled another fish. This time, one petrel zoomed into the water, coming up with its prize in its mouth.

Thank the tides they were fast enough to keep up with the speeding ship.

"Grab a net," I ordered. Hopefully curiosity would make someone help me, at least.

It didn't.

I was running out of fish and the birds were still too far away.

"Stop!" Strong hands pulled me from the ship's edge. This time it wasn't Ajax, but two others. "Are you raving?"

I wrestled out of their grip, shoulder throbbing as I wrenched myself away. "No!" I threw my second to last fish over the side. No nets in sight.

Spinning, I spied the rigging. Small squares of rope. That would do, except that more sailors had emerged from belowdecks and stood in my way. I whipped out the dagger from the sash around my waist. "Move or be gutted!" My heartbeat charged through my chest at the threat. I'd done it. This would finally convince them to abandon me, or, at this rate, throw me overboard. My eyes flicked to the partially reconstructed gap in the railing where the Leviathan had suctioned and squeezed a pirate over the side.

No one flinched at my warning, but no one advanced either.

"Move!" I roared, jumping on the ropes. I sliced madly at the rigging.

Curses rang out as more crew members flooded the deck.

"She's destroying the ship!" someone yelled. Daggers and cutlasses bristled from their hands.

I climbed higher, hacking at the tarred ropes. Hands tried to pull me down.

"Mari!" Zete bellowed from above, actually using my name for once. In his shock or distraction, the wind bursting from his hands calmed enough for me to get a full breath.

Terion will thank me.

I stubbornly refused to look above or below, listening only for the cry of birds. The ropes tugged and bounced as someone climbed up after me. A few more mad slices and I fell with a thud as the ropes split. Two thumps on the planking meant someone else had fallen too. I finally looked to see who it was. Seven angry pirates stared me down. But now I had an unwieldy net. Enough to catch salvation for Rhode.

"Stay the fuck away from me!" I cried. Holding the dagger and the net while threatening the others wasn't easy. But I only needed a few seconds.

"Mari, stop!" This time, the deep order came from Ajax. He was first mate, second only to the captain. But I couldn't stop, not if it meant Rhode would live.

"I have to do this," I pleaded.

My nostrils flared in frustration. If I'd been a stranger instead of a crew member, I'd already be dead. I saw the flash of hesitation in their eyes.

Good enough. I flung the last fish into the water by the bow. (I'd stuffed it in my pocket to climb.) Gripping the net, I hung it off the side. If this worked, the ropes would scoop up the bird and I could haul it ashore.

A hairy arm braced against my neck, hauling me back. With a grunt and a scream, I pitched all my body weight forward again. A few more seconds. That was all.

"Kill the wench," someone suggested.

I wouldn't give anyone the chance. "Let go!" I shouted, slicing backward with my knife. "Let go or I'll gut you! This is for the captain."

Hesitation again as the arm released me. I felt them watch me now, as if I were stringing my own noose.

I'd had cockeyed plans before, but this bordered on crazy. I'd get strung up for this. That, or the captain might leave me to drown.

The petrel plunged after the fish. I held my breath. A slight tug as the wings crooked in the net.

I hauled it back up, hand over hand. Every twitch of the bird in the net had my heart battering against my ribs.

The bird struggled, squawking, as I flopped it over the side. In one movement, I ended it with my dagger. Blood bloomed across its nearly severed neck, but I had no time to lament hurting the creature.

"What the hell, Mari?"

I ignored them all, sheathing my blade and gripping the warm center of the dead bird with both hands before running it downstairs.

In Rhode's room, Klep looked sweaty and ashen. His eyes blew wide as I crashed inside.

"The bones," I panted. "If you grind up the bones, it stops the poison." I tried to hand him the bird, but he just stared at me as if I'd grown a second head. Blood coated my fingers"Trust me."

"Mari..." His gaze moved past my shoulder to the doorway, where others crowded to watch, judging from the shifting sound of boots and clicking of metal buttons and blades.

Sharpness bit at the corners of my eyes. Why did no one believe me? This could save Rhode's life.

"Take the bones. Crush them up with water. I promise, I promise…" I couldn't tell him it was a swamp remedy. Most people dismissed anything that came from there as hogwash. "The captain said to try it."

Klep licked his dry lips and gingerly took the dead bird. When he gave a small nod, I sighed, allowing myself to look at Rhode, who hadn't moved. "Okay," I said, weakness seeping in. I had to fix the rigging. If the crew didn't hang me first.

I turned slowly, lifting my chin and keeping my hand on the dagger's hilt. Rhode was dying and Terion was devastated. I did what I had to do, even if no one believed me.

Half the crew stuffed the dark passage outside our room. I didn't stand a chance against so many. These were my shipmates, but now they glared with murder in their eyes.

"I was helping Rhode. She's not—" But no one listened. Now that the show was over, they disarmed me in a flash. Burly arms and tickling cutlasses pressed against me. There was no trial, no chance to explain why I'd harmed the ship and thrown the rations. My blood-soaked hands felt small against the violence of a pirate crew. Insults and curses floated over me. Redley's hands found my throat. He was the short-tempered son of a wealthy merchant. I never trusted him. Always thought he stole. Now, he squeezed with obvious anger. I flailed like a fish outside my own door for another breathless beat until I blacked out.

When I woke up, I lay in a cold pool of bilgewater behind the iron bars of the brig.

The crew would let me out of the brig when we reached Zenia. Probably. Hopefully.

My throat throbbed, scratchy and bruised from being choked. They hadn't strung me up on the yardarm as I had feared. But this wasn't good. I could only think they wanted to check with Captain Terion before they did anything more drastic.

Crew came first, after all, I thought bitterly.

I hadn't been close to any members of the crew unless you counted being friendly with Terion, Rhode, and to a lesser degree Ajax. After this, there was no way they'd let me belong, even if they did miraculously keep me on.

It was hard to tell how long I'd been down here, since I'd been unconscious when they brought me, and the only light was a dim red lantern. I didn't regret a thing, though. I'd kill that bird again if it meant saving Rhode. Without it, there was no way she would have made it all the way to Zenia for the medicinal plant Klep suggested. She was fading too fast, limp and wheezing in that hammock.

So, they wouldn't leave me down here to die, would they?

My mouth already felt gummy with thirst, and my bare feet shriveled white from being in the shallow water sloshing on the floor of my cell. The box of iron grating was too small for me to lie down. I hated to think what would happen if the crew needed to cage Ajax. His gigantic shoulders would probably press against opposite sides at once.

Ajax. He should have listened to me. Should have let me try to help Rhode, but the captain was king on board, and his commands ruled, even when something was clearly wrong with him—devastation at seeing his sister like that? Illness? Whatever it was, he seemed nothing like his normal cocky self.

As he stepped into his quarters, he'd looked almost vulnerable. It was weird even to think the word in relation to him. Still, he'd been all but naked, stumbling, glazed over.

Please let them both be all right.

A new wave of fear took me. The crushed bones of the petrel would help Rhode's symptoms, but what was wrong with Terion? Was anyone helping him?

I pictured him alone in his sumptuous cabin, tried to imagine him afraid or weak, but all I kept seeing was water gushing down his glorious body as he stood from the bath, muscles hard and rippling, ferocity in his determined gaze. Despite myself, my skin heated.

I let out a tiny scoff. I was no better than women on shore who took one look at him and begged to come aboard for a night. Who knew I had it in me?

My drenched clothes clung to my skin. It smelled like sulphur down here. *Should I yell, bang on the bars?* No, I wouldn't give them the satisfaction. They'd find out I was right soon enough, and then they'd set me free.

My cracked lips tasted like salt when I ran my tongue over them. The bars dug into my shoulder blade where I leaned back.

It's not forever.

I closed my eyes and tried to relax. *You're a child who likes snug places. You're not trapped. You're cozy here, playing pretend.*

A footstep splashed in front of the bars. My eyes flew open. In front of me were brown laced boots, loose pants tucked in at the top, a sword dangling from the thick waistband, a bandolier stretching across a thick chest, and a long blood-red captain's jacket.

Terion. He watched me with an inscrutable expression. All his earlier weakness had completely left. Only the swaggering intensity I knew so well remained.

Relief and fear hit me in a dizzying wave. Why had he come himself? Had my plan worked? Was he here to end me himself? I stood, wincing at the pain in my waterlogged feet.

"Rhode's fever's broken. She can breathe again," he said, oddly calm after everything that had happened. "Klep told me you brought him the remedy."

A rock lodged painfully in my damaged throat. Rhode would live. "I told him about it," I mumbled in a hoarse voice.

"And you mangled my ship."

So my actions had only earned me a stay of execution, not a full pardon. He loved the *Lusca* more than he did most people. I made a face. "Well, that's..."

"Thank you." His eyes glowed in the darkness. Even more than he had on the trip to Dio's island, or during the steamy moment we had afterward, he seemed to look at me without seeing anything beyond. Only me.

The intensity of his gaze made my throat constrict even more. "Of course. Crew comes first."

A tiny smirk teased the corner of his lips. "You can't fix the rigging from in there." He produced a key from one of the many pockets of his jacket and fitted it in the rusty lock. "You sound terrible."

"I know, Captain," I croaked.

My chest loosened when the door eased open on squeaky, groaning hinges. The fear I'd bottled for the past few hours surged up and I shivered violently.

Terion's hands landed on my shoulders, both propping me up and stopping me before I could move past him. "I owe you a captain's favor."

His scrutiny felt uncomfortable, as if he touched more than my shoulders. "No, it was... I would have done it anyway." Honestly, I wanted to fade into the background, without giving him the slightest reason to resent me or owe me another debt. Plus, the crew resented me already.

I had to admit, I liked the way the words sounded in his mouth, though. And the way he looked at me. His attention and approval felt like sweet liquor. I almost took back my muttered words.

"You've earned a favor," he repeated. Then he grimaced, releasing me. "You smell like death, Mari."

"I've been stuck down here," I protested. "Is the crew still angry?"

"I explained enough. You don't look like a lunatic to me. If anyone lays a hand on you, I'll lash them to the mast."

Still angry, then. But I bit back a smile. My gamble had paid off after all. Rhode would live, and Terion would whip the next person who hurt me.

His fingers drifted up to the side of my neck. He wore gloves with the fingers cut off, so rough bare fingertips traced the bruises. "Starting here," he said, jaw squaring. His gaze latched onto mine. "Who was it?"

I had the mad urge to lean into him. Terion wasn't soft, but he felt like a safe place just then. It felt good when I pretended to be his lover at the party and got to snuggle my head against his chest. The idea of gripping his waist, smelling his sea-salt sweat, as he leveled a blade at the scallywag who choked me...

I shook off my crazy thoughts. "Redley," I said breathlessly. "He thought I'd gone raving."

Terion straightened suddenly, sneering down at the evidence of what had happened to me. "Don't defend him."

I didn't need him to say it twice.

"We'll pick up another sailor in Zenia," he declared simply.

My blood cooled, then heated. After a beat, I asked, "Is that my favor?"

"No, no. That's a pleasure."

My heart beat crazily behind my ribs. One moment, I expected to be treated like my aunt would have treated me—with disdain before abandoning me—and the next, the captain himself reinstated me in place of somebody else. My wounds mattered. *I* mattered to him.

I chewed my lip. "And... are you all right?" I asked in a voice that barely resembled my own. Terion had been shaken or ill too the last time I'd seen him.

"Always." He flashed his signature grin. "Wash up, fix the rigging. We land in Zenia in a few days. I want you ready to be my shapeshifter again."

I hadn't imagined his struggle after seeing Rhode unconscious in our room, but if he wanted to ignore it, I could do that. At least he hadn't come down to execute me for disobeying orders. A captain's favor, he'd said. My curiosity burned despite myself. "You have a new plan when we get there?"

"Working on it." His coat swished as he turned to walk beside me to the exit. "We're taking more than money. After this, what Father just pulled..." He slowed.

"You'll hurt him."

His gaze snapped to mine. "I'll torture him." His voice went low and threatening. Ice slithered down my spine. He meant it.

I owed Captain Terion everything for giving me a chance, and I wouldn't blow it by hesitating now. "Tell me what to do."

His lips parted—maybe nothing—then closed again. "Oh, I will."

My mind hurtled back to the fragments I remembered from that night when we'd gotten drunk. How he told me to free myself from his grip. How I'd never been so turned on in my life.

But that had been a game to him. Only a game. He didn't mean for those words to sound so seductive. What was wrong with me? The past couple days had simply thrown me off balance.

I needed to get out of here. It was gratefulness, relief, that made me read into things. He didn't have lust in his eyes when he touched my neck. It wasn't jealousy that made him threaten to kill my attacker. His words didn't refer to the mysterious, rough sex he had in the secret room. He had no interest in fucking his little backwater thief.

Still, he said he'd torture Redley for touching me...

"Good," I said as I reached the ladder. I didn't wait for a response before climbing up.

13

TERION

If my panic hadn't lasted a godsdamned hour, I could have helped Mari before that traitor Redley choked her and threw her in the brig. I heard the shouting and thought my *Lusca* was under attack. But I couldn't move. I struggled to force air into my lungs as I shook and held myself like a fucking coward. My mind feasted on dread until it simply wore itself out.

I watched Mari top the companionway in front of me, my mind so full my skin felt on fire. Rhode would live, but Mari had bruises on her neck, and all because I hadn't been there to stop it. My fist closed on the hilt of my blade as I followed her up.

Philamon was the first sailor to pass. I yanked him forward by the front of his shirt until our faces were a breath away. "Where's Redley?"

Mari spun, a concerned look on her face. Below her down-turned mouth were finger marks.

I gave Philamon a shake.

"Hauling water for dishes," he stammered.

My eyes snapped up. Yes, there, near the side. I released Philamon.

"Mari, get new rope for rigging and bring it here," I said, striding toward Redley's back, light-skinned and bare in the sunlight. He was a strong man but didn't grow up like I did. He didn't scrape to earn everything, get called a waste and monstrosity, bargain and borrow to start a life on the sea. He didn't earn a reputation as the most feared pirate on the ocean by decades of ruthlessness and cunning.

But I did.

"Redley," I greeted.

He turned. Then dropped the bucket in his hands when he saw my expression.

My lips curved into a bitter smirk. "Wasting water."

"What do you n—?"

But I was already on him, pressing the tip of my blade to the underside of his chin. By the time I walked him back to the main mast, Mari had returned with the ropes. I hadn't noticed she was limping before, and the observation only made me murderous.

"Tie him," I ordered, nicking Redley's chin as I flicked the cutlass away and shucking off my jacket. No need to get my favorite coat dirty.

"The hell?" Redley cried, jerking his arm away from the trunk of the mast, refusing to be tied. He stared at Mari, newly freed from the brig where he'd left her.

"I told you," I said, losing all patience, "Mari saved my sister, with no help from you rats."

"You should have seen her, Captain!"

"With your fingers wrapped around her neck like this?" I grabbed him with my free hand. He went still. "Crew comes first," I growled into his ear as he wheezed, struggling for a breath.

The rattling noise reminded me too much of my own breathing an hour ago. I let go of his throat and forced his arms back around the mast. "Wrist, wrist," I instructed Mari, pointing where she should tie.

Unlike the other sailors gathering nearby, her round eyes showed no horror. She did as I asked neatly and thoroughly, with good knots. A question formed in her face when she looked at me for more instruction—*are you really going to do this?*

Hell yes, I am.

The prospect of hurting Redley seemed to excite her. Damn it, I was excited too. I circled the villain, running my tongue over the sharp edge of my teeth. Mari backed away. They'd all seen me take care of people like this, just not among our own crew.

Redley stopped protesting. He knew what was coming. It showed all over his milky pale face.

"You see this?" I said, not raising my voice. I didn't need to. Everyone was already listening, frozen in place.

Mari chewed her lip almost unconsciously as she stared at the man bound to the mast. It was as if she feared he might disappear. A piece of short dark hair fell over her forehead. I could almost see her disbelief like fog that someone would do this for her. Her expression almost made my wicked grin falter.

She put up with shit from the others. I knew that. She had to earn her way up, like all of us. But she was a good sailor and an even better thief.

When I found her, she needed someone to focus her talents. I was more than happy to oblige. She started out awkward but was finding her way. The fire in her, that was what first caught my eye. She was tough and quick-fingered. Perfect for the *Lusca*.

Aboard my ship, I doled out punishment. I was king. And I had to make it clear that here was an edict—no hurting Mari.

Redley's bare chest wavered with shaky breaths. This piece of scum laid his hands on her. He treated her worse than Dio, who paddled his fingers along her hips. Redley had almost killed her.

I rolled up my sleeves and flexed my palm on the hilt. This man was no crewmate of mine.

"This is a man," I said slowly, relishing the moment, "who followed Mari to hurt her." I slashed at his calf.

Redley let out a bellow of pain. Blood gushed down his leg like a red sock.

"She saved my sister's life. But what did he see?" I cut a deep X through one of his eyes. Delicate work with a blade the size of mine. Redley's shriek almost drowned out my next words. "A crazy girl. A stupid girl. An excuse"—I kicked the wound on his leg—"to choke the life out of her with his bare hands." I hacked at the hands bound behind his back. Blood scattered through the air.

Mari stood just behind me but I didn't look at her. Wrists had tendons and bones and blood and took full-body force to chop free. I stopped at one.

The stump of his arm released, no longer held by the ropes. Redley gave a constant stream of guttural moans. I pictured him throttling Mari again and paced to his front.

"No one touches her." I almost added *but me*. That didn't make sense, so I swallowed it back. "Those hands," I continued, "wrapped around her neck and squeezed. I bet that got you hard, didn't it? You sick son of a bitch." Real rage started blackening my vision. I had to end this. He was already chum for the sharks. I'd make it official.

With a final slice across his throat, I left him lifeless, hanging by one arm in Mari's knot.

"Throw him over," I said, the rush already subsiding.

I plucked a handkerchief from the pocket of my jacket on the ground, careful not to get blood on the coat, and ran the cloth over the filthy blade. For a few seconds, I swiped the handkerchief back and forth. The smell of blood tanged the back of my throat.

There was a splash by the side of the ship. I looked up again.

The crew acted strangely quiet, but Mari met my eyes with something like eagerness. Hope, even. Power thrummed through me again. I couldn't help her in that godsdamned panic, but I was happy to defend her now. I raised my eyebrows at her. She was one of us, and she needed to know it.

She also had to fix the rigging she'd shredded to help my sister.

I indicated the bloodstained deck and ropes. "Those are for the new rigging," I said.

"Yes, Captain," she answered sharply, barely any hint of the rasp I'd heard from her in the brig.

The words set my blood heating. I watched her bend to gather the bloodstained rope, flexible as an acrobat. A tiny smile flirted on her lips.

Suddenly, I wanted to give her more for saving Rhode today, wanted this feeling of power to continue.

Had she said where her ex lived?

❧ 14 ❧

MARI

Several long days of repairing the rigging and the railing left my feet and hands aching. Captain Terion strode the deck like he did every day, hovered closer to me than usual, like a watchful shark defending its territory.

He'd already made his point. Loudly.

Redley lay in pieces at the bottom of the sea, all for strangling me. He hadn't killed me. My voice was better, though a little raw. And still, Terion made an example of a crew member just for me.

I was so shocked as I watched that my thoughts didn't make sense. Afterward, though, I felt like a weight had lifted off my back. Until then, I had no idea I carried weights around. Each day was simply a new job with new focus. Fix these ropes, spy on that nobleman, take the spyglass to the crow's nest, find Dio's money and take it back to the ship...

As I worked my fingers red with repairing the ropes, other weights settled in my mind, appearing like deep sea creatures lurking in the darkness. They were ugly. My aunt blaming me for my mother's death, calling me an abomination. Learning to hide my swamp accent so strangers didn't tighten their lips and swerve to avoid me. Feeling grateful when a mark smiled at me like a friend because I'd convinced them I was someone else. Calix finding out I'd faked it with him every time.

Salty breath grew thick in my lungs and my injured throat. Again and again, I found myself searching for Terion's confident form, that blood-red captain's coat that matched his head scarf. Watching him for a second loosened my hitched shoulders and swirling thoughts.

The crew didn't pay attention to me, or if they did it was mostly to scowl or heap more work in my lap. Ajax stayed aloof. The rest felt sour that I'd been right and they were wrong. I wasn't crazy. I saved Rhode and the captain knew it.

He believed me over them.

After another day of repairs in the sun, I had a turn on watch. The sea lay calm and Zete slept, probably exhausted. (He hadn't threatened me when I cut up the ropes, though he probably would have if he'd gotten permission to stop blowing the sails.) The *Lusca* sliced slowly through the blackening waves. All I had to do was check every hour or so that we hadn't drifted off our straight course toward Zenia.

I held the watch right before we were due to spy land, so we landed along Zenia's coastline after I fell asleep. Klep gave me ointment for my feet that smelled like perfume—captain's orders. I'd fallen asleep in seconds, soothed by the sound of Rhode's even breathing in the hammock nearby.

"What the—?" Euporia cried.

I cracked my eyes open. Something must have really startled her. Euporia rarely spoke, always tinkering with the water clock or small carpentry jobs.

She stood in the doorway, looking down at something. The

tail of the blue sash she wound around her head reached the middle of her back, a couple rogue blonde strands escaping around the edges. She hadn't retied the scarf yet like she did every morning. So, she'd just woken up too.

She turned to look at me in a question. In her hands was a plain wooden box.

"What's that?" I asked quietly, rolling out of my hammock. The mix of excitement and insecurities that roiled beneath the surface yesterday left me hollow and irritable this morning.

She thrust the thing toward me. The box was about the size of the cups in the mess. I lifted the lid and let it snap back again.

I glanced at Euporia, who shook her head. She didn't know where it had come from. Something in the wary gesture told me she didn't like how violence among the crew seemed to follow me around.

Maybe she was right to be distrustful.

Inside the box were two severed fingers. Both were still bleeding.

Were they Redley's? No, I'd tossed the hand overboard myself. Besides, the coloring wasn't quite right. It looked familiar, though.

Was the crew all right? Was this a message? And, if it was a message, why was it delivered to us instead of Ajax or the captain?

I had to show someone. Maybe they could make sense of this. Hopefully everyone's fingers were accounted for. I jogged out of the room and up the companionway. The crew's bad mood could go to hell. The incident was behind us, and I needed to know whose body parts these were.

I peeked again into the box. The fingers were large, probably male, with mid-tone skin. Only a light tan. That meant they weren't Terion's, at least. The nails were clean but the knuckles had grime.

Wait.

I halted halfway across the main deck, Euporia at my heels. These weren't...

"I see you got my gift."

My head snapped up to see Terion, no coat, trotting down from his quarters. Around us, several other sailors attended their business.

Terion offered a wicked, toothy smile. "You're welcome."

"What the hell is this?" I demanded.

So many emotions warred inside me that I felt coiled tight, ready to spring. My defenses locked into place, but did I even want them?

Talking with Terion was one of the only times I could be real. I felt cornered, seen. And at the same time taken advantage of—again.

"I had some... irritation to burn off." His eyes sparkled. "I thought you'd be happy."

"You couldn't just fuck someone at the port? 'Cause this is—"

"Calix, yes."

My blood went cold. I sensed the crew looking at me. "Is he alive?"

Terion rolled his eyes. "Euporia, go."

She obeyed.

"Come with me." He stalked back toward his quarters. I had no choice but to follow him.

This was the favor he promised for helping his sister? He

thought he could just kill my ex-boyfriend without telling me and I'd be *glad?*

Had my face as I watched him torture Redley given him this idea? I hated the thought. Calix was a bastard, but the arrogance of assuming this was what I wanted topped even Terion's normal level.

The cold of shock gave way to the heat of fury by the time we set foot in his cabin.

The bank of windows overlooking the rocky cliffs framed him as he turned. "Mari," he began, "don't disrespect me in front of the crew. You make it difficult for me to defend you." He gestured toward the box. "That was hours of work. For you."

"I don't want it."

Terion's eyes darkened. "Calix treated you like shit."

"Is he alive?" I held my breath.

"I took his hand and one of his eyes," he answered casually.

"His *eyes?*"

"I take it this is not the favor you were hoping for."

"Redley... was different."

"How?" he demanded.

"He tried to hurt me. I knew you were going to do something. We talked about it."

"I don't need permission to enact punishment."

"And I don't need a favor."

With every word he spoke, I sensed his condescension. This... *gesture...* should have made us closer crewmates, but it didn't. I didn't need anyone to fight for me. Yes, it was nice with Redley, but I could make my way without him randomly stepping in to fight my battles for me.

"You do need a favor," he said, expression hardening again.

He prowled closer. "You do, Mari, because you saved my sister's life. I guess this time, I sliced up the man for pleasure."

Last time too. We both knew his coy answer about taking one eye wasn't the whole story. Calix was definitely dead.

I set down the box on a chest pressed against the wall. No part of me should have been glad that Captain Terion attacked Calix for me.

"He deserved it." Terion checked his cuffs. "And I did have some fun."

I pressed my lips together. Suddenly, I wished he had woken me up so I could have come along. The captain shouldn't have assumed what I wanted.

"He never took your pleasure into account," he continued.

Why were we back to this? And in Terion's quarters, of all places? The strangeness of the past few days washed over me, and a crazed laugh struggled to get out.

Terion eyed me. "Did I say something funny?"

"No."

"You had to pretend with him. He made you miserable."

"Yes." I couldn't last any longer. I covered my mouth in a silent fit of giggles.

Terion leaned back on his heels. "So you do like the gift."

"Yes." I barely got through the word.

"I knew it. Bastard."

"I mean, no one's *ever* made me come." My laughter died. I had not meant to say that. Not at all.

Terion blinked at me. "Never? Are you fucking kidding me?"

The air seemed to tighten around us. He didn't need to look at me like that, like I was a specimen. Especially not when he acted flushed and volatile after dismembering two men on my behalf.

"I thought it was just that one selfish asshole," he said.

"He was a selfish asshole." *But that asshole was right about me.* "Terion, it's—"

"Do you want to?"

The question hung in the air, thick and dangerous. I went hot all over. He wasn't saying what I thought he was saying, right? No answer felt fitting. No? Yes? There was no safe way forward. Hopefully he'd say something so I didn't keep standing there like an idiot.

"You're not sex-averse?" he clarified.

"Oh!" I gasped. "No." This wasn't his business. Our job at Dio's was over, so there was no reason to return to the topic of my sex life. Before the day of the party, it hadn't come up.

The way he was looking at me, considering.

Gods.

What did he see? Our recent encounters had been jobs, drunken dares. Nothing suggested he was actually attracted to me. Maybe I represented a challenge to him. He could have no idea how much of a challenge.

"Mari," he finally said, business-like, "I still owe you a favor, since Calix apparently wasn't enough. You can say no. Would you like me to give you orgasms?"

For a second, I left my body. Terion was offering me orgasms, *plural?* I sputtered without forming any real words.

"Not romantic," he added, oddly detached. How many of these kinds of negotiations had he made over the years? "There would be rules. I've been frustrated lately and having a... partner onboard would be good for me too."

But what if I can't? I didn't voice my concern. And why the hell was that the first concern coming to mind?

He watched me levelly. Terion could have anyone. So why was he offering?

"You're awfully confident," I managed, my lips curling in a grimace-like smile.

"Yes." His simple answer simmered beneath my skin.

Could he really do it? Did I want him to try?

This was pathetic. Terion had just rescued me from the brig, defended me to the rest of the crew. He knew I was at the bottom of the pecking order, the scrappy thief from the swamps. Only noticed when I was useful. Only cared for when I pretended. My insides twisted with layers of pain. "I don't need pity," I croaked.

He chuckled. "I wouldn't offer out of pity."

My stomach churned with anticipation and apprehension and a wild mix of what-the-hell-is-happening. "You said there were rules."

What am I doing? What am I doing? What am I doing?

"Yes." His posture straightened, shoulders back as he watched me squirm. "No telling the crew, no kissing, no feelings involved."

I waited. "Is that all?"

"No." But he didn't elaborate.

Memories of waking up in Calix's bed hit me hard. When he wrapped his arms around my bare waist, I'd thought I loved him. "And no spending the night," I added.

He beamed, a flash of white teeth. "Obviously."

My breathing shallowed to the merest taste of air. Was I actually considering this? And if I was, so what? It was just sex. Nothing that would harm my place on the crew. If Captain

Asterion wanted to try making me come, why in the Realms would I say no?

We stood face to face. He could have easily reached out and drawn me in, done the opposite of what happened the other day when he ignored me in his washroom. I could belong with him in this one way. This one very hot way.

"Then... we can try it." I clenched my thighs together. Just the suggestion made me wet and achy.

Terion's eyes traveled down. He'd noticed. Oh gods, he'd noticed. A slow smile split his face. "Good. You'll see what you were missing out on." So confident. Little did he know. He took a step back, and my lungs didn't feel so tight. "So you know, I would have chopped off that bastard's hands anyway. Did it to one of Rhode's partner's before too. No one messes with my crew."

He winked and pushed past me to the door. "We start at seven notches. No one finds out."

I nodded.

He didn't have to explain where to meet. Tonight, I'd get my first glimpse of his secret room.

15

TERION

I pierced the needle through the skin of Calix's finger before drawing it up and pinching the ends of the thread together. A swift slice of my knife—freshly cleaned—and I tied the ends together. The severed finger would hang in the window of my quarters until it dried.

Despite Mari's protests, I was surprised she'd left the box with me. If she didn't want her ex-boyfriend's fingers, I'd take them. They'd make a good necklace.

Maybe I'd wear them as I fucked her.

My mind did something funny at the idea. Thoughts tumbled over each other like waves in a storm.

I shouldn't have done that.

She's sexier than I thought.

She's never come.

I'll make her.

I shouldn't have done that.

She was Mari, for gods' sake. I did feel my debt to her in my bones, but I'd made good on that promise already by punishing two of the men who had wronged her.

My gaze flashed back to the fingers hanging grotesquely in front of the window. With a flip, I sheathed the blade across my chest.

I had practice satisfying women without letting emotions get involved. This would be no different. Mari would scream with pleasure by the time I was done. But, did I jump at this idea too quickly?

I donned my captain's jacket and loosened the strings at my throat. Strangers always wanted to play, then leave. Perfect. Mari stayed aboard, though. Part of the crew. Thoughts of her were... stickier.

My lips curled. *Like the honey.*

Once. I'd try it once and we'd only continue if we kept to the rules. No feelings past our working relationship. For her work lately, she deserved to know what it felt like to shake and see stars.

Fuck it. I was primed for another session. Had been for days. Between Rhode getting attacked and Dio's party, I needed release. I needed to be in control again.

Knock knock.

I swung the door open, one hand on the sword hilt at my hip. Cool air swept across my face. The *Lusca*'s black sails were bound while we anchored in one of our secret alcoves. To get to the shore, we had to use lifeboats and scrabble over rocks, but the city of Iupiter was only ten minutes away. Harder to do in the dark, but the ocean was in my blood. Literally.

Ajax lowered his fist.

"Friendly winds?" I asked.

"Aye, and gold on shore," he confirmed. "We have a lead."

I released the hilt. "What is it?"

I'd sent Mari out to do reconnaissance in the city before

our tryst this evening. Had she found something better to loot than the little tidepools of beachside manors? I needed a sea of treasure, if we could find it.

"Pretty good," Ajax grunted. "But a rumor."

I cocked a brow. "Reputable?"

"Is any rumor?"

My lips twisted. Good point.

"Mari spoke to people at the market. They said there was rumor of treasure buried on the Bridge."

I buzzed with questions, skepticism, but that old excitement shot through me too. "How much?"

"Gold the weight of four horses."

A sigh escaped my lips, almost erotic. *That might do it.* "How sure is she? I need to talk to—"

Movement made me squint past my first mate. Klep was topping the stairs. Seeing dark rocks rising behind him instead of sea and sky felt wrong.

"Yes?" I prompted, heart kicking up.

"Rhode's awake and talking."

I darted past Ajax before I realized I'd made the decision to move.

Klep tripped along to keep up with me. "She's able to keep soup and water down, but nothing solid," he explained breathlessly.

"Are you still giving her the powdered bones?" Mari had gotten shit for offering that remedy, but it was the only thing that had saved my sister's life.

"Now that we're here in Zenia—"

"Keep administering them until they're gone."

"It's a rustic solution. I don't know about side effects."

I stopped at the top of the stairs, turning the full force of my attention to Klep. "Did you hear me the first time? Until it's gone." I lowered my voice. "I don't give a fuck about sophisticated medicine or whatever the hell you're implying. Do what I say or I'll find a doctor who will."

Klep went ashen. "Yes, Captain."

Clenching my fists, I jogged down the companionway to the level below. "Rhode!" I called as I opened the door.

I'd hoped she would survive until we reached land, but I hadn't been able to talk to her yet.

The smell inside made my throat tighten. It was like a bucket of fish innards. Rhode lay in her hammock, but her head tilted to look at me when I opened the door. Her forehead sheened with sweat.

Behind her stood Mari, half out of the gentleman's clothes she'd worn to shore. All she had on were brown trousers and white cloth binding her breasts. She shot me a look of hesitation that wasn't like her at all. Locking eyes made the truth simmer between us of what would happen this evening. I was hardening before I could stop myself. I hadn't seen so much of her since the party.

I tore my eyes away from the expanse of light skin at her belly and shoulders, caught off balance.

Kneeling, I took Rhode's hand, looked her in the eye. Divine seas, it was good to see her. "How did you not see the Leviathan coming?" I asked.

Rhode smacked my arm hard. "Asshole!"

I laughed, dodging her next strike. In that one motion, she revealed how much the toxin had weakened her. Clumsy on land but never in the water, Rhode could strike fast. But not today.

Mari turned away and began unwrapping her cloth. If I kept watching, she'd get totally naked as she changed clothes.

No, I'm here for Rhode. No lusting after Mari till later.

I gave Rhode a half-smile and rested my forehead against hers. She closed her eyes. "Don't ever die," I murmured, running a thumb across the scales on her cheek. "Swim in tanks on board the ship. Wear five layers of clothes so you don't bump into anything sharp."

Rhode pulled away, half-laughing, half-furious.

"I'll execute every shark, scorpion, snake…"

She pounded my chest with both fists.

"…sailor who coughs or looks at you wrong." Finally, I sat up straight, grinning down at her.

Her shoulders shook with wheezy giggles. "Terion," she sighed, and her eyes went soft. She'd missed me too.

I tipped my mouth, a lump thickening in my throat. "I'll get Basileus for this." It came out as a threatening growl. "Don't worry."

Her eyes slid away from me. Did she not think I could?

Mari had put new clothes on finally—a dress, maybe to give me better access later…?—and was stuffing things into all the bags and pouches around her everyday outfit. I jutted my chin at her. "You found a way for us to get close to him, didn't you? Ajax said something about that."

"I heard about treasure buried in the Bridge. Nothing about Lord Basileus." Her wide eyes were distant now, as if our earlier conversation had never happened. None of that sense of getting caught. She all but ignored me, easily as slipping on a new disguise.

I didn't like it.

She fluffed her hair from the slicked back style of a Zenian gentleman back to the girl I knew. It was like watching someone when they thought they were alone. Indecent and for some reason arousing. Knowing what was coming tonight made me aware of every tuck of her fingers, every bend and stretch and adjustment of her shoulders or waistline.

"Terion."

My attention snapped back to Rhode, who fixed me with a knowing stare.

"You're not planning on paying our father *yourself*, are you?" she asked.

"Of course I am."

"And what? He's immortal."

From the shadows, Mari's keen eyes followed us closely. No more pretending disinterest.

"Did you think I'd send someone else to deal with him?" I spat. "He needs more than payment and a kick in the ass. After all this time, and what he did to you? I'm Captain fucking Asterion. I'll put him in his place."

Rhode watched me, a whole conversation passing over her face. *Treasure won't be enough,* she seemed to say. *Not after what happened.* She was one of the only people on my crew who was there, who knew what really happened. My father's pride was at stake.

I raised my chin, not taking my eyes from my sister's. "Mari, did you believe the people who told you about the Bridge?"

"They believed it, at least," she answered.

"Whose treasure is it?"

"Thenios. Something about contingencies. Emergencies. I think it's meant as a bribe for Hades if diplomacy breaks down."

I broke into a laugh. "Wait." I met everyone's gaze in the room—Rhode, Mari, Klep, who hadn't said a word since I'd threatened him. "The God-King buried treasure meant for Hades? *That's* the money you learned about?" *Impossible.*

If Hades didn't sentence us to Abaddon, the God-King would. If we didn't wreck in the treacherous water near the Bridge.

But... our father was known for his jealousy, like most rulers of the Realms. If I brought him a king's ransom taken from both of his brothers, who had more powerful reputations than he did, that might be enough to save me and the crew.

Who would miss a treasure buried for obscure contingencies? This could be perfect.

I clapped my hands together. "Get well, Rhode. We'll stay anchored long enough to restock the ship, and then we're bound for the Bridge."

"But..." Klep's protest died.

"Was that the only mark you followed, Mari?" Rhode asked, craning her neck back to where Mari stood by her hammock. The white breast-binding cloth lay in a coil by her pillow. The sight made me think of ropes and... other things.

"The biggest score," she answered, shrugging.

That's my girl.

Our next voyage would be danger, payoff, and reward. The promise of open seas with unthinkable treasure at the end made me half-hard again. Freedom was close enough to taste.

"Then we're doing it," I said.

I'd tell the crew to have their fun while we were anchored near such a profitable city. Surely, they'd bring in odds and ends while they were off having their jollies. A happy crew was a loyal crew, and we'd had some rough seas lately. They'd earned a rest. Soon, I'd ask them to attempt the impossible. It wouldn't be the first time they followed me to the end of the world, but I shouldn't push my luck. With every lost crew member, a part of me died with them, so I stopped getting close to new recruits.

I didn't look at Mari when I left.

16

MARI

Sharp barnacles clung to the metal door handle of Terion's secret room. On every other surface of the *Lusca*, barnacles were regularly scraped off. I'd always thought of these like the thorns on a rose. They wouldn't kill you, but they discouraged you from touching them.

My pulse raced. Seeing him with his sister earlier, excitement lighting up his face because of my tip... I was a good actress, like he told me before, but acting like we hadn't just had a conversation about sex challenged my limits. My nonchalant attitude felt forced. Rhode must have noticed, but she hadn't said anything to me yet.

When I left our room, I didn't tell her where I was going. That was easier than keeping up an alibi, and besides, I regularly came and went without anyone checking up on me.

Down here, it was hard to gauge time. It had to be close to seven notches now, right? The last time I checked Euporia's device, that was what it read.

The longer I lingered near the forbidden door, the stupider I felt. What if Terion decided not to come? What if he realized the ridiculousness of his offer and considered his debt already paid?

What if the captain does come and you can't perform? He'll know you're a cold bitch with an impossible list of needs before you can come.

Even Captain Asterion might not be enough. *I wouldn't mean it as an insult, but—*

Footsteps behind me meant Terion approached. This was supposed to be secret. Should I acknowledge him? Suddenly, all the stealth that came naturally to me frayed away. I stood stock-still, facing the door.

His footfalls neared until he stood so close I could feel his soft breath on the back of my neck. My spine prickled. Challenge, he had told me. I actually felt a wet pulse between my legs—something rare, but that he'd managed to arouse multiple times that week.

Anticipation charged through me as he scanned the hallway, reached past my arm and opened the forbidden door. "In."

I darted inside with him, both of us silent. The door shut behind me, leaving me in utter darkness. Was our tryst going to be like this? Completely blind?

Terion was too vain for that. He'd want to see the effect he had on me. This way, there was too much danger of fumbling. For someone so confident he could get me off, he'd need more precision than this.

A scrape, a fizz, and light blossomed in his cupped hand. He set the match on a candle wick, methodically moving around the room until we were surrounded by a ring of shadowy orange light. Finally, the room came into focus.

The dark skin of the *Lusca* wrapped around a space that smelled like musk and sea salt. The root of a mast plunged through one side of the room. Scattered around the space were leather instruments and odd pieces of furniture whose purpose I could only guess. It looked like I imagined a dungeon. If a dungeon made my mind flare with a hundred sexy possibilities that set my heart beating faster.

My mouth dried, but I didn't want to let Terion know how much I was already affected. "That's a lot of drama for people who come down here."

"Captain."

"What?"

"You will refer to me as Captain in this room." He wasn't joking. The smolder in his gaze meant this was part game, part order.

I'd play along. "All right, Captain."

He stalked back toward me, coat swinging lightly behind his knees. "If you're not sure you want to do this, you can leave now."

I frowned. "What are you talking about? I don't want to leave. I know the rules."

"There are more."

"No kissing, no spending the night, no falling in love," I counted off. "What else is there?"

He made a noise that was half-purr, half-growl, deep in his chest. My body went more alert, wanting more of that sound.

"Captain," I added.

He licked his lips. "In this room, you will call me Captain and you will obey my every command."

I was about to retort that the same pretty much went for outside the room too, but I could tell he meant something else. This was instant obedience. He was the master in this room.

"Noted, Captain, " I answered instead.

"It can get... intense," he continued. "So if you want out, you have to choose a word."

"What word, Captain?"

His beautiful lips curled. The candlelight played against the iridescent scales on his face. He had more on his chest and arms—I'd seen them before. "Any word you like."

"Constellation."

"Constellation, good." He spoke like he'd practiced before. I couldn't tell if I was jealous or excited because he clearly knew what he was doing. Every movement and angle of him was in charge here, totally confident in his abilities. Judging from the items in the room, those abilities were varied and considerable. "Say the word constellation at any point of our interaction, and I'll stop what I'm doing."

He made it sound like a business deal. The beat between my legs grew fainter. Frustration surged through me. I wanted this. That drunken night had been the most turned on I'd ever felt, and now I was going to see what Terion could do when he had me all to himself. I should be dripping. I should want to tear off his clothes. But those feelings were ebbing. They had been there, I would swear. Could Terion get them back?

I wanted to know what women felt when they begged and screamed their pleasure. I wanted to be enough.

"Okay, I'll do that, Captain." I wouldn't, though. No matter what Terion did to me, I'd hold on. I wouldn't break and say the word aloud.

"Constellation," he said again, eyeing me. He probably knew what I was thinking. Damn him.

"Yes, Captain."

"Last chance."

"I won't leave, Captain."

He pursed his mouth, unsurprised. Then he reached for a pair of black leather gloves sitting on a crate and tugged them on, replacing his normal fingerless gloves. *Wait.* He was putting on *more* clothes?

"Then we'll begin," he said, gaze not on me now.

My breathing shallowed, waiting for the challenge he promised. Any number of the things in this room could hurt me, push me to the brink. Maybe one of them could pay off the promise of that night when his body pressed close to mine...

"Stand over there." He pointed one leather-clad finger to the corner where a large wooden oval leaned at about the angle of a mirror. Straps bloomed around its edges.

"Yes, Captain." My heartbeat kicked up as I obeyed. Was I supposed to be in a certain position or something? The uncertainty coupled with the reality of what we were about to do made me almost dizzy. I was glad to be able to lean against something.

After a moment, he followed. Somehow, he looked bigger in this room, all his power, beauty, and cunning magnified. My eyes darted down. Was he as turned on as I was? The fabric wasn't helpful for seeing whether or not he was hard.

"Bad girl. No looking," he said, crouching down in front of me. His face was barely a breath in front of my body.

Was he going to...?

No, he started to bind my wrists at my sides with the straps. He barely touched my skin at all, even avoiding it. Finally, he straightened, standing so close to me I could feel the warmth of his body. Without making contact, he secured one final strap around my neck. He was more careful with that one. The bruises from Redley's fingers had faded, but my throat still felt tender. Terion's restraint didn't choke me, but I couldn't move at all.

Nerves licked through my veins. What if I needed to escape? I never put myself in situations I couldn't get out of. But now I was willingly placing my safety in the hands of Terion. Probably not my smartest decision.

Another part of me relished the lack of control. I was the pawn and he was—

A sting lashed against my hip. I refocused on him. From his hand dangled a small whip.

"You didn't acknowledge my command."

"Yes, Captain."

"No looking unless I allow you to. Do you understand?"

"Yes, Captain."

Now my rebellious eyes didn't want to look at anything but his crotch, but I kept them up.

"Good girl." His eyes went dark and his breathing heavier. The moment felt weighted down with sex. Seconds passed like minutes. "You said you wanted a challenge. I'll give you one. Don't come until I allow you to."

Disappointment and relief chased each other through my body. That wouldn't be a problem. I'd never had a full orgasm before. It would make this challenge easier, but hadn't he promised to give me orgasms? What was this secret meeting for, if not that?

"Yes, Captain."

His capable hands twisted the handle of the whip. I clenched my abs, but then he simply set it to the side.

What kind of game was he playing? I couldn't keep the frustration out of my expression.

Terion leaned close, his lips practically against the

exposed part of my neck. His ocean spice scent intoxicated me, his breath sending chills down my back. "You think I'd make it that easy on you?" He made that same growling, purring sound. I shivered. "No, no. We'll start with something else."

Hopefully that something had him naked soon. I was ready to take him and try my luck with the challenge.

Moist air teased my ear, my neck, my collarbone. Terion never touched me—bastard—but he got maddeningly close. Open-mouthed sighs lowered until he reached the ties at my neckline. With barely a movement, he could take them between his teeth and expose my chest.

Finally. This foreplay already felt like ages. All my former lovers were more eager to get to the good part. Was all this waiting what turned Terion on? It must be. He liked the control, the obedience.

"Oh," he said, as if disappointed. "Pity." He stopped, quick as anything, and turned away.

My mouth opened to protest, but I snapped it closed just in time.

He glanced over his shoulder at me. "I'd like to see those ripe breasts sometime. You know what I would do with them? You may speak."

Jarred, I stayed quiet. We'd teased and told dirty jokes, but Terion had never said anything so sexual to me before. I didn't know what he wanted me to say.

"Answer the question, Mari."

"Breathe, Captain?" I guessed, disappointed and aroused at the same time.

"No. I'd pluck your nipples until they turned purple before I sucked them better."

My breath gusted from my lungs. The idea was so erotic I flexed my thighs.

"Do you want me to do it?" His tone was so measured, not even that husky from arousal. Utterly in command of himself. And me.

"Yes, Captain."

"Then you have to earn it."

My chest heaved, eager. Maybe he could make good on his promise after all. "How, Captain?"

"Tell me how this feels. Every sensation. Leave nothing out."

I felt like an experiment. A sexy, sexy experiment. I searched him, but couldn't tell what *this* would be. "Yes, Captain."

17

TERION

Mari still had all her clothes on, but the way she obeyed me, tied up like that, had me fighting for breath. Maybe she didn't feel *that way* about me, but she was ready to play. So we'd play.

Too bad she'd only dated selfish assholes who weren't willing to find out what was good for her. I'd find out if it was the last thing I did.

Well, maybe not the last thing. If I didn't pay my father back, we'd all be in the shit. The second to last thing. This, with her, was the perfect distraction.

I stood for a minute, deciding. Normally, I wasn't this scrupulous about my next move. I knew how to reduce my partners to a shivering mess before I fed them, watered them, held them a bit, and sent them on their way. Mari was different, though.

No earth-shattering orgasm in her whole life? That sounded impossible. She'd already admitted that she wanted it but had never gotten there. Now that I'd started looking, she had such a gorgeous, tight body. Such intelligent, beautiful eyes. She was layers I hadn't found the end of.

So I'd peel off the layers.

My balls clenched at the challenge. Searching for a way to get her off was already hotter than other encounters I'd had in this room.

"If you stop being able to talk," I said coolly, "make noises so I know what it's doing to you."

She flushed. "Yes, Captain."

I exhaled. I couldn't get used to those sweet words coming out of her mouth. "But no coming."

"Yes, Captain."

"Good." I reached beneath the wooden platform I'd strapped her to and cranked a hidden wheel. The platform lowered horizontally. It could turn upside-down too, but we'd start here.

She swallowed down a squeak of surprise as it moved.

I stopped when the oval platform reached an angle just before full horizontal. All her weight still pulled toward her feet, but barely. It was an angle designed to disorient enough for the submissive to lose themselves in the scene, to doubt whether they were lying down or were propped up.

Start slow. Start slow. My brain was already leaning toward the whips and blindfolds, furniture, binding material, and mechanical devices strewn around the room. *Let her look. Let her want it.*

I removed her boots, one by one, then her socks. That simple act changed her breathing. I allowed myself a smirk. "Tell me what you feel." I removed one glove and touched her bare ankle.

Bindings first. I indicated for her to separate her legs so I could bind her ankles.

Laying a finger just above the strap, I let my power blossom against her skin. It was limited to what I could touch, but I'd gotten good at directing the moisture where I wanted it to go, and in what form. Icy water raced up the inside of her leg, skimming past her pussy and running all the way up to her bound throat.

She gasped. "That's…"

When she didn't say more, I picked up the small whip I'd set on the crate by my thigh and cracked it once against the soles of her feet.

She let out a sound that had my dick harden against my seam.

"Tell me how you feel," I commanded.

"It's… I don't know if I like it, Captain."

"Then we'll do it again, slower."

I touched her ankle again, but this time, I didn't pull away. With one finger, I traced an icy path up her calf, up the inside of her thigh. Her skin was impossibly soft and warm enough to melt my ice as soon as my finger trailed upward. Ice-melt dripped over her leg. Was she dripping for me yet too?

She shivered. "That's better, Captain."

My hand was still under her dress, not quite touching the sweet spot we both wanted. "Open wider."

"Yes, Captain." She spread her knees.

"You want me to touch you, but you aren't ready for that yet." I could hardly hold myself back from doing it, but this wait seemed to be doing something to her, so I drew it out. Anticipation was more than half the battle. If I could arouse someone enough, make them want it enough, then they'd come at the first touch as hard as if I'd fucked them into a wall. That kind of power thrummed like liquor through my veins.

I shoved the strands of the whip under the skirt, letting them linger close to the apex of her thighs.

She shuddered. "I like that, Captain."

"Of course you do." As a reward, I pressed the head of the lash, where all the strands connected, between her legs, and rubbed.

Her mouth ratcheted open. "That..." She struggled. "That's more."

I moved the whip carefully, digging in around the area of her clit, though I couldn't see and couldn't feel exactly where it was. Watching Mari pant as I touched her made me want to stop, climb on top of her, and spear her with my cock instead.

"No coming until I say," I directed mildly.

Her hands became fists at her sides. "That feels good, Captain," she gritted out. "You make me feel good. You're good at this."

Praise. My body responded to her words, just like she knew it would. She was making a bid for release. She wanted me to fuck her. But I wouldn't do it yet. The tension I saw on her face was too delicious.

"Tell me more," I said.

"I want you to touch me with your fingers next," she gasped.

I retracted the whip. The head of it glistened. "Ah, you don't get to make demands here. You just get to take it like a good girl. Can you take it like a good girl?"

"Yes, Captain." The disappointment was obvious in her

voice. She still breathed heavily, but her clenched fingers relaxed.

Time to wind her up again.

The smell of her sex made me dizzy, but my methods weren't working as well as they normally did. Not a problem. There were many options in this room, but I suddenly didn't want most of them. I set the whip aside. Crouching, I cranked the wheel under the platform again.

I could indulge if I wanted to. I was in charge here. And fuck if I couldn't wait a second more to taste her.

The platform rotated, turning upside down. Not fully vertical, since that would put too much strain on the bindings, but almost.

Mari watched me with avid eyes. "I feel curious, Captain," she said, with a challenging edge in her voice that sounded just like her. The submissive was gone and the card-playing, mast-climbing, gold-stealing shapeshifter was back.

"Mm." I tucked her skirt in so it didn't fall around her face as I left her legs exposed to the waist. Finally, I stepped back to see that pretty pussy. My heart thundered. Was it too soon to give in to what I really wanted to do?

Before I could censor myself, I gave a new command. "Praise me."

"Yes, Captain," came her instant reply.

I could tell from her eagerness that she knew the effect that would have on me, that I wouldn't be able to resist getting one or both of us off. Fuck, she knew me too well.

"You're a better sailor than your father and the most feared pirate on the Corae Sea. You were the handsomest one at Dio's party. You probably have the biggest dick, too. May I look?"

I breathed a laugh through my nose. That last one sounded

a little too sarcastic, but the question somehow was genuine too. A puzzle, my little Mari.

"Soon," I said, deeper and raspier than before. Damn. She'd known how even that much praise would affect me. I was rock hard, and my crotch was all but in her face.

I knew exactly what I wanted to do.

"Tell me how this feels until you can't talk anymore, then keep your mouth open."

Her eyes flared wide. It was the last thing I noticed before leaning forward and pressing my face between her legs, desperate for the taste, the scent, the wet slickness of her. Desperate for the praise that erupted from her lips.

"Fuck! Oh! That feels so good. I love what you're doing. Yes, that pressure, Captain—it's perfect. Keep going..."

I found her clit and sucked hard. She made a straining noise, interrupting her stream of words.

I disengaged. "Mouth open."

With my tongue back on her, in her, I wrestled with the front of my pants, struggling to free my pulsing cock. It was hard and straight and big, and I doubted Mari had ever taken somebody this way before. She was going to now. I took the base in my fist and found Mari's lips. Her wet mouth was hot and tight. I growled against her sex and she made an echoing cry. Okay, she liked that. My thoughts fuzzed, sharpening to the feeling of my head at the back of her throat and the musky wetness I lapped up between her thighs. I rolled my hips, growling again, more animal than demi-god.

Mari was forbidden to come, but I wasn't. I could feel release coursing through my balls, waiting, close.

No. No no. I wouldn't break first. Not in front of her. This was supposed to be a reward for her, not me. Even if I was close to paying off my father after this next mission.

The idea brought me hurtling toward the edge.

I pulled out, shaking, and stepped back. I was so hard I could barely see. Mari's open mouth glistened with spit.

I forced my dick back into my restraining pants and knelt without a word to crank the platform back to its original position. I needed every turn of the wheel to bring some sanity back.

When Mari stood fully upright again, I untucked her skirt, letting it fall back to her bare calves. Her eyes were lidded.

"Good girl," I said softly. "You didn't come." And neither had I. Later, in my room, I'd need some time alone or else I would explode.

"That felt really good, Captain."

"Of course it did."

She gave me a teasing look that, in any other context, would have come before a smack in the arm. I began untying her bonds. First the ankles, then the wrists, and finally the neck restraint.

Uncharacteristically weak, she stumbled into my arms. I held her up, sweeping her behind the knees and carrying her to the mattress in the corner.

"Stay here," I murmured, setting her down.

"Yes, Captain." The response was automatic now. My balls tightened again.

I smoothed some hair away from her forehead—her eyes were closed—and slipped out to get some water and rations to revive her.

Moments later, I returned. She was already half-asleep. "Mari," I coaxed. "You have to drink something."

"You didn't keep your promise."

Her slurred words didn't register. "What do you mean?" I helped her sit upright and handed her a cup of fresh water. "I'm warming you up. I'll let you come soon."

She took a deep breath as if waking up. No more 'Captain' now. She understood the scene was over. Sitting on the bed was my thief Mari. It was a little disorienting, as if the past minutes had been a dream.

"You said if I was a good girl, you'd pluck my nipples."

A laugh burst out of me. "Gods, Mari..."

"You did, though."

"That's true. My promise still stands, as long as you obey."

She sipped the water. "Shouldn't be a problem."

"Even alone."

"Okay." She said it so easily, as if she didn't need to get off as soon as possible, like I did. This part was important, though. Mari had to feel safe if I was going to demand her unquestioning obedience, in sex and in everything else on the ship.

"Did you enjoy that?" I asked. "It felt like you were getting close."

"I always edge close." She looked away and focused on the water again.

Edging and edging with no release. What a hellish sex life, and a stupid thing to be embarrassed about. Her suddenly distant attitude made me angry. Who were these people who made her feel like she wasn't enough? Good thing I'd killed Calix. I felt like killing him again.

I shouldn't make her wait too long before I gave her what I offered. Honestly, I didn't think I could. She was a better partner than I expected, eager for everything but taking no bullshit. Should have guessed. It was that no bullshit attitude that made her submission sweeter.

I could try out all my kinks on her to find the right fit, the challenge that would make her break. My dominance and her release went together.

I had to stop thinking. All my thoughts swirled around how good our sex would be, and I was already close to coming in my pants.

It felt different watching Mari, someone I knew, rather than a stranger from a foreign port. Mari would walk out of this room. She'd pretend nothing happened here. I couldn't keep her locked away like my other secrets.

I curled a lock of short hair behind her ear. The gesture felt out of place now that she was normal Mari again, not submissive Mari.

I lowered my voice. "Don't tell the others what we're doing, but if you're a very good girl next time, I'll push you off that edge. You'll have no choice."

She gave me a tentative, vulnerable look, almost wary. More nerves than I'd seen before any mission. "You didn't say this would take multiple times."

"I said multiple orgasms."

Her look hardened, turning impish. She lowered her cup to her lap. "Well, you do have a reputation."

I grinned, running my tongue over the points of my teeth. "The offer stands. I'm easing you in slowly." I laid my hand on her thigh and leaned close to her ear. "You followed orders very well, so next time, I'll give you more. When you're begging me to come, when you can't hold on anymore, then I'll let you. I'll *make* you. I promise."

My mark chose The Royal Crab for a drink. I couldn't protest without calling attention to myself. It didn't matter that this was the pub Calix and I frequented whenever the *Lusca* docked here. For this, I needed to be invisible. A nameless Zenian gentleman innocently asking about a more exact location of the gold buried along the Bridge.

Besides, Calix was dead. Terion saw to that.

His rash attack on my ex followed by the night in his secret room was enough to make wonder... but no. That was ridiculous. Didn't mean I couldn't dwell on memories of Terion's mouth in the silent spaces between conversation.

Above us rose the sign hammered into the side of the stone and wood structure—a blue crab with its claws raised, a crown on its head. The crab wore a toga. A lot of people in Zenia wore togas. To me, those seemed outdated and silly, but the God-King Thenios famously wore them, so today, I wore a toga too. The draped style made it a little easier to hide my bound breasts, but my toga felt loose under the armpit. Had I tied it wrong? Was the pale fabric going to gape?

I laughed at something my mark said, inwardly cringing as we passed under the sign. The familiar smell of sour beer and buttery crab meat hit my nose. Dark, claustrophobic clusters of stools and counters filled the space. It felt a tiny bit like home, except for the big, fancy windows along the back wall, overlooking the ocean. And the lack of that peppery, mustardy, smoky spice blend that the swamp had everywhere. And the patrons that obviously had money.

We'd always sat right there, to the left, against the bar. I almost expected to lock eyes with my ex when I glanced that way. Thank the gods I didn't. Or, one demi-god in particular.

I shouldn't feel glad that Terion had killed Calix, however he managed to do that without being seen, but I couldn't help puffing a tiny sigh of relief. Captain Terion didn't think I was a cold bitch because I hadn't come for him last night. He'd ordered me not to. It wasn't just the mechanisms and whips that turned me on down there in his secret room—it was that order. Something about it was understanding. Caring, even. It made me glad we'd struck this deal.

"Haha! Here, I'll order us a drink." My mark bustled forward, pulling at his trimmed beard. His name was Ferimond, human probably. The last time I'd gone ashore for information, he had gossiped endlessly, prompting me to steal a map of the Bridge right after I left them. I currently had it tucked in the folds of my toga. If he had the connections he claimed, he might be able to point us in a more precise direction toward the gold. Terion needed a heading.

I pressed toward the bar with his other friends. "Aw, let

me!" I cried, jostling the man next to me. I stood as tall as the rest.

"No no," Ferimond declared, pulling coins from the folds of his toga and slamming them on the counter. "Service!"

A woman appeared, wide eyes irritated, mocking, and curiously hospitable at once. "Yes? What can I get you and your friends?"

"Drinks all around!" And, quieter, "And a bowl of broth. You know how it settles my stomach."

"It's all those spicy fritters you eat," she bit back.

"Pshaw!" He waved his hand. "Do you have any left?"

"Sold out at lunch."

Ferimond scowled and turned back to the group. We found seats by bullying a couple of men from their spots. Here, we could look out at the water.

"They never have fritters at sundown," one of Ferimond's friends complained, fingering the empty bowl at the center of the table. All the tables had them, scored with the God-King's lightning mark.

"We should go somewhere else!" Ferimond exclaimed loudly so the woman at the bar could hear.

She appeared from the back to make a rude gesture at him. "Shut up!"

I chuckled along with the rest.

"I swear this might as well be the Nalian swamps, for all the service we get."

My insides clenched hard. This time, I couldn't muster a laugh, but I stretched my lips into a smile at the comment. It was too close to what I'd thought a moment ago.

Memories rushed back, about a bar like this one, closed in to keep out the wet, smelling of mold.

Another demi-god, like me, entering in an outfit that promised full pockets.

A quick flick of my fingers to lift the loot.

Only after I got out of the bar that day did Terion grab my wrist and demand it back with a smile and an offer. I was too desperate to say no. We talked the whole walk back to the *Lusca*, his cheerful optimism grating against my hesitant pessimism.

No way I could have guessed what we'd be doing together in two years...

I blinked, refocusing. I couldn't afford to get lost in thought, even if that thought was the way Terion's tongue had lapped up my taste while I hung bound to that table, bunching, getting close...

I shifted my weight to help the heat pooling at my core. One look at the men around me started undoing that effect.

The woman from the bar plunked tankards on the table in a circle so she could hold all the handles in one fearsome grip. I murmured something as I dragged mine closer. The frothy, bitter smell of ale rose from the mugs.

I raised mine to my lips. When I lowered it again, everyone stared at me. My eyes dropped to the bowl as I swallowed. *Shit.* A thin layer of ale sloshed at the bottom. Everyone else had poured out a drink offering. I'd forgotten.

My heart jogged in my chest. Too late, I poured my offering into the bowl.

The bearded man caught me by the wrist. "Do you mean to disrespect King Thenios?"

The others growled in approval. Despite their polished demeanor on the street, they had the look of brawlers now, as if I'd insulted their children.

"Too long at sea," I said with a smile. "I lost the habit."

Ferimond's brows lowered further. Not good.

Basileus and Scira—the rulers I was most familiar with—didn't demand drink offerings with every meal. I was pretty sure they were only required in the presence of the deity themselves. I should have paid more attention to Zenian customs. There had to be a way to salvage this.

"At sea?" Ferimond scoffed.

"Yeah," I answered as breezily as I could. "My crewmates are heathenish assholes. It's good to be back somewhere civilized."

Every expression around that table dripped with suspicion. Had I not explained my slip away already? What more did I have to say?

"Had to venerate the God-King in my own quarters..." My words ran thin. I took another tentative sip of ale.

That only seemed to aggravate the others. I set down the mug, mentally counting the knives I had strapped under my toga.

"Van-rate?" one of them mocked, exaggerating my accent.

My blood froze. It was a northern Nalian pronunciation. I'd only heard the word a couple times and apparently I'd botched it.

Time to get out while I could. No way they'd believe I was a Zenian gentleman now. *And I said I spent time on the water.*

Fingers of ice crawled up my spine. "Fine," I said, trying to keep my male Zenian voice intact even though I knew I'd cracked that illusion like a mast in a bad storm. "I don't pour out offerings most of the time. More ale for me. I'm a selfish bastard, what can I say? Don't tell the King."

Ferimond reared from the table, purple with rage.

I jumped up and stepped back.

Even the woman who'd served us glared daggers at me. "Get out or I'll report you to the nearest patrol!"

All this over a sip of ale? *King Thenios must be a petty piece of work.*

The group all stood, fists clenched.

I didn't waste time. In seconds, I was out the door.

"Worthless swamp daughter." "So all swamp-dwellers are idiots after all..."

Words I'd hear my whole life rang in my ears. They doubted me, and this slip-up would seal it. All I had to do was follow the customs, something I'd done in a dozen places a dozen times. How many times had I poured a drink offering to Thenios when we were docked here? Dozens. Where was my focus today?

I didn't get a more accurate idea of where the gold was buried in the Bridge, and now I'd lost my mark. Clues would have to do.

Footsteps hurried behind me.

I held my breath, tilted my head. The men from the bar. Every one of them followed me, striding with purpose.

Crap.

I picked up my pace. Should I return to the *Lusca* or try to misdirect them? I ducked into an alley between stone buildings and began climbing the wall.

"Oof!" My foot slipped on the loose fabric draped around me and I fell the short distance to the ground. My jaw flexed. No climbing in this damned outfit. My options were running out.

All I had to do was pour out a godsdamned drink and pronounce a word correctly, but I was too stupid for either. At least I'd sauntered into a cartographer's shop before meeting up with the men.

Overlapping voices showed the men weren't even trying to be quiet. Among the words was one that stood out like a bell.

Pirate.

I'd compromised us. Compromised Terion.

Again.

There was no way he'd keep me on the *Lusca* after this. He'd killed Calix for less—not that he'd kill me. We were past that. But he didn't have to keep me on his crew or in his secret room. One less person meant more spoils all around. The others probably wouldn't miss me.

"...aunt was robbed the last time pirates came through here."

"You really think he was one of them? Maybe just a—"

"*My* brother got a blade to the ribs. I'll send those pirates where they belong if I ever see one of those..."

"...the coast. Maybe the *Lusca*..."

The voices grew closer. Had they seen me enter the alley? These humans had no chance against the *Lusca*'s crew by themselves. Ajax could probably skewer them single-handedly. Terion would enjoy sending them to the bottom of the sea. If they had more than seaweed for brains, though, they'd alert authorities, and *that* would be a problem. A good covert docking spot was worth a pile of treasure. If they found it, I'd be in huge trouble. On top of that, we still hadn't collected necessary food and supplies. Not enough, at least. The crew could be caught unaware and—whether they cared about my fate or not—crew came first.

My forehead scrunched with impotent frustration as I

gazed upward. The alley ended in a dead end. It was go up or get caught.

I'd blown our secret, but at least I could warn the crew before authorities surprised them and tried to sink the ship. Drawing a few quick markings on the map to indicate the likeliest spot to find the gold based on the hints I'd gathered, I kept one eye on the street. It sounded like the angry group would come in sight any second.

Yanking off the pale fabric of my toga, I hurled it to the end of the alley and stuffed the parchment map in my teeth. One hand in front of the other, like I'd done on the mast a hundred times before, I climbed up the stone wall in only my underwear and bindings. Hard sunlight slanted overhead, drowning me in dark shadow.

As I climbed, I made small adjustments to my eyes and lips. Focusing on my power wasn't easy while climbing with a dirty map in my mouth. I sucked greedy breaths through my nose.

Widen the nostrils. Thicker eyebrows...

I couldn't change everything about my appearance. Outfits and mannerisms finished off the illusions. But I could do something, at least.

If the men couldn't find me, they couldn't hurt me, and I could still warn the crew to ship off before angry authorities arrived.

I gripped the top of the wall. Sand gritted under my palm. Hauling myself up, I finally spat out the map and peered cautiously over the edge of the building. Zenia had too many clean lines and stately mountain vistas. I couldn't poke my head too far over the edge without being obvious. Back in northern Nalia, the trees twisted, moss swayed in the wind, vines climbed up cliffs, and a maze of shallow waterways meant everything looked like it was moving all the time.

There were the men below me, walking past the alley with my discarded clothes. *Shouldn't have done that...* Now, I'd stand out just because I was half-naked.

I could still hear snatches of their conversation, but not much. I peered in the direction of the *Lusca*. Buildings and rock formations hid the ship from view. What bothered me was that the men weren't walking in that direction. They had turned north, toward the mountain, toward the authorities and the hub of deathless residents who could actually do some damage to Terion and the crew if enough of them attacked.

It did no good to picture Terion's smirk if he saw a mob coming. He would survive, taking many other lives to ensure that happened, but what about the rest of the crew? What about the *Lusca*? Foolish to think of that ship as my home, but if I had one, it was there.

Something caught my eye. I furrowed my brow to see better. Was that...?

A trident.

The symbol of a trident stamped into a door a short walk from here toward the water.

That meant an Asterion-suna. Terion told me once that the places where his cults met were called "Captain's quarters." I rolled my eyes at the time. Demi-gods (if they were famous enough) all had followings. I should have guessed Terion would have a suna here.

I jumped over the small gap to the next roof. From there, awnings and barrels formed acrobatic stairs down to the ground, away from the street. Huge lemons hung from branches crawling up the awning poles. I plucked one as I ran. Habit.

Sunlight glared down on me as I scurried up to the trident door and banged on the door.

Wait. What would I say?

When a young man opened the door and stared at me, I still hadn't figured out a coherent plan. The human had dark, curly hair and looked no more than twenty-five. And I'd assumed everyone participating in Terion's suna would be women. Silly, in retrospect, since he had so many fans, not only of his looks and charisma, but his lifestyle of piracy.

The young man's eyes traveled down my half-naked body, to the map rolled in my hand, and backed up.

"The captain needs your help," I blurted. Some shapeshifter I was, when I couldn't think on my feet. At least I had the presence of mind to use an accent. With a thought, I'd given myself features that were closer to the traditional look someone from Kantharos would have—mid-toned skin, rounded eyes, a cultured aspect.

His eyebrows arched. "Who are you?"

Two women appeared at his side. They were gorgeous. All three of them wore long jackets instead of the trendy togas. One of the women even had a scarf tied around her head like Terion usually had. An odd jolt of automatic dislike shook me before I packed it away.

"I overheard men in town threatening the captain if he dropped anchor on your shores," I said, ignoring their question.

"No one hangs the captain," the woman with the headscarf said.

My lips curved. "Right."

"Is he here?" the young man asked.

At his question, all three of them became so excited and antsy it looked like they'd shoot out of there any second and find the ship. I couldn't compromise our safe docking spot.

Or maybe I already had.

"Not with me," I answered. "But he needs your help."

Their faces fell.

I jutted my chin and pointed to myself. "Sailor on the *Lusca*. Here, I'll prove it. Ever heard of Calix?"

The young man's brow furrowed.

Good enough. I had no time to elaborate. "The captain is here and I need you to distract those men over there." I pointed. "They're heading from The Royal Crab to the docks. Distract them. They're looking for revenge because of what Terion did to Calix. You'll know them right away."

One of the women gave a determined, eager nod. I briefly wondered what she expected to get in return.

"Perfect," I said.

It wasn't, but it was the best idea I had. Right now, I needed to bolt back to the *Lusca* and warn the captain.

Zete held a piece of black sail in both hands. With the sails furled against the masts, it was impossible to tell where the rip was, but clearly a section of the topsail was missing.

"I need another day for repairs, captain," he explained. "We've been speeding all over drowning creation. This was bound to happen."

"Don't know that we have another day." If anyone cared about that piece of rotten seaweed, Calix, they'd ask questions, maybe look around. We couldn't be here when that happened unless we wanted a fight.

As fun as fights were, they often tore sails or hurt the crew.

And crew came first. Just above treasure.

I planned to send out another group of sailors overnight to take the last of what we needed. No sign of wide-leaf penthesilea yet. Mari, who often stole the most, was the only one on shore, busy securing the location of that gold for our next voyage.

"Captain," Zete pleaded. He'd been working on this since

morning, past his naptime. There was no better speeder, but he was exhausted and snarky for a couple days after every burst of rushing wind. I knew I'd pushed him past his limit. But Rhode's life had been on the line.

"We leave tomorrow." My focus strayed to the craggy rocks Mari had jumped over to get into town. She had to be back soon. Hopefully she found what she needed. We had to get a score bigger than what we'd lost at Dio's. My father was clearly getting impatient.

So, for that matter, was I.

Zete squared his bearded jaw and adjusted his sitting position on the barrel. Must have been difficult to find a comfortable spot with those wings. "I only have enough thread for this patch. If something else happens, we'll be fucked."

"Noted." *Not like that would be anything new.*

The word hurtled me back to last night, though. I itched to return to the room belowdecks to make good on my promise to Mari.

"Captain." Ajax's urgent tone cut through my seductive thoughts. "The shapeshifter is back."

My groin responded before my mind caught up. She sprinted over the treacherous rocks, sure as a water bug.

In only her underwear and breast bindings.

Well, shit. That wasn't good.

"Ready the sails," I snapped.

"Shit," Zete breathed, tossing down the torn piece of sail. "Yes, Captain."

"Weigh anchor," I told Ajax.

I flew from one side of the deck to the other, issuing orders. Everyone jumped to attention, pulling ropes, hauling cargo, setting a course.

Mari made an impressive leap from a lumpy rock ledge to land on the main deck in a roll. Her skin looked slightly darker than before, her eyes slightly bigger, but her real self bled through even as I watched. Her eyes found mine. "Authorities are coming." She immediately closed her lips.

I knew that tell.

With a curse, I loomed over her. "Here for a party?" I growled, helping her to her feet.

"They know we're here. I... I got the suna to distract them."

"I hope you sent them my regards." Inside, I roiled, dangerous as the waves. What in the Stygian Sea had gone wrong?

Mari avoided my look, busying herself with setting sail.

I caught her arm. Her skin flinched from my touch. The movement didn't improve my mood. "What happened?"

"I promise I'll tell you, but right now, they're coming."

A rolled parchment in her hand caught my eye. I snatched it up, unrolled it. "Map?"

"To the treasure. I think."

My shoulders relaxed a fraction. If she was right, this map was worth more than its weight in gold. I pointedly rolled the parchment back up and tucked it down the front of my shirt. "Whole story. Later."

"I promise."

"Zete!" I bellowed. "West!"

A string of foul curses erupted from where he stretched, undoing the knots holding the sails in place. A powerful flap of his broad wings, and he was aloft. Hopefully that tear in the fabric wouldn't slow us down too much.

We had a treasure to find.

Mari moved fast, but the whole crew avoided her. I didn't blame them. Here we were, running again. Something she'd done had caught the notice of the authorities. It was no use to stand and fight them—enjoyable as it might have been—when all we could gain in Zenia were a few supplies we could pick up anywhere. Not when there was a treasure at stake that could pay my debt.

Rhode was getting better. Maybe she didn't need the healing plant.

We should have just looted the city when we had the chance. Would have made everything worth it.

My focus slid to Mari again. Something about her disconnected movements said embarrassment. What had she done?

I narrowed my eyes. I didn't want fractures in my crew. This thing, whatever she'd done, had better be fixable. First, the party, then the rigging, and now this. I understood what happened at the party. The rigging had ultimately helped Rhode survive, so fuck anyone who still held that against her. But this?

Irritation ran black in my veins as the ship bobbed and then jerked forward in the opposite direction of the wind, thanks to Zete. The *Lusca* shone black and conspicuous in the sunlight.

On the rocks behind us, a yellow ball of flame materialized. Someone's deathless ability. For a second, I wondered who it was so the next time I was in Zenia, I could recruit (or kill, if they were only a demi-god. I wasn't picky.) The fire ballooned to the size of my head before rocketing toward us.

"Incoming!" I shouted.

The *Lusca* dipped as it picked up speed. We didn't attempt to swerve—that would create a bigger target—but stayed on course, straight out from the coastline. We weren't moving fast enough.

I tilted my head back to see the ragged black strips of ripped mast fluttering madly in our speed. A growl stuck in my throat at the sight. Could we move fast enough, or was the *Lusca* like a fish already caught in a line?

The fireball splashed and hissed only one ship's length behind us. My eyes found Mari again, my lip curling.

I'd killed crew members for less, and she knew it. My hand wandered up to my necklace of her boyfriend's finger. It was oddly soothing. Releasing a breath, I refocused. No one was killing Mari today. I sure as hell didn't want to, but she had fucked up in a way that had cost us more than supplies. That docking spot was burned. We couldn't use it again.

We'd get out of this. No matter who stood on those rocks hurling damned fire at us.

Above the noise of the wind, a tearing sound split the air. Light from the sky behind the sails bled through a bigger hole. Despite Zete blowing with all his effort, we slowed.

Another fireball launched toward us, fast and sticky-bright. I clenched my fist over the hilt of my cutlass. This shot went further than the last one.

"Out of the way!" I bellowed, hurtling myself toward the object.

I hit one knee to the deck and smacked my palm down, summoning all my power. It only worked when I was touching an object—no summoning waves to crash against the fuckers. Hopefully this would be enough.

Crash!

A blob of flame collided with the deck, sticking like algae. It wasn't green or white like deathless flames I'd seen that wouldn't go out. It was orange and hot, like ordinary fire. And it was burning my ship.

Water slicked from my fingers at a maddeningly slow pace. Straining, now with both hands, rivulets guided themselves toward the flames. I couldn't get closer unless I wanted to touch the fire itself. I suspected that wouldn't be a good idea. I wanted to keep this face.

"Don't use the drinking water!" I ordered. We hadn't gotten any more from Zenia. And we were moving too fast to catch water from the sea in time either.

A hiss erupted as the water from my fingers reached the base of the fireball. I glanced up to make sure no others were coming. Nothing—at least, not yet.

As if it was encouraged by touching the flames, the water running from my hands finally gained power. I'd kill to have a river at my command right now, but I had to work with this. Rivulets became a sheen covering the entire part of the deck between me and the fire. The sheen became a layer of water that grew thicker, deeper...

Ajax took over giving basic commands as he trimmed the sails and resecured the sheets.

Once I had enough water, I commanded it all to cover the fireball. As if a clear gel rushed over it, the fireball turned black where it had been bright orange with flame a moment before. Half the projectile, three-quarters, and at last the entire thing. It extinguished in furious steam.

Another fireball splashed into the sea, this time farther behind us. We'd finally sailed out of range.

I rose, eyeing the black mass of fireball still stuck to the deck. Another thing to fix. I couldn't summon the excitement I usually felt getting out of a scrape.

How had Mari compromised us? I didn't want to punish her in front of the crew. I didn't want to leave her on some forsaken spit of land. I wanted her around. I wanted her strapped to something downstairs.

This was the wrong time to think about that. The vertebrae on her back stood out as she crouched down to secure items to the deck. Suddenly, all I could think of was getting the rest of her skimpy things off and showing her just how frustrated I was.

But that wasn't how I operated.

Two ships, tiny in the distance, appeared to pursue. It would be easier to take them on. If they caught us, the crew knew what to do. Not the brightest, sending their ships after us.

"Ajax, show them who we are if they get close." I doubted they'd overtake us with Zete pushing us at his speed. "And find me so I don't miss the fun."

My first mate grunted, straining at the ropes.

Good enough for me.

The ships didn't gain on us. I watched them for a few minutes from the raised quarterdeck, until the rocky cliffs became only a smudge on the horizon.

Down to more pressing business. "Mari," I boomed. "My quarters. Now."

The others scowled at her as she lifted her chin and obeyed. No "yes, Captain" this time.

"Zete, we're far enough. Full sails."

The ship dipped as it slowed. Waved slapped the hull. A sigh, as if from someone holding up a huge object, escaped Zete's lips as he careened back to the deck. If he'd had more energy, he would have cursed Mari to Abaddon, based on the sweaty glare he hurled. But he was too exhausted to pull in his wings fully. Talking was out of the question.

Mari ascended the steps mechanically, almost defiantly. I waited, unmoving until she reached the top.

When she did, I produced the key and unlocked my cabin door. "In."

I didn't offer her anything to cover up when we stepped inside. Instead, I closed the door and angled the rolled map toward her face. "Speak. How did this happen?"

Tiny movements changed her expression to a thousand different things. The last remnants of her gentleman's disguise melted away, leaving her face and skin distinctly Mari. She ground her teeth, sharpening her jaw. I swallowed.

"I forgot to pour out an offering for Thenios."

My brows ticked downward. "Forgot."

"Yes."

I glared.

"Captain."

The word couldn't help but sound like sin in her mouth. I wanted to grip her chin and suck it out of her. "You forgot a common custom that every child in Zenia knows?"

She didn't look away, but all the openness had left her face. In its place was a blankness, a hardness.

Maybe that was all for the best.

"I did," she said. "And my accent came through. I didn't mean to compromise us." A slight tilt of her head made her look regal. The corners of her mouth turned down.

"Captain," I snapped. "You will call me Captain."

"Yes, Captain." But there was no life in it. No seduction.

I circled her, a shark around prey. I had to punish her. Map or no map, she had nearly gotten the crew killed. We needed more supplies. We were compromised with a ripped sail Zete hadn't had the time to fix. I would have tossed a lesser sailor overboard for this kind of incompetence.

Why not Mari?

I set the unrolled parchment on the table beside my bookshelves. It sparkled at the edge of my vision, ready for me to chart a course to the treasure coveted by the most powerful gods. Now, thought, I had to deal with this storm of a problem with Mari.

"You're a professional, Mari. How could this happen? You are a shapeshifter, *my* shapeshifter."

"Yes, Captain."

For once, it wasn't the response I wanted from her. Her large eyes didn't have the life in them that I coveted, *needed* at this moment. "Are you listening? The crew expects me to punish you. I expect that too. You've fucked this up."

"Yes, Captain."

I smacked my hand on the table with the map and halted to face her dead on. "Mari, you need to get your shit together. I made a promise to... reward you after you saved Rhode, and I will always keep promises to the crew, but this cannot happen again."

"Understood, Captain."

I wanted her to fight, to protest, to take off the small remnants of her clothes... something! Not this damned repetition. The tension made me angrier.

"You will man the helm for the next seven nights. All night." That meant exhaustion and isolation. I knew. I'd started at the bottom too. "I'll tell Euporia to alert you when you're needed."

But that was more of an inconvenience than a true punishment. There had to be more.

"Yes, Captain. I'll begin tonight, if you want," she said.

I hated the distance in her voice, her face, everything. My skin heated with the force of wanting all that distance gone. My jacket, bandolier, shirt, even fingerless gloves added layers between us. The necklace could stay.

"Not tonight," I found myself saying. "Your challenge just got more difficult." I stalked toward her. She took a few steps backward. "No sound. No coming and no sound and no telling the crew."

Her bound chest rose and fell more quickly. Finally, I got a reaction. Relief crashed over me as I realized how much I'd craved one.

"And I can touch you whenever and wherever I want." I raised my eyebrows to give her an opening to agree.

She met my eyes, hair falling out of the gentleman's style over her temple. The sight drove me crazy. The force of this— whatever it was—took me by surprise. Well, attraction wasn't love. That was the really dangerous thing. If I played with her in public, tied her up, made her scream, it was only to release the tension of the god-targeted pirate's life we led.

Mari nodded, small but earnest. "Yes, Captain."

My heartbeat swam faster. "Tonight, downstairs. Tomorrow, the helm."

"That's..." For a moment, it looked like she was going to protest.

My mouth curved. She clamped hers shut. Tonight, I'd make her open up.

We both released a breath and stepped back. I couldn't risk staying here with her any longer. Our interactions only became more fraught with simmering tension that tempted me to care too much.

"Get dressed," I said, opening the door.

The ships in the distance still hadn't gained, even with our ripped sail. Too bad. A fight would have been welcome.

The *Lusca* had seen better days, though. Its dark, scaly skin gleamed in the harsh light, scorched by the fireball. Debris littered the deck from our speedy escape. "Then start scraping that godsforsaken mess off my deck."

🖈 20 🖈

MARI

What was someone supposed to wear for a secret sexual rendezvous with a pirate captain?

The pants I had on were scuffed with tar and the remnants of that fireball. My back ached from cleaning it off the deck. The fire had left scorch marks on the main deck, which I'd sanded down by hand before mopping fresh tar over it. Exhaustion had me panting by the time I got the first coat on. Ajax, trying not to look friendly since I'd just screwed them all again by alerting the Zenian authorities to our hidden docking place, nudged me with his mast-sized biceps and told me to get some rest.

I rummaged through my clothes. Not much to choose from—different disguises I wore to various ports, but I doubted Terion wanted a nobleman to show up instead of his faithful spy. The idea made me bite my lip. The look of surprise on his face if I did...

"What are you doing?"

I jerked my head up. Rhode sat upright in her hammock, eyeing me. The crushed bird bones had given her enough strength to do that, at least. Because of me, she probably hadn't gotten the rest of the medicine they planned to gather in Zenia.

"Just changing," I said. "You look like you're feeling better."

She narrowed her eyes and swept green locks of hair from her face. "Going somewhere, then?"

I schooled my breathing. Rhode didn't know anything. I hadn't destroyed the secret Terion wanted hidden. For some reason, even though I was angry and sore, I desperately wanted our secret trysts to remain hidden too. "The mess for some food," I answered. "Want anything?" I bent toward my small trunk again, drawing items out. There was the gold film of a dress. I was absolutely not wearing that.

"Not hungry," she answered. "Not after swinging so hard through that entire... scene!" She rolled her eyes. "I'm done with this hammock. Once I can swim again, I'll have it shredded to little pieces and sleep on kelp all night."

I snorted a laugh through my nose. Rhode and I were friendly, but we didn't often talk. She felt a little like royalty to me. Sparkly, sweary royalty. A little like Terion. "That sounds like a great idea."

"Yes," she said, flopping down again.

I breathed a covert sigh of relief that she wouldn't be judging my clothing choices.

Why did I feel like I had to change anyway? Terion saw me all the time. He knew what I looked like. The entire crew had seen me in that barely there dress he'd gotten for Dio's party, so they could all picture me naked, no problem. I wasn't as if Terion and I meant something more to each other. We had an agreement. That was all.

Sudden anger propelled me to my feet. I'd wear what I had

on. I'd make his job harder. Even as I thought it, I knew my anger was largely directed at myself, but a sliver wedged into my thoughts of him too. So confident and... *more* than me. I could hold my own, but he didn't have to. He could simply stand aboard his ship, surrounded by a crew who worshipped him, would die for him.

I would die for him too.

And now, this. When we went to the party and then afterward, when we'd touched each other, and then—the memory pulsed loud in my mind—when he'd bound me to a table and eaten me out upside down... Feelings tangled me in their nets. I couldn't stand it. The sight of the mainmast at a certain time of day reminded me of Terion torturing and killing one of his own for me. Remembering turned my blood hot.

I didn't know if I could ever come for him, but he intruded in my mind more and more. How far would he worm in? Was this only a game or punishment or reward for him?

Hopefully he'd let me go soon.

Hopefully he'd never stop.

Don't stop.

Ah, ah! No topping from the bottom, Mari.

Yes, Captain.

I drew in a deep breath and swallowed, stuffing down my fantasies. A glance at Rhode told me she'd been watching my face that whole time.

Damn it.

Hopefully Rhode hadn't found anything suspicious in the way I held myself. Had my mouth softened or fallen open when I lost myself for a second thinking about what Terion might do to me? Normal people did that when they weren't thinking about sex, right?

Instead of honing my skills as a shapeshifter, life on the *Lusca* had made me softer, if anything. My next meal didn't usually depend on my ability to keep an expressionless face. At least in front of Terion, I didn't have to mindlessly agree in order not to get beaten. I didn't have to pass as someone else to sneak into rooms. The crew wasn't warm and fuzzy toward me, but most were civil. Ajax had noticed I was tired. The difference between my past life and that small kindness justified any discomfort I experienced by staying here. I was a pirate. Terion's shapeshifter. I would remember how hard life had been before and serve him better. I wanted to be proud of myself somehow.

I didn't say anything else as I left our room to head down the hall to face a locked door. Halting in the middle of the hallway, I perked my ears to hear anyone else approaching. The ship creaked and tilted lightly. Voices rose within rooms. Footsteps sounded on the planking above. No one near me here.

Closing my eyes, I summoned my power to change my appearance. I added a more golden tone to my skin, covered the grime on my hands, gave myself long pointed nails, changed the shape of my eyebrows, my jawline. I became something sharper, more deadly. Someone who didn't make such godsdamned stupid mistakes as letting my swamp accent show through in a group of men I needed to infiltrate. This version of myself felt more powerful. This version could look Terion in the eye and was allowed to be angry.

For some reason, that turned me on. I inhaled slowly.

"You look ready to devour someone."

I whirled carefully and found Terion smirking at me.

He strode closer. "I hope it's me. Makes this more fun."

"I thought this was supposed to be punishment," I murmured.

He whispered in my ear. "Your silence is punishment." Straightening, he glanced at the ceiling, as if revising. "A complication you brought on. A challenge." He opened the door.

We hurried inside.

I wrapped my arms around myself as the mysterious equipment materialized in the gloom. I couldn't guess the purpose of half the items in here. Okay, sex. But the *specific* purpose.

Terion lit more lanterns so the place glowed with smoky orange light.

The veneer of my arousal earlier remained, but doubts crowded in like a rising tide, stopping it from growing any stronger. If anything, that pulse, that yearning, subsided. I couldn't give Terion what he wanted in here, unless he just wanted someone to play with. Maybe he just wanted to get himself off.

Terion's hand closed over my upper arm. He turned me to face him.

My changed face clung half-heartedly to my features, its power sapped by facing another of my weaknesses.

"Do you like this look?" he asked, but his furrowed brow meant he had a different question underneath.

"As much as any." I let it slip off like a mask.

He released me, regarding me in a searching way. "If you think this is really a punishment, Mari, then we won't do it. I wouldn't touch you like this. We both have to agree and get pleasure from what's happening. I won't force myself on you."

"It's..." But I had no idea what to say. It felt weird to talk about my complicated feelings surrounded by bondage ropes and spanking paddles.

Terion, on the other hand, acted far more open than he had when he confronted me in his rooms. He sat on a sort of half bench, his body language softening. "You know that, don't you? I wouldn't force you?"

It was a simple truth, but so important that I felt my insides loosen. I hadn't feared that he would do something I didn't want to do, but his reassurance—pausing when I didn't seem ready—meant more to me than he knew.

I looked forward to this role as his co-challenger. He'd try to get me to come. I'd try to hold off. But no matter where I went or what I did, I always had a set role. I was a tool to be used, not a person to chat with about feelings.

"I know," I said. "We can get started."

"No, no." He patted his knee. "If you're afraid I'm still angry..." He quirked his lips. "Yes, I am. But I also looked at that map and you've circled the perfect spot to hide a treasure. Out of the way, but not impossible. No one would stumble on it." His eyes glowed. "It's there. We can get it."

The roguish way he looked back at me, as if to invite me into his excitement, made me give in and sit on his lap. He felt strong under me. My side pressed against his torso. As if it were nothing at all, he slung his arm around my back to hold me in place.

This wasn't like the last time we met here. This wasn't a fever of lust. This was a casual, friendly ownership that lit my insides. I blinked once, surprised, to find I was growing wet.

His dark, handsome face with all its hard panes and soft edges stayed close to mine. The red scarf on his head folded slightly slower on the left side as if he'd adjusted it. Yes, that eyebrow stuck up a little more than the other...

"So tell me," he coaxed. "Do I need to make you suffer a little? Force your silence?" He pursed his generous lips. "Call it off and I won't bring it up again."

I gnawed my own lip. His gaze followed. He adjusted his sitting position just a little—enough to accidentally rub between my legs with his thigh, and enough to show that he could pick me up as easily as luggage. The combination flushed me hot. He set me further down his leg.

Why not up, closer?

Oh...

I glanced down at the growing bulge in his lap.

He didn't seem the least bit self-conscious when I looked up and he'd clearly caught me staring. "I'm serious," he said. "I was looking forward to some fun, but it's all your decision."

With Terion's face so close to mine and his firm legs under me and his arms around my back and his attention fixed as if I were the only thing in the world, it didn't take long to make up my mind. "I want this."

"Are you sure?"

I hesitated for a second, glancing around the room. All these things designed for pleasure and pain and domination. For a hundred reasons, I answered, "Make it extra hard, Captain."

"Extra hard?" Terion smirked, his eyes growing black and molten. He snapped into his old dominance with ease. Adjusting his fingerless gloves—arms still wrapped around me—he asked, "The challenge or my dick, Mari? Because one's halfway there."

Sweat broke out on my neck from his nearness. He was showing me more mercy than he should. Favoritism, almost.

Confusing.

I reached for my strength again, that ability to change my appearance, appease anyone I met, blend in, disappear, and then run like hell. The fact that I had to reach for it at all—that it wasn't automatic—showed how soft I'd gotten. How I'd fail again and again. Conquering Terion's challenge felt like a win I needed. I'd be his best submissive. I wouldn't come, even if he took off all his clothes now, wet and naked as that time in the bath, and sucked me dry. I'd build up my endurance and focus again so there were no more slip-ups.

I'd get better.

I'd get...

Slippery. I felt it when Terion eased me off his lap. I exhaled. "Both, please, Captain."

His chest rose and fell in measured waves. I stood in front of him, positioned between his legs, opened wide as he sat. "You want me to do my best to make you come, then not allow it?" His question sounded professional again, almost detached.

Confusing, confusing.

"Yes, Captain."

"You can say no to any part of this and face no repercussions for insubordination. You agree to bondage?"

"Yes, Captain."

"To whipping, spanking, or marking you?"

I struggled to stand still with him right there saying things like that. But I did. I didn't move a muscle. "Yes, Captain."

"To my touching you, with or without my power, with my hands, mouth, or body?"

"Yes, Captain."

He arched his back in a stretch. No matter how many times he'd taken women down here, this couldn't be normal for him, could it? He looked so casual. No. He looked in control. Like a predator that feared nothing, had done this all before.

He cleared his throat. The sound sent cracks down the image of control he presented. "No kissing, of course."

I'd forgotten. On his lap, we'd been so close. Until he said that, part of me had yearned to lean in. Good thing I hadn't. That was one of the rules for good reason. We were here for sex, not closeness or love. Challenge for me, and release for him.

"Right. Yes, Captain," I responded.

"Do you agree to penetration?"

My heartbeat skittered and sped. He hadn't broken eye contact, so neither would I. "Yes, Captain."

We stared. I felt half-wild. My chest heaved.

"Please. I want you to."

He still didn't move.

What the fuck? I was still learning what he liked, but I knew him well enough to guess and hit the mark the first time. This was his secret sex room. He was supposed to initiate things here, and yet he sat still.

I glanced at his hands. They lay on his thighs, where I'd been sitting. He gripped lightly, but not as if he felt the level of awkwardness I did.

"Treat me like a dirty girl," I said. It felt wrong even as it came out of my mouth.

Terion's lips made a wry twist. "A dirty girl?" His voice was gravel.

"Yes." I jumped at the chance to keep him talking or, even better, moving, so we could end this conversation. "I—"

"Who are you right now, because you're not my Mari."

My Mari?

Why did he have to be so godsdamned confusing? Did he speak to the rest of the crew like that? I couldn't come up with a time he'd said "my Ajax." It wouldn't be wildly out of character, though...

"I am me," I answered, too defensive.

"I've seen you as many people, you remember." He stood. Finally. "When eyes aren't on you, what do you want? I'd bet five gold pieces it's not to be treated like a 'dirty girl.'"

There was the dangerous captain I knew. The more his professional questions faded and this raw, demanding, reckless side came out, the more my emotions boiled high. I was vulnerable, a silver fish in sight of a bird, but this was also the part of him I connected with. I couldn't reach his business-like side. But I understood this.

I just didn't want to answer.

"Isn't that what you want, Captain?" I asked, making my voice sweeter than it ever was outside of jobs.

"A dirty girl?"

"Yes."

"I want someone who can let loose and enjoy themselves with me. Someone who likes me being in control. Who likes wild sex. If that's a dirty girl, then sure. But our... agreement doesn't include you pretending to be someone you're not."

I gave the room a pointed glance. "You don't pretend in here?"

Terion's jaw flexed. "You're pretending before we've started. I want to know who I'm fucking. Is it Mari, or some person pretending to be okay with this?" His words had an edge sharper than they should have. Maybe because he was obviously still turned on. He lowered his face to mine, almost touching.

If I moved my chin, I could kiss him. My insides went cold, then blazing hot.

"Why do you want me to do my worst?" he whispered. How he managed to sound menacing, sincere, and gods-damned sexy at once, I had no clue.

I gazed back at him. "I want to withstand you. I want to know I can."

"No one can withstand me." He didn't move his face from mine. And now, his body was close too. Gods. I was used to him teasing, but he wasn't teasing now. He wasn't only talking about making me orgasm, either.

"I can," I whispered back.

Laugh lines flickered in his cheeks.

"Because I'm the Terror of the Seas," I finished. I wasn't teasing either.

Staring him down like that, whispering what I wanted to be true, connected us as surely as sex. Maybe, dangerously, more.

"All right, then," said Terion, pulling back and giving me room to breathe. At last, maybe, he understood what I needed. "Let's begin."

﷯ 21 ﷯

TERION

"You remember the word to say to make me stop."

Mari nodded.

"Say it."

Her lips twitched before she said, "Constellation."

"Good girl." It was already hot in this room. My layers weren't helping. I shucked off my long captain's jacket and slung it on a barrel near the door. "Say that if any of this becomes too much."

"It won—"

I held up a finger. "Say the word again."

She held my gaze. When I didn't do anything but stare back, she relented. "Constellation."

"Captain."

"The word is constellation, Captain."

The word slid under my shirt, clinging to me like sweat. Familiar power pulsed through my fingers. I had to use them. I grinned wide as a barracuda.

Then Mari, my girl, gave me a wink. No, only a glint in her eye, which was just as good. She was ready too.

Finally, we could begin.

"Take off your clothes while I reiterate the rules," I said, staring at my gloves instead of her.

"But I know—"

"You won't speak except to answer my questions. You will address me every time as Captain."

From the corner of my eye, I saw more and more lean, pale skin. Scarred and beautiful and distinctly Mari.

My gloves weren't that interesting.

It was fine. This would all be fine. I could drink her in all I liked. It wasn't as if we weren't going to fuck anyway. What harm was there in admiring a beautiful body? I had one. She had one. We would use them for as much pleasure as I could muster.

It would be fine.

My blood raced. The way her hair fell over her forehead like that as she bent to strip off her pants was particularly fetching and—

Holy fuck.

"If you have to scream, scream my name," I added, my voice a little hoarse. Did I still sound in control? Like this was business or something? I couldn't tell. My mind was screaming *look look LOOK!*

So I looked.

Mari had never gotten fully naked in front of me before. She had little secrets. Not anymore. Her breasts were just large enough to hang down, with brown nipples dotting each one. They looked like the perfect handful. She had marks along her ribcage and stomach. Old wounds. Some of them I knew about. Others, like a small bluish bruise, were new. Her legs had defined muscles I somehow hadn't noticed when she wore that gold dress. For some reason, that soft line dividing her thigh up and down along the sides struck me as important. I had to send my water there, and my fingers, and my mouth all the way up and up. And her naked feet touching the black skin of the ship sent my gaze trailing back up before I did something stupid.

Her shoulders were slim, collarbone another tempting line. Safer. I drew closer. Her pupils flared when I did.

"You will do anything I say, and, no matter what I do to you, you will not come." Our faces paused a breath apart.

Her lips rolled inward in a smile that wasn't quite a smile. Mari against a challenge. Scurvy things had happened lately, but in that showdown, I put my money on Mari. And I never lost.

"Yes, Captain."

Another shiver ran down my back to my cock. I released a breath. "We both know you've been a bad girl. Done bad things." I flicked my hand toward the bench in the center of the room. We'd start there. See what she thought of it.

Obediently, she moved toward it, but it was obvious she didn't know what to do. This was delicious. So different from the other encounters I had with more... seasoned partners. I didn't expect it, but our shared history gave this session a new flavor. She knew me just as I knew her. That fact dulled some of the mystery I usually felt, but mostly, our knowledge of each other heightened what was about to happen. I had information to draw from that I usually had to guess. But the crux of the encounter, the climax—that was still something I had to learn and forcibly give her.

Against most challenges, my gold was on Mari. But when I formed the challenge, she stood no chance.

I directed her to straddle the board in the middle of the bench and put her knees down on the padded sides, facing away from me. Once she understood what to do, she moved easily.

I didn't need more light in the room to see her glorious ass. It was even better than I thought it might be. Another handful to slide between and—

I needed to get control of myself. These thoughts belonged to a younger, stupider version of myself eager to jump in bed with anybody. That wasn't an option now. Basileus—fuck him—would cut my heart out with his curse.

For a second, I looked at the darkened wall past Mari's head to center myself. I was captain. I was king. I would make this woman experience pleasure all her bastard partners had never bothered to give her. They must not have appreciated that ass, or the line of muscle on her thigh.

"I am going to make you wish you could come," I said, low in my throat. "You'd beg me, if you could say more than my name. Since you can't beg"—I whispered in her ear now—"you'll break, and the game will be over."

Her jaw clenched. Good.

I straightened and reached toward a few instruments hanging from the wall nearby. A paddle? Maybe not. A plug? I ran my fingers over the items. Finally, I chose a thin, complicated chain. Lifting it with one finger, I turned back to Mari, who was already looking at me. Her scrunched forehead told me she couldn't identify the chain. Guessing would keep her on edge, just where I wanted her.

Last time, I'd turned her on by strapping her to the rotating table and teasing her. Today, I needed to test more of her boundaries to see what made her squirm. If I could leave her shaking and satisfied for the first time in her life, she'd forgive me for losing our bet. My cock lengthened every time I imagined her crying out my name, especially now, with her bent over in front of me.

The chain and miniature clamps—courtesy of a public house at a friendly port—slithered into a pile on the bench next to her knee. I grabbed a pair of soft leather cuffs next.

"Hands behind your back," I ordered.

She obeyed. Her bare back rose a little more quickly. It wasn't fear. The flush along the nape of her neck said I'd started off with a good decision. Of course I had. This wasn't my first time pleasuring someone who wanted a kinky challenge before I made them climax.

I wrapped the cuffs around her wrists and bound them together. Her hands rested just above the divot in her lower back that looked even more tempting than the line of muscle on her thigh. I wanted to pour liquor onto it and lick it off.

"This," I continued, picking up the chain again, "will make you feel every tiny movement you make. Any flex, any shift, any time you arch into me, trying to get more, will bring you closer to coming." I arranged the thin chains to drape over both her shoulders. The first clasp connected to the wrist cuffs. "But I forbid you to come." The second clasp closed over one of her hanging nipples.

Mari bared her teeth, obviously uncomfortable. For a second, I nearly ripped off my gloves to palm her and make her feel better. Instead, gripping the tiny clasp in two fingers, I avoided touching her soft skin. My erection strained against my pants, hard and sensitive. *Soon. You have to calm down first.*

I moved the clasp a couple times until Mari's expression showed lust with only a little discomfort.

She exhaled a bracing breath. "Yes, Captain."

I smiled, connecting the third clasp to her other breast. She hissed. I shifted my weight so my cock didn't press against the seam so hard. "The final one," I said, pulling the last connected chain down her body, held suspended above the table, "is for your clit."

Her bound arms gave a slight shiver, and she looked me squarely in the eye. It was a lot of... connection. Normally, my partners leaned into the sensation and didn't look at me until it was time to pay attention to what I commanded them to do. Half of them reacted with their eyes closed, soaking in the water I ran up their bodies or the restraints I used to hang them up. Mari looked at me.

Her expression wasn't particularly submissive, but she didn't wear her defiance either. It was measured curiosity, determination. It said, "Do your worst. I can take it."

"How does that feel so far?" I asked, pausing with my hand and the chain near her belly button.

"Like a lot, Captain."

"Do you like it?"

"I... don't know, Captain."

A truthful answer. I'd have preferred a gasping "oh yes, Captain!" But her truthfulness was helpful. I'd deduce exactly what would make her quiver and gasp and scream, wet and desperate. Hell, I thought she was the one who liked challenges.

I'd try the final clasp and see if this was the right direction for my shapeshifter's pleasure. Mouth dry, I stroked my free hand between her legs where she'd lowered flush against the table. With a little coaxing, she raised herself again far enough that it was easy to knead her folds to find what I wanted.

Mari's stomach muscles tightened at my touch. She wasn't sopping, but she was a little slippery. Enough for now. I drew the thin chain down and clipped it gently.

Mari gasped.

"Better?" I asked.

"Yes, Captain."

I caressed her hip as I released her. "Good." Okay, this could work.

There were so many tools in here. I'd just guessed what Mari would like last time. A good guess, but everyone was different.

I prided myself on dominating very, very well. My reputation at the docks was earned. But I hadn't done something like this since *before*. I barely learned the names of the women I invited into this room, and that suited both of us just fine. Mari, though...

I cleared my throat, letting my eyes slide down her form. "You're going to be a good girl for me?"

"Yes, Captain."

"We're going to try two things, and you tell me which one you like more."

"Yes, Captain." She sounded eager.

Very good. "Arch that back for me."

She did, not even making the slightest whimper, although she twitched as the slim chain moved.

I stalked to the front of the bench, grabbing the leather whip I'd used the first time with her. That ass stuck in the air. She was bound, responsive, ready for me. "First, gentle." I trailed the strands over her mouth, coaxing her lips to go slack. Slowly, I moved to the line of her collarbone, then lower, teasing the chain attached to her breasts. Her eyes glazed and slid away from me.

That was what I wanted. Only feeling. None of this extra eye contact unless I asked for it.

I dangled the strands of the corded whip lightly around her side and over her back to her round ass. Her body flushed harder. I moved the leather as soft as breath over her skin, caressing it. When her eyes began to close, I repeated the pattern, lulling her into a comfortable, erotic rest.

"How's that?"

She sighed. One corner of her lips tipped up. She wouldn't be smiling if she were on the verge of orgasm. She knew she had control.

I flicked her lightly.

"I feels good, Captain. Just fine."

I scoffed. Nothing I did was *just fine*. She knew the comment would bother me. It was time to give her more, to show her who controlled her pleasure here.

"That's one. Here's the next thing we'll try."

I drew back the whip and cracked it down on her bottom, hard enough to sting but not cause too much pain. Not yet. She jerked in response and cried out when the chain yanked on her nipples and clit. The noise turned into half a laugh. So, she wasn't hating this, then.

I hit her harder, leaving a red mark. My mark, that she'd have tomorrow when she worked on my ship. Only the two of us would know the secret.

Suddenly, I wanted to mark her whole body as mine. My aching cock spasmed. *When she sits down tomorrow, she'll know you were there.* My breathing quickened. The danger of continuing should have stopped me, but the danger made it better.

"That's it," I whispered, and struck her again.

"Oh!"

"What?"

"Just a noise, Captain. Not a word."

I smirked. Smartass.

After a few more strokes, her bum was laced with markings. Her head had fallen forward, but she gave no hint of protest. She liked this.

Divine seas, the things I wanted to do with this woman. It went beyond enjoying the dynamic of being dominant. I had a bone-deep desire to see her break, to give in fully to pleasure that I provided. To make her feel better than she had in her life. She'd done enough for me, and suffered enough at the hands of careless assholes who didn't see what a treasure they had in her.

As much as I fucking yearned to free my cock from my pants and plunge it inside her wet hole, she had to be getting sore staying in that position for so long.

"Which one did you like more?" I asked, putting the whip away.

"The second, Captain."

"I know."

She shot me a look over her shoulder, wincing at the sudden pull on the chain.

I gave her a crooked smile. "Up."

Her eyes darted, as if unsure how to do that bound as she was. I leaned over and unclipped the chain attached to her cuffs and reattached the chain to itself like a long, exceptionally kinky necklace. Then I undid her cuffs.

She climbed off the bench.

Well, fuck me. If I thought she was sexy before... This

version of Mari, raw and tousled, with chains pinching her naked skin, was enough to make an ascetic break a vow of celibacy.

"Get your hands in the air," I commanded, too fast.

She raised them slowly to adjust for the sensation of the clasps.

Fuck, fuck, fuck.

My goal was to make Mari break, not myself.

I repurposed the cuffs to attach her to the ceiling. The new position was meant to feel like a good stretch. Judging from the noise she made as I hung her up, I'd accomplished that mission. When I backed up, the whole length of her lean frame stretched in front of me, tantalizing as gold itself. She glistened between her legs like an invitation. And how had I never noticed how delicious her mouth looked until now? That bottom lip, hanging slightly open, was my kind of sinful. Just slightly darker than the rest of her skin, it begged to be sucked.

My desire spiked even higher. It was a wonder I still had my clothes on.

Don't kiss. We can't kiss.

Mussed hair fell into her eye.

Thank the gods we can fuck, though.

"Comfortable?" I asked, finally removing my gloves.

Her eyes tracked the movement. "As much as I can be in this situation, Captain."

It was good to have the old Mari back again. Earlier, when she'd spoken like a shell of herself, I felt cracked, like there was a hole letting water aboard the *Lusca*.

"You're not being perfectly submissive, Mari," I observed.

Her eyes refocused, sparkled. "No, Captain."

"Should I do something to change that?" I set the gloves down. My hands rarely went without them, so every sensation whispered over them. It was like being naked. The humidity of the room, the relative coolness without the leather pressed against skin...

"Yes, Captain."

I could barely look at her without surrendering. I let out a growl of acknowledgement.

Normally, I could let foreplay go on longer. I won battle after battle of who would come first. The woman always did. I left them all barely able to stand.

But right now, I had to get inside Mari. It was like I became someone else. My head was a storm.

"Sit on this." I brought over a stool tall enough for her to sit on while her arms still hung above her head.

Since she couldn't use her hands, I scooted her so she sat at the edge. My bare palms against the soft give of her hips had me feral.

When I looked up, she stared back at me, cheeks flushed. Was it my nearness that turned her on so much? My hands positioning her?

Usually, I played longer with my prey before I got to a version of this part. I'd stretch them to their limits and then, right before I fucked them, I made them mad with praise.

"You're beautiful," I muttered, but it was automatic. Mari wasn't a temporary playmate from the docks. I gazed at her, close. She seemed to like that. "You're beautiful," I said again, meaning it more this time. "You've been such a good girl for me."

Tell-tale signs of arousal bloomed on her body. I flicked the chain attached to her nipples. She flinched, but didn't look away. Our faces were close enough for moist, shallow breaths to mingle between us. Her dark brown eyes wanted more.

"In every shape, with every face, you make me want to kill for you."

Was that too much? I gauged her reaction—she hung on every sound I made. And it was true. These erotic scenes used pretend, but true praise was important to me. It's what I would want.

"Right now, you're so slippery and wet for me." I leaned in closer, our cheeks almost touching. "I want to plunder you until you forget everything but me. I'm so hard for you."

The heat from her cheeks made me so hot I thought I'd burst.

"You've been so good. Do you want me inside you?"

A throaty whisper. "Yes, Captain."

"Why?"

"Because you'll make me feel good, Captain."

"Why?"

"Because you're so good at this."

"Why?" My dick throbbed, and the question felt like a risk, but this was always part of my process. Make them beg. Make them praise me too. Mari had guessed right without ever being in this room.

"Because you know what I like and... you're beautiful too."

I pulled away far enough to see her face again. Honesty and intensity lived there. If I tilted forward, I could kiss that bottom lip. I could drown in her.

Instead, I said, "Do you want me?"

"Yes." It was desperation. A confession. "Captain."

Lust roared and I tugged down my pants, freeing my stone-hard cock. "Open your legs, Mari. That's it."

I pushed inside her soaking pussy with a grunt. I had to work to fill her tight space. Her fucking partners hadn't treated her right. A wicked smile crossed my lips as I remembered Calix's severed finger hanging around my neck. The idea made me even more savage.

Mari's mouth opened as I forced myself deeper, deeper. I clung to her hips as I thrust forward, working all the way in. Her walls squeezed me so tight I almost came right there.

No. Mari first.

I ground hard into her. The chain attached to her clit stimulated my groin. Every time I tapped it, Mari sucked in air and her raised arms tensed. She felt so fucking good. My thrusts grew wilder but her pleasure didn't spike any higher than when I praised her.

I needed her to break. Now. Because I was about to explode any second.

I took her chin in my hand to force her to look at me. Every time we made eye contact, she seemed to get more aroused. She stared at me, lust-glazed, while I pumped into her. Her lower belly flexed. I felt it in my cock.

Grunting with each thrust, I managed to unclip the chains from her nipples and take the handful I'd wanted, soothing that spot with my palm.

She whimpered. Watching her was impossibly hot.

If she didn't orgasm now, I—

I slipped out of her with a guttural cry, gripped myself, and came on her belly and thighs and the chain still attached to her swollen clit. Sweat dripped down my temple. I fought for breath.

That was... different.

Mari panted too. She still hadn't looked away. Her entire

front glistened wet, a mix of my cum and her arousal and my power exploding from my fingertips.

Was she thinking the same thing I was? That I'd said too much, let myself go?

She'd called me beautiful. (I was, but she didn't go around telling me every day.) Beautiful. And she trusted me to make her feel good.

I'd told her the truth, too.

Fuck. We might have to stop doing this.

As the tide of my lust lowered, I realized I still hadn't made her come. I'd gotten her damn close, though. If I'd held off a minute longer...

I glanced at the pink between her legs. "I'll—"

"That's all right, Captain," she said quickly. She sounded less breathy and hoarse than before. Her chest heaved and she grinned, sloppy and real. My guts clenched with want. "I win."

22

MARI

Things were awkward between us in a new way after Terion uncuffed my hands from the ceiling restraint. He brought me water, which I drank. I put my clothes back on—he'd never taken his off.

That was... My mind wouldn't settle down. The way he'd whispered to me and whipped me and looked into my eyes as he plunged into me over and over...

I felt drunk.

"Stay in here as long as you want," he said. The smell of our sex still filled the room. All the strange furniture and ropes and objects looked like treasure I needed to collect.

"Rhode will notice I'm gone." I tightened the sash around my waist.

He nodded. "She will. You're right." His shoulders and words were tight, rigid. Terion usually acted so cavalier. Was he angry that he couldn't make me come? I'd gotten closer than I ever had in my life. That was an accomplishment he could boast about to himself.

Damn, the way he'd made me ache and spasm. And his

eyes... like he wanted to make me all his. An almost angry need.

The space behind my ribcage felt empty. I wanted *that* again, even if it left me bloody and screaming.

But Terion was bustling around, cleaning and rearranging all his equipment for the next time. Based on the way he avoided my eyes, I suspected the next time wouldn't be with me.

THREE DAYS LATER, I RUBBED MY WRISTS AS I CLIMBED THE steps up to the helm. No marks remained from Terion's cuffs, of course. Only memories. He'd been careful, even as he became a creature of lust as he drove into me. I felt the markings on my ass, though. They made sitting on the stool sting for two days afterward.

I hated how much I liked it.

Even now, topping the steps, my pants rasped against the hidden lashes. Terion had been there. Had actually fucked me. It felt like someone else's dream. Especially since Terion had barely spoken to me since.

Night air hung heavy and moist over the ship. From where I stood on the elevated deck, palming the helm, I could only see fragments of the mist-covered water and the ghostly outline of the dark ship itself spread out before me. Waves sloshed lazily against the hull.

It was late, but about half the crew sat around a lantern —the brightest spot for leagues, since clouds covered the moon. Zete had gone to bed, of course, but Ajax, Rhode, and even Euporia passed bottles of rum among the group. Seven sailors all huddled around cross-legged as if the light were warmth. A typical night aboard the *Lusca*, with the type of camaraderie I'd envied when I'd first signed on. I still envied it. At least I hadn't fucked up too badly. Although, I could see where the fireball had landed on the deck, we had a heading, Rhode was alive, and Terion's "punishment" was... well...

Terion presided without even trying. He wore the red scarf on his head and guffawed with laughter any time someone told a bawdy joke. In the dim light of the lantern, his eyes crinkled and then sharpened with intensity and awareness. Everyone checked his face for a reaction, even when they pretended not to.

He didn't look at me.

As if we didn't just have feral sex in his secret room.

I couldn't hear most of their conversation very clearly with the water slapping and the sails fluttering. Bottles clanked, shanties were sung, and then music.

"Up!" Terion commanded, helping half-drunken crewmates to their feet. I perked up, but the word wasn't meant for me. Did any of the crew know about our arrangement? No one looked my way, so I guessed not.

Invisible again. All for the best, since lately, most had looked at me as if they'd rather see me in the brig than on the deck. Or maybe ripped from prow to stern. *That* would have been a threat, unlike Terion's command I keep silent if he touched me in public. That sounded more like a dare.

"In every shape, with every face, you make me want to kill for you."

I checked our heading and shifted, growing wet again at the memory.

Rhode poised a fiddle underneath her chin, and a lively tune danced across the deck. I knew this one. It was a joyful, fast, chaotic tune.

"When the rum's all out and the gold's locked up,
Then the pirates come in the dead of night.
When the birds all call and the waves are high,
Then the Lusca's *crew readies for a fight."*

They began clapping, faster and faster, for the chorus.

Terion gave a smirk and started a dance popular on Nalia, with lots of hopping and spinning. The others joined in, even Ajax, once he saw participation was inevitable. His scowl made me purse my lips to seal out my laughter. Seeing Terion dance shouldn't have made my stomach twist. But he was all lethal grace and dangerous joy. What I wanted to be.

My soft shoe bobbed against the planking in time to the music. The second verse included lines people only sang when they were too drunk to know better. Things about stabbing and fucking and getting away.

But all that friendship didn't include me. The singing grew rowdier.

"You can't escape. No, you can't escape
The Prince of the Ocean, the god of the tides.
Take up your weapons, grab all your knives.
No one hangs the captain. He'll get out alive!"

Terion's jacket swung as he danced. Euporia took a swig of rum and followed the rhythm, in her own world. It was rare to see her on deck at all. She was always tinkering in our room, marking time.

What if, one day, I figured out how to amplify my power

and change my looks with more than a nudge here and adjustment there, and I infiltrated this crew again? Would things be different?

Your swamp accent gave you away.

I swallowed down my bitterness and checked the star measurements again. Still on course.

My eyes traveled back to Terion, skipping with the rest. Soon, he'd leave. He always left at unexpected times. You couldn't count on him unless he made a solemn promise to a member of the crew. He was like the sea itself, dangerous and beautiful and unpredictable.

But suddenly, watching him, I gripped the helm tighter with annoyance. He shouldn't mess with my mind like this. I had nowhere to go, and he had suna from here to the Beyond. I couldn't understand him anymore. Was he attracted to me, like I'd felt in the breathless words he whispered in my ear, or did he just see me as a distraction or—worse—the chance for a power trip?

I heaved wet air into my lungs with the difficulty of a bellows. I didn't deserve to drift alone like this, to be used when called for. I wanted to be down there with the fiddle music and the dancing and the savage joy of piracy.

Terion was maddening. So why did I want him to come up here, stand beside me, and test my ability to be silent in front of the crew? It was sick. Kind of like Calix's severed finger dancing on the string around Terion's neck. Maybe I was the same type of crazy as he was. Seeing that finger bob on the string as he ground his hips against me only turned me on even more.

Yeah, definitely sick.

The song ended and Terion took a long draught of rum

before passing off the bottle. Mist wreathed around him. When he swaggered in my direction, I tensed. In a breath, I calmed my features. My heart shouldn't hammer at my captain coming closer, but everything had gotten so complicated. We were ropes gnarled together. Even if I wanted to get free, I couldn't. The knot was too tight.

Just like the knots when we—

"We're going to Anemos," he slurred at me, leaning very close and grinning. One of his partially gloved hands wrapped around a knobby handle of the helm. "Supplies."

I paused, half-scowling. I already knew our heading. The pirate-friendly island formed a natural stop on the way to the Bridge. The way he said that, though... Was he rubbing in my failure, since I'd prevented us from getting more supplies? I was usually good at reading people. But Terion, lately, was harder and harder to understand.

My eyes fell to the gruesome necklace he wore, and my belly flipped. Forcing my gaze upward again to meet his, I pushed all these stupid tied-up emotions aside in favor of the one he deserved.

"Aye," I ground out, sounding like Ajax.

"Ah ah!" he sang, holding up a finger.

"Yes, Captain."

"That's it."

His breath smelled like sweet liquor. I wanted to taste it, to see if it was even possible to feel better than I had a couple hours ago. So far, he hadn't made good on his promise to make me come. Dark enjoyment at my victory was overshadowed by a small voice saying, "But don't you want to see if it's possible...?"

"Angry?" he guessed, his eyes sharpening with new focus.

"No, Captain."

"I see it in your face. Do you think I'm treating you unfairly, because I assure you..."

"No, Captain."

He circled me slowly. The faint breeze lifted the tails of his coat. He looked far too self-satisfied. Any pleasure I'd experienced from the marks on my ass faded to soft disgust. Why didn't he look at me like he did before? Why was he acting so catty? It felt like my insides were crashing in chaos. Simmering to the surface came hurt and annoyance. I shoved one down and lived with the other.

"*No one hangs the captain,*" he recited. "Know why not?" His voice had lowered so the sailors on the deck couldn't hear us.

"Because you're the most feared pirate on the seas," I guessed.

"With my Terror." He beamed. "Yes. What else?"

"The best fighter." I wasn't in the mood to stroke his ego right now. Instead, I wanted... I didn't know what I wanted, but it started with him not looking at me like that.

"And?"

I closed my teeth in my mouth. "*And* I don't know."

He clucked his tongue, stepping up so he stood right beside me. "And I can tell who my enemies are before they strike. I pay attention to their hands." He placed his lightly over one of mine.

I relaxed my tight grip.

"I pay attention to their eyes."

I'd been avoiding his gaze, looking straight ahead, but I turned. The blue-green scales on his cheek gleamed dully in the light of the single lantern below. Around us was darkness. It was as if nothing existed in the world but the two of us. A jolt of what passed between us before struck again like lightning.

He released my fingers. "I pay attention to their mouths."

My lips, which had half-curled into a snarl of irritation, relaxed too.

His eyes lingered long enough for me to imagine a dozen things he could do with his mouth. But he was playing with me. It wasn't fair.

"All these things, you see," he said, closing the small distance between us, "show me who's delighted to see me, as people should be, and who's ready to strike out." The final words whispered in my ear like a threat. He stayed there, his rum-hot mouth by my ear, his fingers secretly finding the place between my legs and rubbing it over my pants. "Why do you look ready to strike out?"

My breathing turned unsteady and mouth went dry. My guts roiled worse than fish in a whirlpool. "I'm angry," I confessed.

"Keep steering."

"Wha—?" My brain couldn't tear itself away from Terion's fingers and his threatening words.

He backed away, so it looked like he simply stood next to me while I controlled the ship. From below, it would be diffi-cult to tell that his hand kneaded my sex just out of sight. I tried to focus on our direction again.

"You're angry because?" he murmured. "Was it not good for you?"

Fucker. He knew it was good for me. I obeyed his command not to come, but—for the first time in my life—it was truly difficult.

"Because I don't know what you want from me. I don't understand this."

Miraculously, the others didn't look up here, but they would if the captain stayed much longer.

The fingers stopped, but I still throbbed where he had touched. That didn't improve my mood.

"It's a distraction I think we're both enjoying." His *s*'s slipped into softer noises. He was drunk. I ground my teeth. "And it's reward. And punishment."

I fought the urge to shush him. The others would find out if he kept talking so loudly.

"Would you rather I leave you on some spit of land for destroying the *Lusca*'s ropes and sending those idiots after us in Zenia?" he asked.

"No, Captain. That's... no."

He swallowed, touched the necklace of Calix's severed finger almost pensively. The rum-soaked haze lifted a fraction. After a moment, the corners of his lips turned down. "I shouldn't have... just now."

"Maybe not," I agreed. But fuck me, I wanted him to do it again. I was a mess. "I'm on course here." I stared straight ahead as intensely as if an island of pure pearl had appeared on the black horizon. Hopefully he'd take the hint.

"I want to know how you taste. I will someday."

"You... have," I said, so quietly I could barely hear myself.

"Mmm." It was a hungry sound. "More."

"Captain," I pleaded. How much more of this head-spinning back and forth could I take?

"You're right." He tapped a finger against his lips. "We'll get the gold and then... Terror of the Seas." He made a theatrical gesture with his hands like an explosion.

"I don't know what you're talking about," I said, sour.

When he didn't speak for a while, I glanced over at him. He winked at me before descending the stairs again, reckless with drink.

My throat worked. This arrangement wasn't working. I had to find a way to tell him that I couldn't handle being his downstairs girl. Either he cared about me or he didn't. I ached with the need for those things he whispered to be real, but, as much as I thought we were friendly, Captain Terion was still ruthless and violently independent. I thought I could handle it, but I didn't want to be his fun. I wanted more or nothing.

Because I would become the Terror of the Seas.

That was one good thing to come from our encounters—the fierce knowledge that I wanted that name, to belong in the ranks of Captain Terion in my own right. *Terror of the Seas, Terror of the Seas...* I scanned the dark waves. I didn't need to put up with this shit. I could make myself more.

The thought bolstered me, even though I knew no one would believe the name. Not with my past.

At least the idea encouraged me until I locked eyes with Rhode, who reclined on the deck by the lantern. One look and it was clear.

She knew about me and Terion.

❧ 23 ❧

TERION

"Terion."

"Yes." I kneaded my forehead. Last night I'd drunk more than I should have.

Rhode glared at me. Honestly, it was nice to see her glare again.

We stood on the main deck in the too-bright sunlight. The island of Anemos was due to come in sight any minute.

When Rhode merely cocked an eyebrow and tossed a length of green hair back over her shoulder, I realized she meant for me to fill in the blanks. "What? Now that you're back to full strength you want permission to swim again?" I gestured over the water. "Granted."

"No! I saw you last night."

"That makes two of us." Was I still slurring? I felt like I was slurring.

Rhode sighed. "With Mari? It doesn't take a brilliant mind to figure out what's going on."

My chest tightened. Nothing was going on. Not really. But I had to admit that *something* had *almost* gone on when

Mari made desperate eye contact while I fucked her. A connection deeper than physical, and the physical was already... well...

Fucking perfect.

"I don't know what you're talking about."

"Yesterday," she prompted.

Damn it. She knew me too well.

"Mari left the room early, and then last night when you talked to her at the helm...?"

I turned away to look over the waves. Piercing points of sunlight stabbed my head. "I talk to everyone."

"Terion!" Rhode stamped a foot. "You can't mix piracy and pleasure."

"On the contrary, I take a lot of pleasure from piracy."

She huffed a breath through her nose.

Behind us, Klep and Zete walked by. When they were out of earshot, Rhode bent closer to me. "You're taking Mari to your secret room. You can't fool me. She's a spy and a thief, Terion. There are so many reasons you should have left her out of it!"

My brow furrowed. Her assessment was true, but not the whole picture—Mari wouldn't betray me. Thinking she would showed a lower opinion of Mari than I liked to hear coming out of my sister's mouth. Much as I loved Rhode, I was still the captain here. She shouldn't attack my decisions so openly. "Go for a swim, Rhode."

"The crew will think you're playing favorites."

"Rhode..."

"And what will happen when you give her up for someone else?"

Tenacious. If there was one word to describe my sister, that was it. "Enough," I growled. "Let me live my own life. And if you tell anyone else—"

"You're not exactly subtle."

"—I'll throw you in the brig while we're docked."

Rhode's eyes widened. Immediately, I regretted the threat. Threats were for others, not her.

But part of me was glad I could say the words. Maybe that meant I didn't love as fiercely. Maybe that meant she'd be safe from the curse.

Mari's panting mouth as I drove into her yesterday intruded into my thoughts. Her eyes. The way she responded to me like she never had to anyone else. Would she be safe too?

"Then I'll only say this, Captain," Rhode hissed, anger written over every feature. The scales on her cheek glinted in the sunlight. "Think about what you'll do with Mari once this flirtation is over. Do you think she'll go back to being an obedient member of the crew? Or do you think she'll resent you?"

My concerns had leaned in the opposite direction, that I'd gotten too close. But maybe Rhode was right. Damn it, she usually was. I fingered my gruesome necklace. Making Mari tremble and come dominated the empty spaces between my thoughts and duties on the ship. If I gave into the pull between us, I doomed her. If I ripped us apart, I lost my shapeshifter—one who knew too many of the *Lusca*'s secrets...

Rhode was right. I needed another drink.

"I'll figure it out," I said, keeping my tone light.

Rhode's lips flattened as she eyed me. Right behind my eye socket, my head pounded. "I'm going for a swim," she said.

Part of me wanted to hold her back. The last time she'd

gone into the water, the Leviathan had almost annihilated her. But the sea was her element, even more than the ship. Her illness had kept her away from it for too long already. "Island's coming up soon," I pointed out.

In quick, precise motions, she removed her clothes and jumped overboard. When she resurfaced, glistening with water and smoothing green locks from her face, she already looked refreshed. "I know. I won't miss it."

Between Rhode swimming again and the sex I'd had with Mari that went far beyond fun, panic fluttered against my sternum.

Rhode slipped beneath the surface, out of sight.

I calmed myself with slow breaths. No attack this time. Not when I was so close to finally paying off my debt and breaking the curse that threatened all of us. The gold on the Bridge. It had to be enough.

I exhaled, too shaky.

Yes, I needed to clear my head, and the island would do just fine to offer a distraction.

❧ 24 ❧

MARI

I strapped a knife to my leg before jogging down the gangplank. Here, I didn't need to disguise my face or wear different clothes. I could be a pirate—ignored, next to Captain Terion's fame, but still a pirate.

Confusion and exhaustion clouded my head as I reached dry land. Men and women crowded the dock, human and deathless alike. Ajax stood menacingly at the top of the walkway to prevent anyone from rushing the ship. His scowl could burn sugar black.

I slipped between the straining bodies, all but unnoticed. Everyone's eyes drank in the sleek black form of the *Lusca*, scanning the railing for the reason they came.

The air around me smelled like sweat and tropical flowers. Heat made the layers of my outfit cling to my skin.

Applause erupted around me.

"No one hangs the captain!" someone began. A chorus rose up from a hundred pitchy voices. The intimate fun the crew had on the deck was totally different than this worshipful roar. As I slithered further away, bitterness clogged my throat. Even

though I was fucking the captain they screamed for, I wasn't a part of either that fun or this frenzy. I stood alone. As I always had.

I'd changed my eyes, face shape, and hair color. It was time to be somebody else. I could take on a new persona as I nicked supplies for the final leg of our journey.

The crowd thinned in the back, and I followed familiar roads that led to the liquor, the food, the medicine, the soap.

"What a welcome!" came Terion's voice.

I glanced back. His arms were raised like a politician's. My gut soured.

Clapping and shrieking broke out again. Uplifted arms in the crowd had trident cuffs or tattoos similar to the captain's.

"It's good to be back," he continued. "No place like this in the Realms!"

More clapping. I turned away.

"We stay until tomorrow. Will you treat my crew well?"

Another rendition of Terion's song rippled through the crowd, petering out halfway through as affirmative answers drowned it out.

Terion laughed, that hearty, delighted laugh that ran through my body faster than rum.

Shoving my hands in my pockets, I quickened my pace, his voice fading into the distance behind me.

"Well then, feast and rum...!"

I rounded the corner away from the chaos of the dock. A few people strode here and there, but the shadow of the *Lusca* didn't dominate every thought. I could breathe.

First, a stop at the pub. A curvy mermaid with a thick tail formed the sign above the door. The Siren's Legs, it was called —a regular stop for all of Terion's crew.

I slapped a bronze piece on the counter. "Shot," I said.

The bartender, a square-faced human in his fifties, slid the coin behind the bar with a finger and replaced it with a small metal cup filled to the brim with liquid. I didn't ask what it was, but I did notice the keg he'd used to pour it. Above the spigot was the burned symbol of a trident. I smothered a frustrated growl and took the shot in one gulp.

Strong, piercing, just like I'd hoped.

Behind the bartender, a young woman washed dirty glasses. I studied her face.

When the door swung open and the man's attention swiveled to new customers, I got out of his line of sight and ducked behind the counter. In a second, I looked like the girl doing dishes. Her stature matched mine close enough that all I had to do was change a few aspects of my face. The young woman I impersonated flitted among the horde of people entering—all coming from the docks, I reckoned. They spoke rowdily and demanded drinks.

I poured several for the oblivious bartender, who reached backward without a word. If he wasn't mute, he certainly expected people to anticipate his every need. After handing him an ale or shot of liquor, I'd pour another for myself into a set of flasks hanging beneath the keg. One for him, one for me. Maybe a few for the crew if I got enough.

"Ale for the captain!" someone cried.

My core tightened with irritation an want.

"Rum," Terion clarified, somewhere in the midst of the crowd. I couldn't see him. He chuckled. The sound cut through the murmur and cry of voices like a knife. I'd recognize him anywhere, in any form.

Two people clambered to buy his drink at the counter.

No wonder Terion liked stopping here. Anywhere else, our sins got us in trouble with the law. Here, he basically was the law.

The bartender reached a thick hand behind him. I set a double shot of rum in his palm. Snatching the next flask, I held it under the rum spout and twisted the spigot.

At the counter, the crowd parted enough for me to see Terion sitting at a table with a busty woman on his lap. Her cleavage all but rubbed against his face.

What the hell?

Red tinged the corners of my vision. Those hands had touched me only yesterday. Those eyes had stared at *me*.

Rum slopped over the rim of the flask and ran sticky down my hand. "Fuck," I breathed, capping it and shoving it into one of my pockets.

That was it. I'd had enough. There were errands to run, and I'd rather clean a boatful of diseased fish than stay here another minute.

Grinding my teeth, I couldn't help one more quick look before I disappeared out the back. The woman whispered in Terion's ear. Whatever she said made a smile curl the edges of his full mouth. Shaking with fury, I stalked out of the pub.

I'd seen this play out a hundred times. He would take her onto the ship. He would treat her to ecstatic sex in his room below deck. He'd drop her off, smiling and satisfied, at the next port.

I clenched my hands. He wasn't forbidden to do any of that. We didn't mean anything romantic to each other, but I thought he'd keep his fucking hands to himself for one stop at least.

With savage efficiency, I gathered, bought, bartered, and

took the supplies we needed on board before we set sail for the Bridge. I passed my crewmates occasionally at fortune tellers or bawdy houses. I didn't speak to them.

The image of Terion with that woman kept intruding over the goods I shopped for. I couldn't focus.

This is pathetic, Mari. You knew this would happen. Keep your emotions out of it.

I smiled at shopkeepers, slipped unnoticed into bars, flirted with apothecaries. I was everyone and no one. Maybe the hurricane inside me made it easier to be someone other than myself. I hardly knew who Mari was anymore. I'd let Terion become too much of my identity.

I'd refuse to let him touch me anymore. He kept saying I had the right to stop our arrangement, and that was exactly what I'd do.

When I returned to the *Lusca*, the crowd had reduced to only a handful of people. Ajax remained on board. I could see him over the railing beside the gangplank. Lugging my latest haul up the wooden ramp, I scanned to see if anyone else remained aboard. Euporia often did. She kept time and tides. But she stayed in our room for the most part.

I put away the supplies quickly, running from the mess to the storeroom to the upper deck and back. My mind churned like an angry sea.

If I didn't tell the captain off, I thought I might burst.

He never promised he wouldn't take other partners.

That thought didn't comfort me like it should have. He'd looked into my eyes and brought me to the brink of screaming pleasure. It wasn't just sex anymore.

Not to me.

I hated how certain I was about that revelation. What

started as a fun secret between captain and crewmate had become so much more to me. He wore my ex's godsdamned finger around his neck, for fuck's sake. Did that not mean anything?

Of course it doesn't.

You're no one. You're a mistake, a liability.

I shut my eyes tight.

You've always known it.

I stood in the center of the deck, staring up at Terion's bedroom door behind the spokes of the helm. Then I looked up. I'd try the obstacles first. I'd beat my time if it killed me.

And *then* I'd confront Terion, armed with the knowledge that at least I'd accomplished a personal goal. Made a small step toward the fantasy of becoming the Terror of the Seas.

Tying my sash tighter around my middle, I glared up at the ropes. Readying my muscles, I counted down.

Three, two, one.

"Careful, Mari!" Ajax shouted behind me, exasperated.

I ignored him. Up, up, up, into the rigging. I swung and jumped, keeping a manic pace. This anger was helping. Without the fear of falling, I kept making every leap. Pain didn't register. I kept going. Fierce joy lit my body. I felt like I was flying, invincible.

The ship was my village, my playground. On a whim, I added a skill. Could I make a longer jump? The rest felt easy.

But then I was falling.

The black skin of the *Lucsa* hurtled toward me.

"Mari!"

I flailed, hands splayed wide to catch anything going by. Nothing. Too fast!

I bounced against the ropes and hurtled out over the water.

One second the sun blazed on the surface and the next I went under, all sound muting.

Because I hadn't expected to fall, the landing smacked against my body. No graceful dive. In a few wide strokes, I reached the surface again, gasping.

"Fuck, Mari!" Ajax roared, looking over the side. "You almost landed on the deck."

I clambered back on board. Although I didn't need help getting over the railing, Ajax seized me with a meaty hand and yanked me forward, doing more damage than the water had.

I stood. Nothing broken.

Well, maybe a piece of my pride.

Ajax scowled at me. "You could have been killed. For what?" He didn't wait for an answer, but tromped back to the top of the gangway, looking fit to murder.

Movement caught my eye. On the upper deck, Terion turned his back and retreated to his rooms.

I bared my teeth. He couldn't say anything to me? Even after what just happened? After *all of it?*

Reckless and soaking, I lunged after the captain who forced me to care about him.

❦ 25 ❦

TERION

"Ooh, Captain," the woman crooned, drawing a line across my jaw with her fingernail. Her smile spoke of wicked things.

I smiled easily at her, but the lush curves pressing against my thighs didn't arouse my regular response. I looked into her pale eyes, but she averted her gaze, looking instead at the triangle of bare chest showing above my shirt.

"What a strong and capable captain you are," she said, voice thick with the accent of the isle. My cock perked up, but I still felt like she was a coat that didn't fit. She leaned against my ear. The rumble of voices around us in the bar, ordering drinks or catching up with old sea mates, covered the sound of her words from prying ears. "I'd love to feel what those strong hands can do. Tonight, you can have me all to yourself." Her long, wavy hair tickled my face. "Mmm, you must want some fun after a long voyage."

I didn't tell her it was a fairly short voyage and I'd had her kind of fun just a few nights ago.

Fun wasn't the word.

I scooted her up my leg, testing. She did feel warm and eager, all soft, rounded curves. I could make that mouth do things it had never imagined. And then she'd leave. And then I'd meet a new partner. And on and on it went like a current leading nowhere. Was there no reward beyond getting off on someone?

I chuckled. The woman took that as me accepting her proposition and boldly kissed me. She tasted like sweet cherries.

She didn't taste like Mari.

I plunked her off my lap. "Sorry, madame. Too many things to do today." I gave her a wink and strode out of the bar. Her glare was murderous. I could have used another good drink, but the air felt close in there. I liked freedom. And my mind itched.

I knew why. It was a stupid reason. A strong reason. Something I couldn't shake off.

I couldn't sink into the woman's kiss because her lips were wrong. Hair, wrong. Attitude, wrong. If I didn't compulsively compare every godsdamned thing to Mari, the woman would have been perfect. She was gorgeous and willing—exactly my type.

But then memories burst to the surface and squelched any rising desire for the woman in my lap, leaving them all for... someone I shouldn't take to my secret room again for her own safety. But Divine seas, the look in Mari's eyes as I pumped hard into her slick hole, the sweat sticking her short hair to her temples, even the way she pretended not to respond when I touched her through her clothes at the helm. That last memory was foggy, tinted with shame. I shouldn't have done that. I'd mixed my love for bold and brazen action with something that could fracture my crew and hurt Mari. Bad idea.

"Captain Terion!"

I slid sideways out of the way of the old woman who had appeared in the path.

"Captain!"

With a resigned smirk, I halted. The woman, a tall, thin palm trunk of a person with long whitecap hair, didn't look familiar. Beads dangled from her bracelets and overlarge ear piercings.

She reminded me a little of Scira, the goddess ruler to the north of my homeland. The one time I'd met the goddess, she spoke in incomprehensible riddles that did not help me locate the merchant ship owned by an ex-mutineer. I found him myself two months later. Scira's cryptic comment about a tail might have referred to the mutineer's pet monkey, which I took on board after skewering the bastard.

The woman in front of me looked ancient but lucid—both of which didn't describe the goddess.

I swept my arms outward in a bow. "Fair winds, good mother."

"I need to give you something."

I grinned. "Kind, but no. I make my own fortune."

She beckoned me back the way she'd come. Behind her was a thatch hut. Maybe a fortune teller.

A little like Scira after all.

I didn't like fortunes. I preferred doing and discovering the consequences later.

"Please, Captain. I see..." Her words cut off in a worrisome way.

"What?" I demanded, getting sour now. I wasn't sure what kept me rooted, listening to her.

She drew closer, smelling like too-sweet lilies. "The darkness around you," she whispered. "The curse."

My nostrils flared with surprise. "You don't know what you're talking about."

"If you don't make amends..."

I closed the distance between us, setting a hand on the hilt of my cutlass. "You speak of things you know nothing about."

She grimaced, but didn't back away. "Do you have a plan to pay your debt before death comes calling?"

My hand shot out and gripped her by the throat. After a breath, I let go. I couldn't murder this old woman just because she knew too much about my secret. First, I had to know *how*, and then I could drop her somewhere away from the wrong ears.

I'd always known this island would only be a haven for so long. My father had so many spies it was bound to be discovered eventually. Or, if not that, then this godsdamned seer would ruin it all.

"Where did you learn this?" I hissed.

"I practice the great art."

"*Where?*"

"It traveled on the air to me. I don't know how it works. I'm only here to warn you."

Her eyes were red where the bottom lid drooped. Her bottom lip protruded twice as far as the top one. Was this woman sent by my father? His tricks always targeted me where I was softest—Rhode, now this elderly woman, whoever I deeply loved...

"To warn me about things I already know?" I growled.

"No. About things to come."

I all but pushed her in the direction of the little hut. She ducked and went inside first while I held the door to make sure she didn't reach for a weapon. Instead, she simply entered and sat down at a small round table covered with mats and candles.

"Tell me," I demanded.

"How do you plan to solve the problem?" Now in the dimness of the hut, she seemed more at ease.

I still hadn't released my hold on the weapon at my hip. One side of my mouth curled up. "That's for you to divine."

Her fingers traveled oddly like insect legs across the tabletop. She didn't look at them.

If she was telling the truth, that she could see the future, I might want her aboard the *Lusca* for our last leg.

When the silence continued except for the little shuffling sounds of her fingers, I leaned against the table. "Any time."

"You sail for treasure."

Not exactly a revelation. Pirate.

Her eyes, which had been unfocused since we entered, grew almost white. "Tell me and, in exchange, I will reveal the fate of the one you love."

My jaw flexed hard. I didn't love Mari.

But that was my first thought.

Did she mean Rhode? If either of them had a scratch by the time I returned to the ship, I'd string up the villain until his guts poured out on the main street.

"Don't fuck with me," I said, dangerously low.

"She will give her life..." The woman's pupils rolled back into view as her gaze locked on mine. "Do you want to know how?"

My cutlass rang out of its sheath. I set it glistening on the table. "Listen, witch. I've killed people less aggravating than you. I leave you your life. You tell me what you know."

"Your destination will bring my knowledge into focus."

I slammed the tabletop. Since our first interaction outside, she hadn't shown any fear. "Do you work for my father?"

"No."

"Do you want to die? Because I can arrange that for you."

"No."

She waited. Just sat there, as if I hadn't threatened her. In a horrible, bone-deep way, I knew I'd stay until I wrung out all her secrets. She knew more about my feud with Basileus than she said.

I ran a hand over the lower half of my face. "We go to find gold the weight of horses."

Her eyes lit up a fraction. "The weight of horses?"

"That's right. Now what do you know?"

"You go to the Bridge."

My heart jerked painfully in my chest.

"Where she will give her life for yours."

I hurtled up from the table. "No one will have to."

"She will die."

Noise built in my skull. "No, she won't." I wasn't even sure which *she*, but I knew neither could die or I'd... *Shit. It happened.* I wasn't supposed to get close to anyone—not close enough for their deaths to destroy me. *Shit shit shit!*

"She will."

I pointed my cutlass at the woman's throat. "I'll pay off my debt before that happens. I'll gut any murderer in my way."

She still didn't flinch. A god-like calm exuded from her.

"She will suffer because of your choice. No gold could be enough."

With a shout, I drove the point of the cutlass through the center of the table. I shot out my gloved hand and gripped the pulse points under her jaw, dragging her toward me. "If I find out that a word of that is true, I will return here and personally feed you to the sharks. Understand?"

She smiled. Nothing that had happened so far was as eerie as that smile.

I should have run her through. It didn't matter that she was an old woman. She knew my secrets, and those of my crew. She could prove dangerous to our mission.

Everywhere I walked, people stopped me with congratulations or praise or promises of the best blowjob I'd ever had. My smile had gone rusty. I needed a glass of rum in my room. When my boots touched the *Lusca*, this sensation like eels squirming in my chest would quiet.

"Fair winds?" Ajax greeted as I went aboard.

"Gold on shore."

But he obviously heard the heaviness in my tone, because his square face compacted with concern. I waved it away, heading toward the upper deck.

I drew in a deep breath of salt sea air, thick with heat. Birds cried overhead. Rum was what I needed. It took a matter of seconds to enter my room, eye the map to the Bridge, and toss back a healthy pour of rum.

It burned and didn't help.

She'll die.

Had the seer meant Rhode or Mari? Did it matter? I'd be damned to Abaddon before I'd let either one of them die. Fights were natural, slices and bruises, but giving her life for mine? Fuck that.

I emerged to look over the length of the ship, a sight that always calmed me. The *Lusca* was like a giant scaly sea creature bending to my command.

Movement above caught my eye.

Mari, wearing a scowl worthy of Zete after a long flight, leapt from one mast to another, a huge distance. My ribcage tightened. She landed gracefully as a dolphin. Her taut form moved among the sails and ropes effortlessly. I'd seen her practice this sequence scores of times, but she'd never looked like this. She was reckless and fast, strong and weightless. She was perfect.

Was she adding elements to her practice routine?

Wasn't that ...?

Shit! Mari flew forward in an impossibly long leap and missed her grip. Her body met air, flailed, went down.

Falling happened so fast, I couldn't jump down the steps fast enough. Air caught in a painful knot in my throat.

Ajax sprang forward with a shout.

Mari fell, toppled...

And splashed into the water.

But I was already hyperventilating. My mind could say Mari was alive a million times and my body wouldn't believe it. I started to twitch, uncomfortable, foreign in my own skin. My lungs had no clue how to work anymore.

Just needed to get to my room.

Damn this day!

Look behind you. Check...

I fought through the panic squeezing my chest and mouth and eyes to turn long enough to see Mari reach over the railing and, with Ajax's assistance and curses, flop onto the deck. Then I all but fell into my room.

I didn't even have time to close the door behind me before I closed into a ball safer than the dread outside, sweating and fighting for air.

"Ter—! Oh my gods, Terion!"

Blackness rounded my vision. The pressure of hands against my shoulder felt like a lifeline.

"Terion! I'll get Ajax."

I shook my head, dizzy. "Shut... door."

I heard it close. "What's wrong?"

I can't breathe, I can't see, and panic's crushing me into powder.

"I'm here," Mari said. "I'm here." I felt her ease down to the floor beside me, wrapping her body loosely against my back. She breathed steadily into the crook of my neck. "I'm here."

erion shook in my arms. My heart couldn't stop galloping behind my ribs like it wanted to get out. I'd never seen him like this, never seen him as anything other than self-assured. Now, he was falling apart.

"I'm here, Captain. I've got you," I soothed. What else was I supposed to do? My sopping hair from falling into the water seeped under his collar.

I forced myself to breathe slowly and obviously, my stomach rising against his back. Matching my rhythm might help him.

Klep and even Rhode had left the ship with the rest. Only Ajax, Terion, Euporia, and I remained aboard. When he'd commanded me to close the door, I knew he didn't want Ajax to know what was happening.

Terion's hand gripped mine convulsively, as if he were drowning. His fingers pushed between mine and he squeezed hard. But his back, which had been twitching against me, slowed a little. I felt him take a deeper, shuddering breath.

Together, we lay that way long enough that I felt like I'd actually pulled him ashore. I was exhausted, my muscles tight from holding him firmly but loosely enough that he could escape if he wanted to. I didn't know if he wanted me to hold him like this. The woman I'd seen in the bar was probably waiting downstairs right now. To think, I'd come in here to tell him off and now it looked like we were embracing on the floor.

I looked over his shoulder at his room. A corner of the Bridge map hung off the side of the table by the shelves. His bed, set into the wall on the opposite side of the room, was mussed, like he'd had trouble sleeping. That made two of us. I looked again at the shelves full of books and trinkets and souvenirs from Terion's travels. I recognized some of the objects—a painted conch shell from the beach on Hyperion, a buckle from a warlord's belt, part of the wooden figurehead from a merchant ship we'd pillaged about a year ago.

Something glinted in the light. What was that? I squinted, but the sunlight from the windows faced toward us rather than falling on the eclectic hoard on his shelves. Intricately sculpted to look like three intertwining mermaids, the metal and gold statue looked suspiciously like...

Oh my gods! I'd heard of that. It was a Nalian national treasure, its lore wrapped in legends of mystical power. Supposedly, it could confer some of Basileus's power to its owner. I'd only heard about it, never seen in it person. That statue alone had to be worth more than everything I owned.

Terion's hand relaxed in mine. I took that as a cue to let go of him. I'd been wrapped so tightly that his entire back was wet. My leg had even curled around his to hold him steady.

I swallowed and stood.

Terion rolled to his knees and got up more creakily than usual. Expression grim, he lifted his chin and resettled his now wet coat.

"It seems we have two secrets now," he said without cracking a smile.

"Are you... okay?" I didn't know if what I'd seen was poison, illness, a curse, or something else.

"Now I am." His dark eyes bored into mine, as if trying to reestablish control.

The look was enough to hurl me back into the anger that had propelled me in here to begin with. "You might have noticed that my first instinct wasn't to mutiny but to help you, so don't look at me like that. Has that happened to you before?"

He seemed to weigh his words. "Yes."

I blinked. "Who knows?"

"Ajax. And now you."

The past few minutes had left him totally vulnerable, not the strong captain everyone on shore knew and loved. He could be taken advantage of like that. He could be killed.

"Does your father know?"

For a second, it looked like he might spit. "Don't mention him to me. No."

I'd never thought of Terion as fragile before. He wasn't born a cocky, bold leader. He'd started somewhere before all that. Against my will, I traced the line of his jutted jaw with my eyes, the light and shadow creating a soft line.

"Don't tell anyone," he said.

"I won't." I put my hands on my hips. "You have a lot of secrets, don't you?"

He slid his attention to his damp, crumpled clothes and began smoothing them. "Heard news about that lately, have you?"

"Terion." My voice lowered in exasperation. "There's me and there's this. You're allowed to have secrets, but I'm getting sick of this."

"Which part?"

"Terion!"

He finally met my eyes. His were ringed with shadows.

"Is that woman downstairs?" I asked.

His brows ticked down. "What woman?"

"The one who sat on your lap at the public house."

He burst out laughing. "What the fuck are you talking about, Mari?"

"I saw her." My cheeks burned as I continued. I had no right to confront him about doing something we'd never discussed. He could have sex with anyone he wanted. He didn't belong to me. I just hated the feeling that I was chained to him while he was free to do as he pleased. I deserved more than that. Maybe the first step in creating my own mythology, after being a crew member on the famous *Lusca*, was taking this stand.

"Who? And when were you in there?"

"Shapeshifter," I said, pointing to my face.

He smirked, slow and sensual. "I knew I chose well."

"Terion." I steeled myself. "I want out of our deal. Whether it was a reward or a punishment or a game..."

Uncertainty flickered in his expression. "Is this about when you were at the helm? I barely remember that. Not sure I should have done that."

It did feel good to hear him apologize, or as close to apologizing as he got. "No, it's... everything." All my ranting thoughts from an hour ago had cooled in the wake of Terion's episode.

"It was good for you, though." He meant it as a question he already knew the answer to. Somehow confidence without the swaggering cockiness.

"I..." I didn't know how to explain. "Is there a woman coming aboard tonight?"

"No." His sharpness eased a little as understanding lit his eyes. "Are you jealous?"

"That's not how I'd put it. Would you like to see me with somebody else?"

"Depends on how long I got to watch."

Despite myself, my lips quirked. "That's terrible."

"Wouldn't have to be if you were enjoying it."

"Terion..."

His expression grew serious. "I said that you could call this off any time you wanted, and it's true."

I crossed my arms. "I do want to call it off."

"And you're sure? Even before I win our bet?" His hand drifted up to touch his gruesome necklace, but I couldn't read his face. Was he disappointed?

"Yes, I'm sure." My gaze drifted back to the mermaid statue on the shelf. Would that not be enough to pay down some of Terion's debt? If he ever mentioned an exact amount, it was never to me.

"All right. No more sessions downstairs. Back to normal crew and captain."

"Yes." But something like regret twisted my gut. This was the best choice, so why did he have to be so beautiful standing there, backlit by the sun, damp from the way I'd held him as he tensed and shook? "Will you be okay?" The question ripped out before I could stop it.

"Without making you orgasm? Yes."

I huffed out a frustrated breath. "No, I mean..."

"Ah. No need to worry."

That wasn't an answer, but it was all he would give me.

27

TERION

I tried to focus on the map Mari had taken in Zenia, but my episode kept intruding on my mind. She knew about my panic. And she'd called off our deal.

Were the two connected?

It wasn't every day she walked in on her captain limp as a dead fish on the floor. I gritted my teeth. As soon as shame reared its familiar head about my weakness, other impressions rushed in too. The moment was a maelstrom. After weakness has seized me by the throat after her fall, she'd done her best to calm me. She'd held me.

I couldn't remember the last time I'd been held. My first instinct was to buck her off, but she didn't demand that I get up, or act superior, or take advantage of my predicament. She was a pirate. She could have scented weakness like blood in the water. But she held me instead until I felt calm.

My partners, when I touched them, typically had their hands tied so I directed their pleasure. I loved how it felt to be in control and learn what made each woman squirm and scream and break. Afterward, I usually held them long enough that their drowsiness either wore off, or they fell asleep.

No one held me.

Clashing reactions fought like rival ships in my chest. Mari *cared* for me when she could have taken advantage of the situation, and then she called off our arrangement. Was it pity? The thought made my lip curl with disgust. Except for her body language a minute ago, I would have been sure pity motivated her decision, despite how good I'd made sex for her. She obviously was attracted to me. But she kept mentioning that woman at the bar. Maybe Mari wanted me all to herself.

I straightened my gloves and returned to the map. Watercolor islands dotted the paper, crisscrossed with Mari's scrawl and approximate locations. If her information was correct, I could shake off my debt and the curse.

Mari didn't know how badly I needed her lead to be right.

And how badly I needed her *not* to sacrifice herself for me.

She shouldn't hold me again. Interesting that that was what kept bothering me, not the idea that she'd tell anyone about my panic attacks. I knew she wouldn't, even after she'd decided against having any more sessions.

She smelled like the sea when her face pressed against the back of my neck. That scent defined me—it seeped from my pores and whispered freedom and ran fiercely in my blood. It was like air to me. More than her arms around me, that scent calmed me down.

Around and around, Mari swirled in my thoughts. She was the scent in my nose and the scratches on the map that could lead to treasures large enough to change my fate. I brought her so close to breaking as she stared, desperate, into my eyes.

Mari, Mari, Mari.

I slammed the tabletop. Enough of her. But even that thought was laced with the way her hair fell over her face and the jealousy that flared like light behind her eyes when she thought I would take somebody else to the secret room.

Mari, Mari, Mari.

This was too far. Basileus used weaknesses like this. He would kill what I loved.

Mari.

I ground my teeth, yanking the necklace of her lover's finger off and tossing it on the floor with a thunk. Mari and I weren't lovers. We were barely friends. She was my shapeshifter. Only. No matter how she looked in a gold dress or how earnest she was about becoming a better thief. No matter how she smelled while she held me while I panicked.

We were nothing.

But I couldn't focus on the parchment. I knew where the Bridge was. We'd head due west and figure out the heading once we sailed closer.

Right now, I needed a drink.

✵ 28 ✵

MARI

I did it. I called it off, whatever this twisted thing was between Captain Terion and me.

When we set sail for the final leg of our journey to the Bridge, Klep said a prayer to the Divine for our safety. Stealing a treasure meant for the two most powerful gods in the Realms was no small feat. We could fail. The God-King Thenios could send lightning to burn us and the *Lusca* to ash. Hades could subject us to tortures worse than anything we could imagine. We could be sent to Abaddon. The options were... not good. Unless we succeeded.

Terion said if we stole the gold, we could be free from Basileus's shadow of threat. If we pulled this off, I could solidify my own legacy as part of the most feared pirate crew to sail the Corae Sea and beyond.

But what if we died for this?

I didn't hate risk, but risking the entire crew? Risking Terion?

I pushed off against the ground with my foot to swing my blanket-filled hammock. I'd been awake for an entire day, between my night shift at the helm and gathering supplies on the island. Exhaustion pressed on my eyelids, but my mind spun. I'd get no sleep.

The promise of riches buzzed under my skin. If I were captain of my own ship, I wouldn't hesitate to sail to the Bridge to find the mythical treasure. Visions of myself flying through the makeshift course among the sails ran through my mind. I'd teach people to know my name.

This wasn't my ship.

That didn't mean it wasn't my fight.

Three days to the Bridge, where we'd make our fates. The answer was simple, but my thoughts wouldn't stop swimming around. Stealing from the gods to pay another meant that Terion might make greater enemies than he already faced. What if he didn't survive this?

I couldn't lose him. He aggravated me so much I wanted to shout, but I couldn't lose him. He had his hooks in my mind and body. He'd become like the air I jumped through and breathed. He knew me with a hundred faces and still gave me that maddening smirk. He made my blood so hot I bloomed with sweat. Fuck him. Even if it meant I'd be banished from the crew, I had to make sure he didn't fail. And the only way to be sure was to find a different way.

I'd brought him the map. At this point, destroying it would accomplish nothing. I had to make a move before we reached land.

I already had an idea. He'd hate me for this, but at least he'd live. I pictured him fierce and beautiful and grinning against lashing rain and waves like hills. *That* had to go on. He had to stay free and vital. Alive.

So what if he hated me for saving him? At least I had an idea that could delay the Sea God's wrath.

The hammock creaked as it swayed against the boards. Rhode was working on the upper deck, and Euporia peered against dim lantern light at her collection of curiosities and instruments for measuring time and elements of water I didn't begin to understand.

My arms felt the phantom sensation of curling around Terion's shoulders. *We have two secrets.*

I'd miss being in his confidence. I'd miss the sparkle in his eye and the trident on his arm. Fuck, I'd miss calling him Captain and watching his eyes grow dark with lust. Maybe I could find a different crew, if he let me live.

There had to be a future without him. Somehow. But everything about him wrapped like tentacles around my throat and made it hard to swallow. Part of me *was* him.

And I was planning to rob him.

HOW TO CONTACT ONE OF THE GODS OF THE EIGHT REALMS? I'd never really thought about it before.

They were so powerful, even compared to our crew, that I figured they were omniscient or something. But that was stupid. Each deathless person had the same shared set of abilities and one other specific to them. I could shapeshift, Terion could release water from his hands, and King Thenios could crisp us all to black with his lightning. Basileus had a wider set of water-based abilities. I could try calling to him. Communicating through the water?

I couldn't believe I'd never considered this before. Terion had to have a way to contact his father, didn't he? Nalia was too far away to walk through the air. That was especially dangerous to do in the ocean anyway. Falling into the water could lead to... bad things.

So, my plan consisted of stealing from Terion, escaping from the *Lusca*, and hoping Basileus would talk to me. Great.

But I was pretty sure he'd accept my offering as part of Terion's payment. He wouldn't have to anger the world's most powerful gods by taking their gold.

I bit my lip. Was this even a good plan? I liked a challenge —as Terion knew too well—but my stomach roiled whenever I thought of this one. It might not work. And it cut me off from being Terion's shapeshifter.

Or being more than that. Forever.

I felt like I was back in the swamps, lifting what I needed to survive. No joy filled me at the thought, just like no joy had followed me in the swamps. Need drove me then and it was driving me now.

Terion needed to live, and this could help ensure that, so I had to try even if it made me a fool or an outcast. Or a corpse.

I was scheduled for another night shift at the helm, my perfect opportunity to strike. Heaviness weighed down my limbs. Night settled dark and thick around me.

The crew hit their beds early after all the partying they'd done on the island. Some slept off hangovers. Apart from me, the main deck lay deserted. Even Captain Terion didn't emerge.

Whatever that panicked moment had been, it rattled him

more than I'd ever seen. He didn't say what had started it. My heart clenched. Hopefully he wasn't sick. Maybe he needed to sleep that moment off too.

Worked for me.

I glanced at the sky. Velvet black, punctured by starlight. Growing up, this was one of my favorite views—the night sky when I was alone. It reminded me of possibility, that the people who hated me were small compared to the Divine. Plus, darkness meant peace. Freedom. No eyes to follow me and whisper about what happened to my mother. It meant sleep, which meant I didn't need to steal to eat. For some reason, tonight it made me nostalgic, of all things.

I wasn't nostalgic for the swamps, that was for damn sure. Maybe I already missed this ship and its swaggering captain. I chuckled drily and ran a hand through my hair. Of course I'd miss Terion. And not only because he made me feel something I didn't think I was capable of feeling.

The *Lusca* eased over the water. I had to stop stalling and do it.

After checking our heading, I left the wheel and approached Terion's door. Locked. But I expected that. Crouching down, I pulled a set of pins from my pocket and fitted two of them into the keyhole. They made tiny scraping noises too small to be heard over the hot breeze and rhythm of the waves. I worked quicky and methodically around the lock. One of the pins snagged.

My lips stretched in a wry smile. *There you are.*

Easing the pins around, I found the right spot for leverage. Just as the lock gave, I coughed quietly—a normal noise to cover up the click. Stowing the pins, I straightened. There'd be enough moonlight coming through the bank of windows for me to see the treasures on Terion's shelf, but that also meant there would be enough light for him to see me.

I realized I'd already changed my facial features to resemble someone else. Not smart. If Terion thought he saw a stranger in his room, he might skewer before asking questions. If he saw me, he'd be angry but wouldn't kill me. Probably. I was planning to take all his most valuable things and sail away with them.

Two slow breaths later, I lowered the door handle. Slowly, slowly... With the door opened just a crack, I slipped inside. Mother used to say I was like an octopus, fitting through holes and getting my sticky tentacles on everything. Little did she know Terion himself would invite me on his ship for those skills. And little did I know I'd use them against him.

His rooms lay thick with warmth and shadows. Windows framed the back wall, but less moonlight got in than I expected. I couldn't see Terion himself on the curtained bed. Not knowing where he was unnerved me. I should have been able to see his outline, at least, but all the blankets made it too hard to tell.

Walking silently, I padded to the shelves. The mermaid sculpture was small enough to carry, but I wanted more than a single item. He had troves of high-priced objects here. After casting a quick glance back at the quiet bed again, I drew out a bag from my clothes made of thin but strong material. I used it often. Reaching through holes in the netting, I eased the statue through. Something soft followed, to muffle the sound as it dropped into the bag. My fingers traveled over the wooden shelves, slipping over the rims to feel for hidden surprises. It was amazing how many people thought that simply placing something out of sight was enough to protect it.

I moved quickly. The gold on the Bridge was worth a fortune, but Terion had been a pirate long enough to have amassed certain treasures of his own. Enough to raise eyebrows, at least. King Basileus had to consider an offer if I gave him all these things. The fact that these were Terion's personal things had to soothe Basileus's ego, and maybe make them worth more in his eyes.

A jewel-encrusted bangle dropped into the bag next. Was that a goblet on the upper shelf—?

With breathtaking speed, I was flung around and pinned against the table. I heard the bag rip and things clatter out. It had never ripped. Was it sliced open? The thought had barely formed before a blade lay cool and sharp against my throat.

Terion frowned in surprise. His face, teeth bared, was so close to mine that I felt his breath. He didn't remove the weapon from my neck.

"What the fuck, Mari?" he seethed. His voice rasped with sleep.

I didn't quail. "I'm saving you from yourself."

"Looks like you're relieving me of all my favorite things. Planning to run?" When I didn't answer, he sighed. "Your timing is baffling. Earlier, I literally couldn't move and you choose this moment to steal from me? I never pegged you as a defector. Or a mutineer."

"That's not what I'm doing."

"Enlighten me." He finally lifted the knife from my skin and gave me space to breathe. Lighting a couple lanterns so we didn't have to grope around in the dark, he looked at my bag bulging with half-fallen treasures. "Let me guess. Two options. One, you think you're a curse on the *Lusca*, so you're taking enough to begin a luxurious and sex-fueled life with Dio. Two, you're planning to give my things to Basileus because you still think he might be merciful."

I squared my jaw.

"My father is not merciful," he continued. For some reason, he wore his entire outfit—jacket, sword belt, and all. Had he been sleeping like that?

"I didn't think he was."

"He's jealous and petty."

"I know. I thought getting your things would hold more weight for him."

He ran a thumb over his lower lip. "Inventive, but handing him the *Lusca* itself wouldn't pay off what I owe, and there's no way in Abaddon I'd consider it."

I deflated. "A side of personal humiliation wouldn't help?"

He smirked. "Humiliation? By having my own crew steal from me?"

"Having *me* steal from you."

"What difference does that make? You're the best thief on board. Why would that be worse?"

"I'm the least important."

Frustration twisted his features. He rolled his eyes. "According to who? Zete? Waves and feathers... You tried to save me just now. Stupidly. And it wouldn't have worked. But still." He approached a couple steps. "By the way, *don't* try to steal from me again. You can still do your duties with nine fingers."

My gaze dropped to his neck, where he'd been wearing the

necklace with Calix's finger. It was gone. He must have taken it off the moment I said I wouldn't keep having sex with him.

My face grew tight. He could have kept it on for one more day.

"But as far as reasons go," he continued, "saving my skin is the best excuse I've heard."

"I don't think you should go to the Bridge," I burst out.

His black eyebrows rose. "Your memory is usually better than this. You gave me the map, Mari. It was the one thing that saved me from having to punish you in front of the crew."

"I know." Now it was my turn to roll my eyes. I shouldn't have felt this comfortable with the captain, but he let me *be* in a way the others didn't. It wasn't my place to advise him, but he hadn't ordered me out of his quarters yet. "Thenios and Hades," I said.

"Suddenly against a bit of danger?" He searched my face. I heated under the scrutiny. For some reason, it brought back the time we'd spent in his secret room. He didn't mean the look that way. He couldn't.

I scoffed. "I'm a pirate," I answered.

"Then what's the problem?"

What did I have to lose? "You! You're at stake if this fails."

"That's usually the case. Dio wants my head. I saw an unflattering poster on the island before we left."

"Terion..."

The laugh lines around his mouth softened. His deep eyes filled with some of the ferocity I'd seen in fights. "We're going to the Bridge. If you don't think your information was good, then we'll—"

"No, it was good." I cut my glance to the side. "I just don't want three gods after us."

He seemed to ponder this. "Good for the legend."

Desperation welled in my chest, even as I admired him.

"That," he said, gripping my wrist, "or we get the gold and we're rid of Basileus forever."

Waves of sensation radiated from his hand all over my body, almost as if he used his power to send out chilly water. "I don't think we should," I managed.

I meant the trip to the Bridge, but we both felt the second meaning hang in the air. Terion looked at me for several beats too long.

He said I could dictate whether we kept up our encounters. I'd said my piece. But this felt like pleading.

I was tired of it. Tired of Terion commanding my body and my thoughts.

Tired of the way my pulse spiked between my legs when I looked at him.

Tired of the way I hated danger now because it meant throwing him in harm's way.

Tired of feeling like I'd never be enough, even for him.

"Let's not do this," I muttered.

He, still holding my wrist, reached for the other one. Damn it, I craved his touch enough to let him take it. I sulked rather than smiled at him, though.

"We're not doing anything. You have run off lately and I want to keep you here."

I want to keep you. He didn't mean that, but the words tumbled through my mind as if he did. Anger reared up again. "I've run off?" I echoed.

"You're the one who snuck into my room in the middle of the night. You can't be trusted."

He was teasing but I was acid. "And you're the one looking

like you never went to bed. Going to meet the woman you lied about?"

His face went darker. "Cut that out, Mari."

"You're right. You deserve to be with whatever harlot you want. Fuck her until she can't see." Pain oozed out of me like blood. I had no right to Terion, no right to say any of this.

He squeezed my wrists harder. "I don't want to fuck her."

"Then don't!" I cried before he could go on.

"If I had my way, which I usually do, I'd be back downstairs with you. Now, I know why I think that's a reckless, bad idea, but I can't wrap my head around why you would think that."

"Don't..."

"I hate that you said no. Because—"

I huffed.

He yanked me closer. I smelled the sea on him, salty and rich with adventure. "*Because* I think you want to be there too, but for some godsdamned reason, you're pulling away."

"You know why," I said quickly. If I spoke fast enough, his words would evaporate. They wouldn't land and pierce me like his cutlass. "We could never work. I don't want to hurt. I want you to live, I want to stay on the *Lusca*, and I don't want to care about you any more than I do. You'd never choose me."

"I did."

"For some twisted game, not *for me*."

"Listen to me, Mari." His eyes bored into mine. "You attempted to steal from me and kept your hands. You were the one to call off our arrangement, not me. I'm still happy to give you orgasms that will send you into another life. You know I can. I'd like to try, because I like the challenge, the grit in your eyes when you practice on the masts..." A smirk curled his mouth. "And the way you call me Captain."

"You don't do relationships," I tried.

"No," he admitted, "but if you'll accept that about me, I want you exactly as you are."

"You don't want me exactly as I am," I snapped, tearing my hands away. "You think you've seen me, but you don't want the girl from the swamp, the one who keeps getting you in trouble, the one with no home and skills that don't even work!" Layers of masks I wore daily felt like they tore bodily from me, leaving me wounded. "You want someone who looks good on your arm, not someone who can't even come." Each word came out jagged, like weapons. The future I feared didn't matter at that moment. Terion would have me or he wouldn't have me, but the truth would be out.

Terion's eyes blazed as he stared at me. "Mari," he began, but I cut him off.

"My own mother didn't want me. You know why?" My face convulsed with the pain of this knowledge finally leaving my head. Captain Terion would know what no one else in the world did.

"I think so."

I fought the urge to strike him. He said the words simply,

without some of his normal bravado, as if he really did know something. Bastard.

"A god raped her," I burst out. "She wouldn't even tell me which one. It ruined her life. *I* ruined her life."

Somehow, Terion was holding my arms again and I wasn't trying hard enough to get away. Everything felt useless and charged at once. I needed the pressure of his fingertips to keep me grounded.

"You didn't ruin her life."

"I was a demi-goddess born into a poor family who never wanted me. My ability was only good for hiding. You'd better believe I ran onto this ship the second I could. Because yes, Terion, I did. And I'm ruining yours."

"You overestimate your abilities."

I roared in frustration. "I can't even do *that!*"

Terion laughed. The warm sound slid into my belly and allowed me to breathe. He straightened me to face him. "You think we're so different."

"We are. You're Captain fucking Terion and I'm..."

"Marica, Terror of the Seas."

I scoffed.

"You have to believe the name before anyone else will." With deliberation, he released my arms and straightened his cuffs. "I was an unwanted child too."

I took in his stature, the way his features looked rough and soft at once, his attitude as he stood with his weight balanced on one leg as if he owned the world. How could someone this confident, this capable and beautiful, be unwanted? Visions of his bad behavior gave me some ideas—he must have been an unmanageable child—but who couldn't want him? Friendly ports had eager partners practically lining up for him to do with as he wished. The crew adored him, even after he killed one of their own.

"Bullshit," I hissed.

He leaned close enough to my face that I felt the humidity from his skin. "Say that again."

I swallowed, second guessing myself for the first time. "Bullshit. King Basileus doesn't want you now, but you weren't an abandoned swamp child."

His lips curved dangerously. "You think this is a competition? I win those."

I cocked a brow.

"I invited you aboard because I wanted a shapeshifter, someone who could spy for me, steal for me."

I knew all that.

"And because I recognized you."

A frown crossed my face. "Recognized me? From what? Where?" Even if I hadn't known Terion's name (impossible, even then), he would have caught my eye. I remembered most faces. At the time, I might not have snapped my neck to watch him, but at this moment it was hard to imagine not noticing his long, powerful stride, or his sculpted lips, or his burning, mischievous eyes full of promises.

"I knew that life," he said. "Basileus forced my mother just like that god forced yours. You were left envied and hated and discarded like trash." He captured my chin in one hand. "You hadn't called yourself the Terror of the Seas yet."

My heart beat furiously in my chest. Terion looked down at me, unmoving but so intense I felt I'd burst into flames. Thoughts blew through my head like a hurricane, crashing and crashing. I struggled to hear a single one. They were alarms. They were desire. He was so close, so close... We hadn't been drinking, but I felt like I had. My head swam. My pulse beat everywhere.

The idea of being thrown overboard for the sharks and serpents hadn't been this frightening. Here, I was caught and seen and I didn't like it.

I shook my head no. Just a little movement. I wasn't even sure what I was saying no to. No to his speech, maybe. To the thought I was more than that swamp girl who lived in my head.

When he stepped back, I panted as if I'd been fighting. In the light from the windows behind him, Terion's throat worked. His profile looked hard, like stone.

"You make your mythology, Mari," he said, low. "Or you let the sea swallow you up like all the other unwanted bastards like us."

Like us.

Us.

"Terion..." Why was he confiding in me? The fact hit me like a wave. "I didn't know." Picturing him as anything less than the captain, as a child who might have picked up crabs in the mud to boil on the beach like I did, twisted something inside me. It made me feel big, like he had handed me the weight of memories.

You make your mythology, Mari.

Terion looked like mythology now, life pulsing through his veins, an outline drawn in gold. The orange lantern light traced his lashes, the set of his mouth. It traced down his chin. His strong chest. The hand he held loosely around the hilt of his cutlass. He was treasure. I longed to run my finger from his forehead down his body and claim that treasure for my own.

But I couldn't. It was a stupid wish, even if it baked my insides warm.

"It seems impossible." My voice fell small among the clutter of Terion's room.

He turned to look at me. His gaze splashed my body with heat. "Why?"

"Who could not want you?"

His dark eyes turned wild. Under different circumstances, that wildness would have meant overwhelming danger, but now it was just... overwhelming. All of him focused on all of me. I couldn't breathe. Couldn't look away.

Determination hardened his limbs as he closed the distance between us. Then his arms were around me. His mouth crushed mine, taking. He didn't hold me—he gripped, he grappled, he took handfuls of me. We couldn't get close enough. I surged against him, tangled up in clothes and arms.

He bent me toward him as he squeezed me closer. Even through layers I was desperate to peel off, I felt the hard outline of his cock. His breath was humid. It was as if he wanted to crawl around under my skin and plunder what he found there. He'd never been like this. The room downstairs was for arrangements, scenarios. Those had all gone to hell.

A growl ripped from his throat. His fingers found the collar of my jacket and tugged it back over my shoulder. I did the same to him. I needed to discover the skin he'd never pressed against me. The rounded shoulders moved like the rest of his body, rolling and pressing and flexing closer. He wasn't careful. The movements that had been so calculated in the downstairs room weren't anymore. Nothing was planned. I just needed him close. I needed him in my hands, on my mouth, and he took, grabbing me by the waist, breathing hard. The layers came off, off, off.

He threw his gloves to the floor. The feel of his palms against my bare skin made me gasp. He gave a hard, open-mouthed kiss as if he could eat the sounds I made.

Frustrated, we wrestled out of the rest of our clothes. Soft thuds followed us to the bed.

He doesn't like using the bed.

Shut up.

Every thought stopped when Captain Terion fell on top of me with an urgency that left me breathless. His skin, hot and hard, moved against mine. The commander of the seas, and now what he wanted was me.

With hands used to command, he pulled apart my legs. I let him, although vulnerability raced through my core. I wasn't only naked, I was wet. Dripping. Flushed and tense with the need for more.

He gave me more. This time there was no foreplay. I realized a second before he pushed the tip of his cock against my opening that some of the wetness came from him. His hands on my skin left trails. He was wet too. His power wasn't directed in some careful way—it leaked from his hands as if he couldn't stop it.

I gasped as he curled his body around me and pressed inside. I was slick and open and he felt *good*. My head fell back. Was this what people were talking about? A whimpered noise of pleasure escaped my lips with each eager thrust.

From the corner of my eye, light reflected off the blue-green scales on Terion's clenched face. He moved inside me with his whole body, not just his hips. Wet hands bracketed my head, then slung around me like tentacles as he fought for better angles, for more, chasing his need. He was a wave taking me under. I fought for breath.

"Yes," he whispered. I wasn't sure if he knew he was doing it.

"Yes," I echoed.

He adjusted again, sliding in deep with a ruthless roll of his muscles.

There. Oh gods...

I was making a mess and didn't care because *there*, right there, was a spearing, aching place I'd kill for him to touch again. It sent my mouth gaping and my fingers grasping for something to hold onto. The blankets weren't enough. I needed something solid.

He did it again.

I cried out his name, begging. I needed his body, his mouth close to mine, his cock pounding just... right...

I gasped hard, stopping myself from losing control.

Terion seemed to take it as a dare. "Yes?" This time the fiercely breathed word was a question. His fingers, slick and warm, found new places. All the places no one touched. All the places that craved the slightest pressure from his hand or his mouth, or even the hair on his chest. If he was a wave, I wanted to drown.

This desire was like hurt. What would happen if I let it take me?

Terion said no more words, but he got louder anyway. It was effort. It was moaned longing. Frustration. Growling to get closer, get further in. He went balls deep, taking me hard, scraping his rough palms against my stiff nipples, reaching underneath and wedging a finger between my round cheeks to enter me there.

Everything was Terion. His leg strained against mine. His back flexed under my hands as I struggled to hold on.

And there, that spot again! I clawed my fingers into his skin.

"Come now, Mari. Break."

I heard half the command before I obeyed. My spine bent and legs shook. A noise like a gull ripped from my throat as I came hard for the first time in my life.

30

TERION

That painful, ecstatic sound and the slip of Mari's cum on my cock made me so hard I could barely see the bed, the curtains, anything at all. Her pale body writhing under mine drove me wild. It was her skin on my skin. It was the dark hair that stuck at weird angles on her forehead.

It was making Mari come for the first time.

I gritted my teeth in a half-grin, half-grimace as I pounded frantically into her. She wasn't only a willing body, but the only body I wanted. I wanted every movement. I lusted for her eyes to roll back again. I would wring another orgasm from her so she knew what pleasure meant. Damn her other partners to Abaddon. They'd never had her like this, spread wide and mumbling incoherently for more.

I liked every version of her. Every disguise. Every defiant moment and every submissive one. I wanted her to have songs, be the Terror of the Seas. And I wanted her on her knees for me.

The last thought made desperation scramble my brain.

Panting, I thrust hard and fast into her perfect, tight pussy. She drenched me. I edged closer.

I didn't mean to keep going—I wanted to give her another chance to come with me inside her—but I didn't stop. I couldn't stop. She felt so fucking good and I had... to...

With a huge groan, I pumped out my release. I kept coming, seizing, giving her more.

Soaked and breathless, I pulled out and bent down to kiss her. We were sloppy, all tongues and faces. I flopped down beside her. She faced me, face and chest red with what we'd done.

Regular sex on a regular bed.

But it had been anything but regular. My sessions in the downstairs room weren't as charged as what just happened.

What just happened...

What just happened?

Mari nestled close to me, her face in the crook of my neck. She breathed half-formed words hot against my throat.

"I know. I'm amazing." I caressed her bare back, but now, as a different head started to think, the truth surged up like a serpent from the depths.

"I am too," she said, apparently not minding that I'd said something asinine just then.

I smiled at her answer. "You don't even know." Glancing down at her short, dark hair, terror gripped my throat. My hand tensed on her shoulder blade.

What have I done?

I held Mari tighter. She felt hot and wet with sweat and the water from my hands.

What have I done?

NO ONE KNEW THE FULL EXTENT OF MY FATHER'S GRUDGE. I could never repay Basileus unless I brought him the palace of Hades or something equally impressive. I'd lost crew members, and that was enough to prove he was serious.

I told no one, not even Rhode or Ajax, about the curse attached to my debt. Rhode guessed, because she was good at guessing, damn her. I loved her so much. Attachment made me vulnerable, but how was I supposed to stop caring about my own sister?

Or about Mari?

I shifted her weight in my arms. Feeling her form pressed against my chest and legs was heaven. Her breathing, slow and safe, flowed over me. We were *right*, like this. I was fore-ground, she was background—a whole picture. People would fear her one day, I was sure of it. She had the same fierce deter-mination I did, sharper and hungrier. But we could joke too. She was a submissive who wouldn't take any bullshit. And *fuck me*, I wanted her more than my own skin.

She stirred. Maybe I'd woken her with my raging hard on.

Hadn't the seer told me Mari would sacrifice herself for me? And my father had told me to my face that he'd made a deal with a witch from Menos just to curse anyone I loved.

Either I got up now and didn't speak to Mari again, or she'd die.

My rage against my father just made me want to fold myself over Mari and fuck her all over again. That would drown out his controlling voice, and replace it with "Terion, please, more, do that, ah! Yes, Captain!"

I eased a hand between us to deal with my painfully rigid dick. Everything in me wanted to wake her up and feed myself into her pussy again, or her ass—I wasn't feeling picky. Every part of her was divine, and I'd barely started to explore her.

I ground my teeth together. *Either you get your ass out of this bed or you doom her. Don't be a fucking idiot!*

A stream of colorful language erupted in whispers as I stiffly separated myself from Mari's warmth and stood. My lip curled. My cock didn't understand what was happening and ached to return to her. I cursed my father to eternal disembowelment in Abaddon, calling him every name I could think of, and I had a wide vocabulary.

Fuming, I padded off to the washroom. A minute of pumping myself for relief and I came with a groan.

Thoughts didn't have to work so hard to get in my brain. *Kick her out. Now.*

More foul names snarled out of my mouth. But it was true. Every second spent with Mari meant more danger for her. I might still be able to excuse what just happened, play it off like nothing serious.

Lie and say I wasn't obsessively, violently in love with her.

❧ 31 ❧

MARI

I felt Terion get out of bed but didn't move. No light pressed on my eyelids, so it wasn't day yet. The room smelled musty and salty with our sex. Without him curled along my naked back, even the muggy sea air felt chilly.

I wanted nothing more than to feel him around me and inside of me, but I'd learned a long time ago not to hold on too tight. It didn't matter that the pit of my soul longed for Terion to choose me to fight beside. The Captain and the Terror.

Maybe he'd come back to bed. Maybe his reckless passion wasn't a fluke. Just the memory of his lips and tattooed arms claiming me made me sopping wet again.

Labored breathing from nearby suggested he was in the washroom. It was a muted version of the ferocious growls and grunts that burst out of him as he drove hard into me. Was he... Was he already having sex with someone else?

Heart in my throat, I angled up on an elbow. *Don't hold on too tightly. You'll break.*

My eyes fell on the dim shape of the fallen loot I'd attempted to steal. That reminder couldn't have helped enflame his attraction to me. If anything, it would remind him not to choose me after all, despite his low, possessive claims. The fact that I wanted to trade the items to gain more time for him was irrelevant. *No one hangs the captain*, the song said. Well, no one stole from him either.

Terion sighed, a loud burst of air. My skin went clammy. That sound was unmistakable. I had to go.

With a jolt, I remembered that I'd left the *Lusca* drifting for the past few hours with no one at the helm.

Bolting out of the bed, I felt blindly for my clothes lying in heaps around the floor. I tugged them on as quickly as I could, sensitive where Terion's grasping fingers had squeezed and his large cock had filled me. Halfway through pulling a shirt over my head, I realized it was Terion's. It was far too large and smelled like him. The scent caressed me like fingers. One side of my lip lifting in a snarl, I dragged it on and tucked it into my pants anyway. Boots and weapon and I tromped toward the door.

Terion appeared in the doorway of the washroom, dark against an already dark room. I didn't see anyone behind him. I also couldn't see much of his expression. It felt like an invisible hand squeezed my throat.

"The helm," I said, pointing to the door.

"Oh." His voice was groggy and delicious, but distant. "Go check where we are." He didn't come any closer.

"Yes, Captain." The response was automatic, but we both felt the heat in it.

Cursing myself, I flung the door open and gripped the helm's spokes. *Heading, heading...* I checked the stars. They looked off. "Fuck," I muttered, beginning the sequence of tasks to figure out our location again. At least we hadn't run across a sandbar or something.

We were still going to the Bridge. Still stealing gold that belonged to the two most powerful gods in the Realms. Still putting Terion in danger.

The door behind me creaked open. Was he coming out here for me? At best, what I'd heard was Terion getting himself off, but why would he, when we'd just had mind-melting sex? He'd made good on his promise of an orgasm and then some. I wasn't even mad I lost our bet. If he'd let me, I'd scream in his bed every night.

Not so tight.

We'd conquer every challenge. We'd rule the seas.

Let go.

Captain Terion would have me by his side. I'd protect him as viciously as a shark, and he'd defend me too.

Don't.

"How far off course are we?" His tone was unreadable.

"I'll get us back," I replied quietly.

"This wasn't part of your plan?"

"Of course not." *And neither was getting fucked so hard my legs still feel wobbly. But here we are.* I chanced a look at him, finally. He stood shirtless just in front of his door. No arm around my waist, no press of his full lips against mine. Not even a smirk.

"Good." His gaze swept down my body. "That's my shirt."

"I had to get out here to check."

Without a word, he ducked into his room and came out holding my shirt in one fist. "Change. Quickly. You can do it in there." He stepped to the side, indicating that I could enter his quarters alone.

Cold rinsed down my spine. He wasn't speaking like a lover. Something had changed. Now, his expression read like regret.

I wouldn't apologize. He kissed me. He fucked me like I was air and he was drowning. What right did he have to brush me aside like this?

"Fine," I snapped, pulling my shirt from his grip. The lantern light fell on the trident tattoo on his forearm. I stalked into his bedroom but didn't close the door. In full view of Terion, I stripped off his shirt and put on mine. I left his shirt on the floor.

His eyes were nearly solid black when I passed him on the way to the helm. The way the muscles flowed over his chest made me ache. Now that I knew I wasn't broken—I could have dizzying orgasms after all, like I'd wanted—a different part of me cracked. It was as if my body had been waiting for Terion, in all his maddening, talented, confident, beautiful glory. Part of me hated him.

"Get us to the Bridge," he said, and I watched his back as he disappeared once again inside his room.

I blinked back angry tears. He'd said perfect things to me, things that were wrong and tantalizing and vulnerable and savage.

He'd said *us*.

I'd get his godsdamned gold. Fuck, I'd still do anything for him. I scrubbed a hand down my face. Warm tears tracked over my cheeks. Would anyone ever say the same about me?

32

TERION

The mermaid statue was a replica. Mari was right that stories about the original piece said it was legendary. But I lifted this one off a merchant ship selling cheap goods. No way they had the real thing. I liked to see it on my shelves and imagine that I had control over the deep sea water and the huge creatures and could tell them to attack Basileus. Fantasy.

My thumb slipped over the breast and torso of one small mermaid as I put it back on the shelf from where it had fallen.

I'd hurt Mari. Rage and confusion shone like lights from her face just now.

I knew the thought was stupid as soon as it occurred to me—she wouldn't betray me. Her sweat-slicked neck craning back as she came made it impossible.

I squared my jaw.

Stupid.

There was no way I was sleeping tonight, not when we were so close to the Bridge and Mari stood within reaching distance. As if they had minds of their own, my hands kept flexing, wanting to stretch out fingers and draw her back into this room. I'd barely started showing her what pleasure was. And the way she'd made me explode...

The night sailed on so long I expected to see the Far Realm on the horizon. I kept my hands busy with knots and knife throwing and one more frantic session in the washroom. The gloves went back on. One night had never felt so long before.

"Steal from me, Asterion, and I'll kill anyone you love."

I smirked at my father, who was all regal bluster. "I live on the sea. I own the sea. I'm not afraid of it."

"Silence. You are in the presence of the Sea God. Your pathetic abilities won't protect you from the wrath that's coming." He leaned closer, showing off the blue-green scales in his dark skin. Despite his age, which rivaled the oldest of gods, he still looked hearty. "You're insignificant. The most important thing about you is your connection to me, and I wouldn't have known you existed if you hadn't angered me."

"Not very observant."

"If thousands of women begged to share your bed, you'd lose track of bastards too."

"Funny. Most deathless women control their cycles and with humans, well, there's such a thing as pulling out."

"Which I should have done with your mother to spare me of you!"

I glared back at him.

"Anyone you love," he repeated. "You think that your little crew can best me? With no consequences? No. I keep a witch from Menos for occasions like this." He lowered his voice. "Your beloved sea, which was never yours, will rebel against you. And I have already activated a curse that cannot be undone. You'll sail away, but one by one, everyone you love will die. You'll have peace for a week, a month, a year, but I will strip everything from you."

"Why don't you kill me instead?"

"It's far more painful to watch and live on, knowing you caused their suffering. You killed five members of my court and humiliated me in front of my brothers. If you ever have a family, or a lover, they'll suffer most."

Sickness roiled inside me. The fabled pearl-encrusted crown wasn't worth this. "A Menos witch?" I scoffed. But I knew he wasn't lying. Some kind of magic he didn't possess caused the crown to turn to salt in my hands as I ran out of Thenios's palace.

The leaders of all Eight Realms had assembled there for the eclipse. I knew my father would attend, and if I could steal from him under the noses of the most powerful beings in the world, I'd solidify my legacy.

"Check your ship."

It was the worst thing he could have said. I planted my feet to stop myself from retreating. "Empty threats."

"You owe me a debt, and I will begin gathering the toll now."

That was enough. I left my father to return to the Lusca. It hadn't sunk. But five of my crew members sprawled out on the deck, dead.

I cleared my throat. It hadn't stopped after that. People I'd meet in passing would die in strange ways. There was the Leviathan. There were serpents and hurricanes. In all of it, I saw my father's furious green eyes. Decades had passed, and I was done.

When destruction wasn't inevitable, I liked danger. Someday Mari and Rhode and Ajax and the *Lusca* would all burn because of me.

Fuck that.

Father said I owed him. Fine. I'd give him the biggest treasure I'd ever attempted to steal, and from his brothers. If that didn't make him stand down, I doubted anything would.

Compulsively, I cracked the door open to see if Mari was

still standing there. She was. She heard me, of course, and turned. I shut the door again. She was alive and that was enough. Even if the statue had been the famous mythical version, it wouldn't have paid off my debt to Basileus.

He wanted to watch me suffer and then he wanted to kill me. Evading him had felt like a game for a long time, but I was done.

My eyes felt dry and bloodshot by the time the sky lightened on the horizon. Watching the sea shift from black to blue awakened my blood. Hope crested just over the next stretch of water.

I stood, creakier than usual, whipped my coat around me, and stepped out. Mari no longer manned the wheel. Ajax had taken her place.

"Friendly winds?" he grunted by way of greeting.

"And gold on shore." This time, I'd make sure that was true.

Clouds obscured the horizon when I woke. According to the *Lusca*'s location when I'd stumbled off to bed at daybreak, we should have been approaching the Bridge, but there was no way I could see it. Instead of friendly winds, the breeze was chopping and the waters writhing. Looked fit for a storm.

Appropriate.

I felt like shit, a tangle of longings and anger and gods knew what else. I just wanted this mission to be done. Ordinarily, I liked them. But this one felt like a prophecy of doom for Terion. I couldn't exactly explain why.

Maybe that was all for the best. He'd basically kicked me out of bed, after all. If he was eaten by a sea monster, I might be able to move on.

Heading down to the mess for a quick meal, I blew hair out of my face. No chance. Terion was in my blood, and last night he'd been everywhere else too. I'll kill for him to do it again.

The *Lusca* pitched in the surf, not violently enough to take up storm positions, but getting there. The air felt thick and charged with lightning.

I rummaged in a tabletop barrel for a hard biscuit. It wasn't that I had an appetite, but I knew I'd need strength today—to get the gold, deal with this oncoming weather, and not punch Terion in the face.

The biscuit, dry and gummy, stuck in my throat. I coughed and kept chewing. The lantern above the table swung, casting ghoulish shadows. Terion and I had sat there the night after Dio's party. The crazy light made it look like our oversized spirits flickered in and out of the seats.

With a huff, I left. Less nauseating to be on deck than below with the ship bucking like this.

On practiced feet, I ran up the companionway. Zete glared at me when I appeared. His wings looked sodden, but the weather wasn't my fault. I ignored him and walked by. Despite Terion's infuriating mixed messages, he wouldn't let the crew harm me. Redley had proven that. The captain might not love me (although he obviously felt a hell of a lot of lust) but he wanted me alive.

Terion's handsome face circled in my mind like a fucking waterspout, all I could think about, all I could see. Every move he made and word he said. The storm paled in importance to him. Prince of the Ocean. I wanted to stab something.

An enormous swell lifted the prow of the ship up so high I had to bend one leg to keep upright. On the other side, we crashed down. Spray coated the ship, wetting everything in fine mist. At least, I thought it was the splash. Rain started to fall—one of those drenching tropical rains that broke clouds open between one step and the next. They were common in Nalia, but not in this part of the world.

I knitted my brows. Something wasn't right. I knew storms, maybe not as well as Terion, but I knew the Realms too. Storms here should look different.

With heavy steps to keep my balance, I stomped over to Ajax, gripping the helm with bulging arms the thickness of my waist.

"This storm isn't right," I yelled to him above the water.

He didn't respond, but his mouth sneered in agreement.

"Of course it fucking isn't, sweetheart." Zete appeared at my side.

I shot him a look. If he thought so, why didn't he say anything? "Do you think it's magic? Basileus?"

"I don't think it matters until we're on the other side."

I planted my feet. "It matters if King Thenios knows what we're trying to do." The God-King of Lightning wouldn't love the idea of us taking his emergency gold.

Zete's dark face pitted into a scowl.

Ajax shouted directions, but I didn't hear them because the door behind him opened to reveal Terion, looking like he hadn't slept in days. Despite being ashy and drawn, a pale version of his signature smirk twisted his lips. He didn't look at me.

I saw him mouth the word "magic" to Ajax. It was too loud to hear him over the storm.

Fierce justification shot through me.

Right before I was launched forward, smacking my forehead against the wall.

Dazed, I regained my footing. The hull of the ship scraped against something huge with a sound louder than a swamp hawk's scream. Panic gripped my chest. Had we run aground? But I hadn't seen any land.

Terion all but flew down the steps, curses pouring from his mouth. He looked like the sea god he was, full of fury. If this was somehow the gods' doing, they'd targeted the wrong ship. Terion would have blood.

Zete and I ran to our stations. From below, Rhode emerged, followed by Klep and Euporia.

The captain, blade in hand, looked over the side. From where I stood, no land appeared. Only sea and clouds. So many clouds. They thickened, stirring over the water, gaining height and shape as they flowed closer.

The *Lusca* tipped up the farther it scraped against whatever was solid beneath us. Terion's silhouette looked black against the wall of white, armed, jacket waving in the wet wind.

That was my last view of him before he disappeared in the mist.

I felt rather than heard the strange voice in the fog. It stuck to me like a cruel smile. It was big as a Leviathan, proud as Terion himself. And it thought it had won.

I wiped rain from my eyes, straining to see. Without any idea what was happening, I abandoned my post to sprint toward Terion. Somehow, I'd known something terrible would happen.

One of the scariest things was the silence. I felt a voice, but I heard nothing. Not Terion joyfully threatening this entity, whatever it was, or cries from the other sailors. I'd have been happy to hear from Zete at that point. From anyone.

My hands hit the railing, but I still only saw white. The *Lusca* wasn't bobbing anymore. We'd definitely gotten stuck on something. I felt down the length of the rail. No Terion.

"Rhode!" I screamed, having an idea. "Rhode! If you can

hear me, I bet you can see in the water. Find out what's happening. I can't find the captain."

Still, no one answered me.

Heart punching against my ribcage, I flung my arms wide. Someone had to be here. This fog hadn't transported me to some isolated island. I couldn't be alone, because if I was alone, that would mean...

"Terion! Captain!"

He didn't answer.

My drenched skin crawled. "Fuck. Fuck! Where are you?"

By this point, the crew should have been shouting back at me in annoyance. Nothing. Every breath came too fast.

Feeling my way back to the center of the deck, I found the main mast. I'd never climbed totally blind before, but I knew the route by heart. I clung like a spider and sprinted up. Rainwater made everything slick. I was trapped in a silent, white nightmare.

But as I reached the tip of the mast, the clouds grew thin. I could see, not well, but anything was an improvement over blindness. Gripping the rope hard in a shaking fist, I scanned all the way around. Dead ahead and under us was the Bridge, its sandy beach and trees obvious. Something—no, *someone*—had hidden it. Strong wards, maybe? It didn't matter. What did matter as the seconds went by was that the fog dispersed. Below, on the deck, nothing moved.

I was totally alone.

34

TERION

She looked like a palm tree. And she shouldn't be here.

That was my first thought when I opened my eyes.

"People underestimate the Menos witches," the seer said, cocking her head. Beads from her earrings rattled. Any meekness I'd seen on the island was totally gone. Now she had all the confidence of a god. "They have much greater power than you little demi-gods."

I flexed my hand. No blade. My wrists were bound behind my back, tied to my ankles, which were also tied together. The rope was too rough and thick to break through easily. I tested my strength against the restraints. They didn't budge.

We were in a temple-like building with columns set into the round rock walls. It felt like we were underground. No god symbol scored the walls, which meant people either used this building for a rare suna or for Hades himself.

Where was everyone else? Had they been killed like the crew when I'd stolen from Basileus?

Panic didn't choke me, so I stared levelly back at the witch. "I don't know. All you've done is tie me up and bring us somewhere to be alone. I'll admit, I'm usually the one doing the tying, but this is a pretty average day for me."

Her expression didn't change. "King Basileus has chosen this day as your last."

Hadn't she said something about Mari sacrificing herself, though? Funny that that was my first thought. It felt more important than the seer's threat. I'd been threatened many times—rarely this seriously, though. Basileus might be able to do what no one else could. If this meant that Mari and Rhode and the others didn't have to suffer because of me, things could have been worse.

Where was Mari now?

My eyes darted around the witch's frame. No weapon. She wasn't all-powerful. No one was. So what would she use to kill me? She stood out of range for me to lunge for her, and there wasn't so much as a piece of furniture in this round room. Only a fire pit in the center, filling the space with smoke.

Ah. Fire.

"I have chosen this day to live," I said. The stone floor dug into my knees. I let water release from my fingertips, slowly at first, then in more of a rush. I managed to put out the fireball on the *Lusca*—how different could this be?

She smiled for the first time. The sight was eerier than watching enormous sea creatures four times the size of the *Lusca* swim just beneath us on the way to the Far Realm. She looked so pale for a Menos witch. Menos and Nalia usually produced people who looked like me.

"You won't die this moment," she said. "I was merely called to fetch you."

Because they don't want to kill me right away.

The thought, which normally would have been encouraging, unsettled me. They wouldn't tie me up and leave me here unless they wanted me to suffer first. Was I supposed to watch my ship full of my crew die?

I couldn't consider it.

Don't come after me, Mari.

She was foolhardy, lusting to prove herself. Much as I loved that about her, she needed to keep herself safe.

I locked eyes with the seer again. "Fetch me for Basileus, I guess? What's he giving you to help him? I can give you more."

Her lips curled in a mocking smile. "You can give me nothing."

"You have no imagination. I can get you gold beyond your dreams."

"I long for no gold."

My eyebrows shot up. Everybody could be bought for the right price. Most prices were actual prices. This reality had gotten me out of more situations than I could count (before I returned to skewer them and take it back.) "What do you want?" The longer she talked, the more time I had to figure out how to get the fuck out of here.

She ignored me, as if listening to something else. She smacked her protruding bottom lip thoughtfully. The fire crackled behind her. The humid air made me sweat under the bindings.

"Basileus?" I guessed. Facing him after all this time would actually feel good. I'd prefer to be on my feet with a blade in my hand so I could run it through his throat.

Hopefully she wasn't listening for Mari or one of the others.

I raised my voice in case my crew were coming. "Leave me in a room alone with that sea monster and I'll be happy."

Leave leave leave. Air strangled from my throat, not because of the seer but from the panic that finally caught me.

Where was Mari? Where were the others? Would they sink the *Lusca*? Doom pressed on my neck. I couldn't move my hands. Water wasn't snaking into the flames or damaging the ropes, even though I changed the temperature to both extremes.

"You would not be," said the witch, face passive.

"In the room?" I pressed through too thin air. "Happy?"

"Either."

"What is it you want?" Again, I raised my voice. "I, for one, want to be left alone."

If they could hear me, my crew wouldn't obey my implied command.

Mari *really* wouldn't listen.

Breathe. Don't black out. You can get out of this. You're Captain fucking Asterion.

"Order is what I crave and the world lacks," she replied smoothly. "You are chaos."

I gave her a lopsided grin. Hopefully she couldn't tell it was forced. "Thank you."

Her uncanny eyes darkened. "We eliminate such forces."

Behind her, a figure appeared—lean, pale, strong, with short dark hair. Her face was her own. Her fist clutched a knife.

Fuck me, but I felt relieved.

35

MARI

My feet landed on squishy sand. I didn't find anyone else on the ship, and Terion was gone, so I had to search for him.

In one hand, I clutched a knife, gazing into the trees. A hodgepodge of palms and other plants I couldn't name. No building broke up the deserted stretch of land. Just hot, humid air with patches of fog interrupted by green.

I raced low into the trees. Maybe I could find footprints, something that would point me in the right direction. This cursed mist wouldn't have overtaken us if something hadn't willed it. I'd encountered more than my share of magical and deathless beings—this didn't feel like a random attack. It pointed straight at Terion.

We hadn't even found the gold and Basileus was already stealing Terion away.

I wouldn't let him.

The ground, littered with rocks and natural debris, didn't reveal any footprints. I squinted for a final look. Nothing. Spirited away, then. Could I feel the residue of traveling through the air? Normally, there was a faint smell or feeling that lingered right after somebody disappeared in one area to appear in another. I'd never been great at sensing it, but I was getting better.

A faint tang, like shards of metal, glittered in the air. Was that proof of traveling? A ward? Some new creature nearby?

I closed my eyes, focusing on the sensation. *Where are you?* His life filled so much of mine that I could swear I sensed him.

I could die, came an unwanted voice, right before I disappeared in search of the feeling. Fear could go hang.

He could die too, I told myself. *And he's not going without me.*

I walked through the air after the sensation. Because I'd looked at the map a few times, I had a rough sense of the geography of the Bridge. The gold was buried south of here, but the magic compelled me inland.

I emerged from the darkness and landed at the mouth of a cave. Its entrance was low enough that the tide had apparently leaked in, forming pools around the interior. Inside, all was dark. Adjusting my grip on the knife's hilt, I plunged inside.

Stalactites and stalagmites spiked from the floor and ceiling. If I hadn't worn soft shoes—damp now from the pools of standing water—they'd have echoed like the dripping columns of rock. The occasional crack in the ceiling let in shafts of light, enough to see.

Portions of the cave narrowed to claustrophobic tunnels. *I'm a child exploring a cave. This is fun. This is safe.* I kept repeating those thoughts to myself until I believed them enough to duck and sprint forward.

Deeper in, the natural formations took on a more polished look, obviously tooled by living hands. Sunlight was replaced by scattered lanterns bolted into the walls and bowls of fire. I stiffened. This wasn't just proof of past human or deathless activity, but evidence that someone was here now.

I was on the right track. I forged further in, keeping to the shadows.

"...that sea monster and I'll be happy."

The faint voice was unmistakable.

Terion.

My blood raced. Who was he talking to? It sounded like he was just ahead. No sound of distress in his voice, but that didn't surprise me. Besides that time I'd seen him panic in his room, he usually spoke in two ways—either in commands or with roguish good humor. That was his bantering voice.

My legs moved faster. Whoever had taken him would suffer. Basileus himself wouldn't expect a swamp dweller to materialize out of the darkness and carve him open like a fish. But I'd do it. Fuck anyone who got between me and Captain Terion.

An opening in the side of the cave had been decorated with inset bones. No god symbol. For Hades, it looked like.

I crept through where the air grew hotter. Carved columns and more bowls of flame lined the walls.

"You are chaos," said a female voice.

"Thank you," Terion replied.

If I ever needed confirmation that I'd reached the right place...

Rounding a bend, I finally found my quarry. Terion, tied up on the ground, and a tall, white-haired woman standing over him. I didn't know who she was. I didn't care.

Terion's eyes met mine for a fraction of a second.

"So," he asked, oddly short of breath, "will my father be joining us?"

"In a moment," the woman replied.

My throat constricted, but rage fueled my movements enough to overcome the terror.

I didn't ask the woman who she was, whether she was deathless. I didn't make my presence known. I simply attacked.

Air gusted in a wheeze from her lungs as I stabbed her in the back and neck. I'd done ruthless things before, but nothing quite so violent. She'd been about to hurt Terion. That was enough for me.

After a minute of frenzy, I let her body drop. The scent of sickly-sweet flowers and metallic blood lingered in the air.

Chest heaving, feet apart, I faced Terion again. He gazed at me with nothing short of adoration.

"Well, fuck it, kiss me," he demanded.

I rushed to him. His arms and legs had been restrained, and there was something oddly empowering about that. I straddled his lap and pressed my lips to his. Blood from my clothes got onto his shirt. Feverishly, I rolled my hips over his hardening crotch. It felt good. So good.

Reaching behind him, I worked the knots that held him bound, considering just pulling down the front of his pants so we could fuck right here.

Terion moaned, helping me with the knots as he could and grinding back against me. The heat in the room doubled until my skin felt tight. For somebody who'd never had a good orgasm until the other day, I came close just by riding Terion over his clothes.

"So stupid," he murmured.

"So brave," I corrected. I was the Terror, and he was bound beneath me.

He growled. One of his hands flew free and he used it to anchor my hip.

Dully, I remembered that Basileus was coming and a bleeding body lay nearby. But I'd saved the captain. Desperation energized us. I wanted him more than ever. And I'd have him.

"Quick." I shoved my hand down his pants to pull out his hard cock. At the same time, he slid my pants down my legs enough to let him in.

My head fell back as he speared me with one hand still bound behind his back. Whimpered noises erupted from my throat as he savagely thrust into me and I rolled against him.

"Oh, Mari..." he gasped.

"Yes, Captain?"

With a few more breathless, grunting thrusts against each other, we cried out together. It was fast and wild and wrong, and none of it made sense because he wasn't dominant and I wasn't skeptical, and the timing and place were as bad as they could possibly be, but *damn!*

He gave me a sloppy kiss against my open mouth. I stood and undid the rest of his bindings.

"Fuck, Mari. You're insane." He looked to where I crouched behind him, working at the knots. A smirk sinful enough to make me wetter crossed his lips. "I love it."

I gave a small, crooked smile. In seconds, he was free.

Standing, he took my hand. The knife lay by the body steps away. Terion wasn't wrong. I was insane where he was concerned. He'd gotten so fully into my body and mind that I could never let him go.

Terion's eyes fell on the corpse. "How's the *Lusca?*"

"Still floating."

"Crew?"

"I haven't seen them."

Terion's hand tensed around mine. Darkness crushed around me as he dragged us through the air back to the deck of the ship.

When the black skin of the *Lusca* materialized under our feet, I tensed. I'd only heard of Basileus before that, but I would have recognized him anywhere. Even, unexpectedly, aboard our ship.

❧ 36 ❧

TERION

"Impatient, I see," said Basileus, standing on the deck of my ship, surrounded by the unconscious bodies of my crew. No blood—not like there was on Mari and me—but that didn't mean my father hadn't killed them. Cloudy light reflected off the blue-green scales embedded into his cheek and exposed chest.

No revenge was too much.

Only, I couldn't breathe.

No, no, no.

"I was going to come to you in a moment, Terion." My father's eyes fell on my hand, holding Mari's. "But now I don't need to transport anyone. This is easier."

Behind him, Zete's body, gray wings sprawled, rose and fell with a breath.

Not dead.

Not dead.

There was Rhode with her thick strands of green hair, thrown like trash in an awkward position, but her lips opened. Not dead either.

I hadn't panicked in the cave. Why was my godsdamned body doing this now?

"Where's the witch?" His eyes roved around the sleek black decks of the *Lusca*. I hated that he stood here as if he owned it. This was my ship, and I'd lose every limb and organ in my body before I'd give it up to him.

I tried breathing deeply. From the corner of my narrowing vision, I saw Mari glance at me. Based on that look, she knew exactly what was going on.

"Dead," she answered, defiant. Her blood-soaked clothing should have given that away.

The corner of my mouth stretched upward.

Basileus sighed. "I'll find a new one."

Then it struck me. If the witch was dead, did that mean her curse was too? My father's ability didn't allow him to kill someone by thinking. He could only use the sea and some creatures in it. Normally, that was powerful enough, but now...

New purpose surged into me. I could care about my crew, like I had all along, and I could love Mari. My love wouldn't doom her.

"The fuck you will," I said. I felt powerful as the sea itself. Even my breathing began to return to normal.

My father smiled malevolently. "You don't insult me and get away with it. I will kill them all one by one in front of you, and you'll think again before stealing from me. Last will be your ship."

As one, Mari and I jumped forward. Our only weapon was Mari's little knife. Fuck.

Basileus raised his hand with the ease of elemental power. An enormous wave rose on one side of deck and crashed over us, sending us skidding against the opposite railing. Drenched, we stood again. A couple of my crew members lay like puppets after being washed by the wave.

I snarled at Basileus. He wasn't bothered, but my skin was hot with rage.

Another wave took us down. When my head rose above the water again, Basileus lay on the deck, Mari crouched on top of him with the knife to his neck.

I sprinted to her side. I stomped on my father's arm closest to me to hold it down before squatting next to him. My power wasn't much to his, but I had ideas. Fingers found his eye socket.

"Cut him," I told Mari.

She did, deep enough to make him struggle.

I put my other hand against the gash. Blood bloomed around my fingers. "I'm going to send ice through your veins," I said. "And it won't matter if you try to use your power against us, because that will only fuel the pain I'll send through your entire body."

Beneath me, the deck bucked on the churning sea.

"I won't let go," I gritted, freezing the water I sent into his neck and eyes. "I will destroy everything you love."

His face contorted. "You don't deserve to wear the trident."

Mari menaced him with the blade again.

"Let me," I said. My water snaked into him, freezing and crawling further. I gave a crooked smile. "Ah, I see. You'd bring the crew to me in the cave. Mari would come to help. You'd kill them all. Is that it?" I pushed out more water.

My father convulsed.

I tsked. "No one hangs the captain, or his crew, you petty... little... fuck."

His eye itself froze. He never screamed—being an ancient god must have given him a supernatural tolerance to pain—but panic shone in his un-frozen eye.

I continued. "You can go back and pray to the Divine that my shapeshifter won't sneak into your palace at night or that I won't push more ice through your veins while you sleep. Dismemberment..." I tipped my chin. "Do you think that's a possibility?"

"Could be," Mari answered casually.

Good girl.

I got close to Basileus's face. "Leave me the fuck alone, or I will visit so much pain on you you'll wish you could die. There are deathless members of my suna everywhere. Trust me. I'm not worth it." I eased off him. Mari did too. "When you stand, you walk through the air. Four jumps to Nalia, right? Never let me see your face again."

I returned my hands to my sides and kissed Mari.

My crew was starting to stir. My sore body began to ease.

Basileus glared at me. "You upstart bastard," he sneered.

"Prince of the Ocean," Mari corrected.

"That's right," I said, taking her hand again. My fierce little Terror, my anchor and addiction growing every second.

He regarded the two of us, looking again at our hands, at my trident tattoo. His teeth ground together.

And he disappeared.

Mari exhaled. I swept her up in my arms and held her against me. "Perfect," I murmured through kisses. My dick swelled. I had no guarantee my father wouldn't return, but as long as we kept him from making deals with anymore witches, he'd move on to other grudges, other targets. Otherwise, he never would have obeyed my order to leave.

"Is that it?" Mari managed.

I gripped her hair in my fist. Her mouth was hot and wet against mine. "That's it." I wanted to slam her against the railing and fuck her senseless, but the crew was starting to wake up.

I peeled myself from Mari and began helping them to their feet.

"Terion, what...?" Rhode asked, concern radiating in her face.

"Basileus," I answered.

Her eyes rounded.

"He's gone," I said, grinning.

"A fog rolled in," Ajax said, groggy. Even as he spoke, it got wispier, dissipating into the air.

"His witch. Basileus was going to kill you all."

"But he just knocked us unconscious?" Rhode asked, massaging her temples. She touched my arm.

I gave her an encouraging look. "His grudge was against me. He knew it would hurt if he destroyed it all... while I watched."

"Fuck him," said Mari.

"Fuck him," I agreed. "I couldn't have done it without Mari. No, that's not right. She did everything. Without her, you'd all be shark bait."

Zete stirred, giving Mari a look of thankful appreciation I'd never seen before. Maybe he noticed the smudges of blood on her clothes.

We helped a few more sailors to their feet.

"Thank you," Euporia said softly. Others echoed the words.

Mari tilted her lips, not minimizing her role, not fading into the background. I wrapped an arm tight around her waist.

Ajax approached, hulking, with a slight smile across his broad face. "Seeing as there's fair winds now…"

I grinned and kissed Mari on the cheek. "Let's go get that gold on shore."

❧ 37 ❧

EPILOGUE: MARI

Dio's ship was a speck on the horizon. My lips curved.

"I see it!" I reported.

Terion grinned up at me from the quarterdeck. "That's my girl! Heading?"

I drew my gaze from the ship to the position of the sun. There wasn't a cloud. The perfect day for piracy. When I knew the exact direction, I grabbed a rope and slid down to the main deck.

"You look damn good coming down like that," Terion said as I trotted up to him.

I wanted to kiss him but we agreed that I'd wait until after we were done with this job. "Is Rhode ready?"

Terion's dark eyes looked ready to eat me whole. "She should be."

"Then it's time for me to go."

He stretched his jaw and wet his lips. "If you say so."

"Yes, Captain."

He smirked.

For touching me and dealing in human cargo, getting revenge on Dio would be sweet.

RHODE SWAM ME OVER TO THE SHIP WHILE TERION STEERED the *Lusca*. As the sailors stared at the famous pirate ship overtaking them, I climbed aboard.

I had a couple minutes before Terion would demand to board their ship. Enough time to become someone else. This vessel was wooden, not scaly black like I was used to. The sails were white, billowing out with the breeze. Sailors called to each other, craning their necks to watch their pursuers. This view of the *Lusca* made my heart beat faster—it was like Terion's legend come to life. And not just his. Mine. After the events on the Bridge, I'd carved out a little fame. This would add to my reputation as the Terror.

Scanning the sailors on board, I didn't find any with my exact build. But that young man would do.

Crouching behind a pile of crates, I watched him like an octopus waiting for its prey. The chaos of running from Terion and his crew caused enough commotion that no one noticed right away that I was there. The young, beardless man didn't come close. It would be simpler to slit his throat and steal his clothes, since my sopping outfit gave me away.

"Lord Dio, get below!" cried a tall woman.

Dio himself appeared at the top of the companionway, looking around in bewilderment. "What's going on?" Behind him, several men and women, possibly the acrobats from the party, peered over his shoulder.

"The *Lusca*."

Dio paled.

I had options—the young sailor or one in Dio's entourage. I tried out both faces as I half-hid behind the crates. The sailor's appearance fit the best.

I took one more look over the deck. Sailors strained on the ropes. Everyone ran and shouted and hurried to escape.

But Terion and I didn't lose.

"Captain Asterion must want the money on board," the woman explained, trying to pacify the terrified god. If I had to guess, she was probably first mate. She acted competent, but she was wrong.

Terion and I had our fill of riches from the gold horde we'd found on the Bridge. As far as we knew, Thenios and Hades never discovered it missing, so we used it as freely as we wanted. My favorite purchase so far was a gold collar and earring I wore when I didn't have to pretend to be somebody else.

"Keep him away. We can outrun him."

I couldn't stop my smile. Little did they know that his Terror was already here. I drifted out of my hiding place, busying myself with something or other. The less I stood out, the more likely people would overlook a duplicate person on board.

Out in the surf, Rhode's tail flipped above the waterline.

A few minutes later, familiar black sails loomed.

Terion's voice boomed across to Dio's ship. "I suggest you allow us to board. Wouldn't want this to turn into a bloodbath."

After a swift conversation between the captain and mates, Dio's ship complied, drawing alongside the *Lusca*. Dio hadn't retreated belowdecks yet. Even better.

"Arrange yourselves," Terion drawled. Gods, he looked good staring down a ship full of sailors like that. The scarf on his head and his captain's jacket flowed in the breeze. "Everyone on the deck."

I stood obediently among the rest, still sopping wet but otherwise exactly like the others.

Several of the strongest crewmen secured the ships in place, and Terion swung on, landing with a soft thud on Dio's deck. He winked. "Dio, good to see you again."

"I demand you leave my ship," faltered the god.

Terion laughed. "The last time I saw you, you weren't very welcoming. In fact, do you remember my date? Stunning woman, about this tall?"

Dio looked flummoxed.

"Right over there?" Terion pointed at me. And I thought I'd done a good job of disguising myself. It didn't matter what body I wore—he could always pick me out.

As soon as Dio turned, I flew toward him. He barely had time to cry out before I slit his throat open. He fell bleeding to the deck.

Pandemonium erupted.

Savage joy showed in Terion's bared teeth. More crew from the *Lusca* poured onto the ship, all of them making quick work of the people aboard. Some went to find treasure stores.

It took a matter of minutes. We left a few people alive—the least likely to be complicit in Dio's plan to capture and deliver us to Basileus.

"You'll remember us now," I said while two of our pirates carried gold across the *Lusca*. "Captain Asterion."

"And the Terror of the Seas," he finished, sending me a look that made my blood rush hot.

"I LIKE THAT LOOK," SAID TERION AS WE STEPPED INSIDE HIS downstairs room. He drew a finger across my jaw.

"Yeah?" I let the face of the sailor fall away to reveal my own.

He ushered me deeper into the dark room, his hand on my lower back. "Yes, but I like this one better."

"Good." I turned to face him.

"Gods, I love you," he murmured, expression darkening into something dangerous. "You're ruthless."

I bit my lip suggestively.

"See? Turn around," he ordered.

"Constellation, Captain," I replied out of habit as I obeyed.

"Very good." He sidled up close behind me and growled a frustrated, admiring breath in my ear. His hands ran roughly down over my hips. The growl turned into a chuckle. "I get to fuck the Terror of the Seas."

"That's right, Captain."

"Not unless I ask you a question."

"Of course not, Captain."

"Don't make me punish you."

"No, Captain. I'd hate for you to do that." I stretched to look back at him.

"Bad girl," he breathed in my ear.

The more he stood like that, possessing me but not nearly enough, the only points of contact his hands, the wetter I became. But I refused to move or complain. We knew by now that this was always a competition. Terion would tease and dominate and strain me to the point of breaking, or I wouldn't come.

Terion was right. He won competitions. But I was rooting for him to win this one.

"Know what someone found on Dio's ship?" he whispered low in my ear.

"No, Captain."

One arm snaked around my waist while the other rummaged in his pockets. He held out a paper. I took it and read.

In the center was a drawing of a blank face with short dark hair, only a hint of where the nose, eyes, and mouth would be. "Marica, Terror of the Seas, shapeshifter, known to sail with Pirate Captain Asterion. Do not approach alone. Five thousand coin reward for capture or death."

"Now, you wouldn't happen to know who that is, would you?" Terion asked, his voice so hoarse I knew he was straining to let himself loose on me.

"No, Captain." My cheeks warmed with excitement and validation. Terion was proud of me too. My stomach flipped with anticipation of all the ways he would show me. "But I'd love to keep this. Maybe I could meet them one day."

"You'd be lucky. I hear she rules the seas with the captain."

"Yes, Captain."

"Again."

"Yes, Captain."

He made a noise deep in his throat and walked me to my favorite apparatus. He'd picked it up just for me to try. A chair, but it held my legs open and the backrest curved so I could arch. And, of course, a series of restraints lashed my ankles and knees in place with options for my wrists and neck as well. I loved being opened for him. I was already dripping, and he hadn't begun any of his real foreplay yet.

I smiled against his roguish grin as he grunted commands, a mix of the detached dominant he'd been at first and the savage lover he'd been in his room. The mix suited us both. "Clothes off. Sit. Open. Lay back."

I did as he said. He hummed hungrily, dark gaze roaming over my splayed form. His focus heated me like a fire so close it could burn.

He took off his clothes. I got slicker, flushing and straining as my nipples hardened to painful points. His wild grace, like a sinuous, charming, dangerous creature rather than a demi-god made me crave him to the edge of endurance. I needed his cock inside me, his trident-marked arm reaching around to pull my hair.

He watched me a while longer. He knew exactly what he was doing to me. A wicked smirk crossed his features. "Do you want something, Terror?"

"No, Captain."

He leaned over me, a whisper away from my skin. "You don't want me grinding into you, making you come so hard you can't see? Hm?"

"No, Captain." Damn it, I was totally breathless, already so turned on, I could barely think.

"You don't want me shouting your name this time?"

I couldn't answer.

"Say something. You don't want that?"

"Terion," I groaned, squirming.

He laid a finger against my lips. I licked it and his smile widened. "You know to answer my questions. I'll have to punish you for breaking the rules. And then"—he drew even closer—"I'll wring orgasms out of you like water, Mari."

I was already panting, and he'd barely touched me. I feebly shook my head no. This wasn't a fight I would win. At least it was the only one I was happy to lose.

After Terion used freezing water from his fingers and my favorite whip, he finally positioned himself between my legs and rolled his hips into me. The slide of his thick cock into my slippery opening made me thrash against the restraints. He didn't say anything else as he picked up his pace to something primal, thrusting hard. His hands found my shoulders to jam himself more fully inside. I was winded, desperate, riding the waves of his body against mine.

"Look at me," he ordered.

I pulled my head up to lock eyes with his. I bobbed frantically against the cushioned backrest.

"Who am I?"

"Terion," I huffed. "Captain Terion. Best... ah!... most feared pirate in the Realms."

He fucked me harder.

"In the world!" I gasped.

"And you... are?"

I writhed as he edged me closer. One of his bare hands reached between us. He hadn't broken eye contact. "Tell me, Captain," I gasped.

Sweat dripped down his neck. "I don't take... commands."

"You—oh fuck!—take them from me. Say it."

"Terror. The Terror of the Seas."

"Again."

"Mari." He ground deep and hard.

My chest rose with quick breaths. I released the chair I'd been gripping and reached for his tattooed forearm.

He groaned. "Fuck, Mari. Fuck! You feel so good. Keep looking at me."

I'd closed my eyes, neck flexing backward. When I opened them, Terion's were savage and honest.

"Look at me when you come," he growled, obviously close himself.

"Say my name."

"Fucking demanding."

"Do it."

He circled my clit with his finger and rubbed ferocious circles. I couldn't hold on. "Let go, Mari. Come for me."

"You first." Every muscle in my body went taut at the combination of everything Terion was doing.

He grunted, close to slipping. His thrusts grew faster, chasing his own release. "Mar—" He couldn't get my whole name out. His teeth gritted and he poured himself into me as pleasure crested through my body. Between waves of orgasm, I heard him shouting my name.

This first book in the Deathless Love series welcomes you to the Eight Realms, where danger and desire lurk in every corner, and mythology isn't quite as you remember it.

Join the Foxy newsletter and read this book FREE!

What if Icarus left the Labyrinth to work for the Sun God?

When ambitious inventor Icarus volunteers for a position in the Sun God's court, he doesn't expect to fall for one of his consorts.

Chosen for his beauty, Jacin has spend his entire adult life in the palace. Although the Sun God has never spent the night with him, he wants Jacin ready at all times. That includes a command that Jacin never be touched by another living being on pain of death.

When an accident leaves Jacin in need of constant assistance, Icarus steps in to help. Their growing attraction makes it nearly impossible not to touch. Luckily, inventing solutions is Icarus's specialty...

With deadly heat growing between them and danger looming outside the walls, can their love ignite without taking the palace with it?

Roshan knelt in front of me, painting my calf gold. The paintbrush tickled. Or maybe I was simply on edge because the King finally wanted to see me.

I held my hand out, rotating it slowly in the lamplight. It shone brighter than everything around it, the gold shining in contrast to the dark red room where I spent most of my time. I looked like metal compared to the soft hangings and pillows and baskets of "accentuations" that littered the room. That was the name Roshan used, anyway, and the small number of other palace attendants. Really, they were little bottles filled with oils and tins of scent and drinks labeled with things I blushed to look at. Not to mention the objects that set my imagination aflame.

The gold paint had to be part of King Lox's plan. I'd never seen any of his other consorts, but the Sun King enjoyed light. Like the sun, he glowed. His magnificence chased away darkness in the kingdom. I had to be a fitting partner for him.

My stomach tightened painfully.

"Please don't move," said Roshan.

"I'm sorry. I'll try not to."

I stood as still as I could. Only the tip of the paintbrush grazed my feet, never Roshan's hand, and the bristles tickled.

It wasn't just my nerves.

I bit my lip hard, realizing a second afterward that my lips had been painted too. Hopefully I hadn't spoiled Roshan's work. My assistant didn't visit often, except to deliver food and such, and he wasn't talkative. Sometimes he acted like he didn't enjoy his job at all, though he never said that. Since he was the only person I saw regularly, I wanted to crack through his tough exterior so we could become friends.

When he reached a particularly ticklish spot, my foot jerked.

Roshan cursed and reared back. "My excellent ray, the Sun God's favorite," he recited through his teeth, "I almost touched you."

"I'm sorry," I repeated. "My feet are ticklish." I grimaced at him in apology.

He pushed a mass of dark, curly hair out of his face before carefully leaning forward again to finish the job. He had beautiful hair and beautiful skin. I'd learned he had a daughter, but he didn't like to talk to me, so I hadn't learned much else. I didn't even know if he was a demi-god. Or a full god. That thought hadn't even occurred to me. It was all far above a mere human like me, even if I was chosen several years ago for King Lox. Maybe Roshan was a demi-god and that was the reason he didn't want to become my friend. To him, I only lasted a second.

I had to get my mind off my upcoming presentation and ticklish foot, though, so I tried again. "Roshan, is this what you do with all the King's consorts?"

He didn't look up. "I only serve you."

"But you can see more of the palace," I insisted. "Have you seen any other gold people?"

"The gold is just for meetings with the King," he murmured, clenching his free hand into a fist at his side to keep from touching me.

My next question burned my tongue. "For this meeting..."

He slipped the paintbrush between my toes. The most challenging part came next, when I'd have to stand on one leg to present the sole of my foot. That would be even more difficult than when he'd painted my groin half an hour ago. My cock had started to respond to the touch of the brush, but I'd stood still as a statue otherwise. Embarrassment was the only obstacle to get that done. Roshan regularly saw me naked. The embarrassing part was standing this close to someone, having them touch me. Sort of. With the brush, at least.

I hadn't been touched by living hands in six years.

I shut my eyes tight. "In this meeting, what exactly does the King expect me to do? I want to be ready."

Roshan tapped my anklebone with the brush, and I lifted my foot, wishing for something to hold onto. "He doesn't confide in me," he scoffed.

"But you know, don't you?" I pressed.

Finally, Roshan leaned back on his heels and looked up at me. "The Sun God does what pleases him, but I believe this meeting is like all the other firsts."

My heart thumped hard and fast behind my ribs. "What's... usual?"

"He wants you to learn. Watch and learn."

My blood didn't cool at the thought of *watching*, but anxiety didn't sprint so fast around my head. "Thank you." I scanned the room, my eyes skipping to each filled basket. When I first arrived at eighteen, I was told those baskets were for the King should he wish to visit. I'd waited breathlessly for months. Then years. And now, at last, he summoned me. "Are you... with someone? Here at the palace?" I asked Roshan.

"Not at the palace."

I waited for more, but he didn't go on. Instead, he blew the paint dry on the sole of one foot, which felt like torture. His face was too close. My foot wanted to kick out so bad it almost felt involuntary, but I breathed through it, shuddering a little when he instructed me to put my foot down.

In a couple more silent minutes, Roshan finished painting. I was golden for the Sun King. He didn't have to touch up my lip, thank the gods.

After putting away his tools, he led me to the back of my chamber, pushed aside the heavy curtain, and unlocked the door. We were about the same height, which could mean he was a tall human like me, or else a short deathless one. His fingers moved gracefully as he turned the key. They'd never given me a key. In an emergency, they would come fetch me, they said.

My breath shallowed as I followed Roshan. The hallway we entered was blinding bright—white and gold. No heavy curtains or scents. Music filtered through the air. It was beautiful, like the mornings I remembered as a child, when the sun would rise and turn the sky pale blue and orange. The instruments even replicated the feeling the cool dawn air sweeping across skin. It wasn't that I wanted to return home, exactly, but I wanted to see a sunrise again if I could. Maybe I could ask Roshan if that was possible for a consort of the King.

Even as the thought crossed my mind, I knew what he'd say. No. I was too precious to risk. I was reserved for one sun alone.

My throat bobbed. Today, I'd meet my king. This was the moment I'd waited for so long.

The hallway opened into a vast circular room many times the size of my chamber. Stylized golden suns hung suspended from huge chains on the ceiling. multiple stories, maybe seven, rose and up and up. A few of the stories were rimmed in glass, so I could see people moving inside—an enormous array of people, mostly bronze-skinned and dark-haired, which was typical of Hyperion, but there were also half-reptile demi-gods and slender beings taller than any I'd seen in real life.

This palace was the beating heart of Hyperion. The lovely song ended and music changed. It came from a group of female musicians on the opposite side of the room, all pale and curvy, like sisters.

I wanted to watch them, but Roshan led us away.

Men and women stared as we passed. All wore clothes except for me. All of them kept their distance so they didn't accidentally touch me.

I gave an awkward half-smile to a few people, but no one offered a genuine smile back. When I caught Roshan glaring at me, I stopped looking around, focusing only on following him carefully and obediently.

He rounded a corner, then another—how big was this place?—and at last reached an ornate ivory column inlaid with gold and silver. When the light hit them just right, the carvings in the column showed a variety of scenes.

King Lox, larger than the people around him, ordering music to be played.

King Lox rising into the air like the sun itself.

King Lox, glowing, surrounded by worshippers on their faces.

King Lox, mouth open in ecstasy as three people knelt around him, the strongest-looking one clearly sucking on his—

"This is the most excellent ray, the Sun God's favorite, Jacin, who has been summoned," Roshan said.

I realized a woman stood guard beside the pillar. She

looked as war-like as people from Eriset, the kingdom to the north caught in a centuries-long conflict between the ruling gods. Her gray eyes narrowed at Roshan but turned softer with surprise when she looked at me.

"I expected you," she said in a rock-hard voice. Her gaze dipped down my body.

I'd been told not to wear clothes, right? Hopefully, I hadn't done anything wrong. Even though this woman said what I wanted to hear—that King Lox waited for me—her tone said the opposite. If I was the Sun God's favorite, why did this guard look at me with... whatever this was? Suspicion, maybe?

She held out an armored hand. In it was a gnarled wooden staff too short to be useful to her.

I frowned at it. I'd expected her to have a dagger, or, I didn't know.

"Lay your hand on the staff," Roshan instructed.

I obeyed, laying my hand on the knobby end away from the guard's fingers.

The room with the massive pillar sucked into itself like a whirlpool. Right before everything squeezed into breathless, panicky blackness, I heard the guard say, "Don't let go."

I gripped with my fingers, but didn't move my hand any higher on the staff. The darkness crushed, but I could still feel the object beneath my fingertips.

Don't let go. Don't let go.

If I did, I would die. I knew it.

I couldn't breathe. My legs kicked air. I thrashed like a swimmer before—

We landed.

My feet hit solid ground and I gasped for breath, fingers trembling on the end of the staff. I was somewhere else.

"Release the staff," Roshan whispered, as if I'd done something impolite and needed correcting.

Had he just experienced that sensation too? Was this normal? I felt like I was walking around outside my body. So many months of nothing and now this. I almost laughed.

I forced myself to let go and take in the new space. The pillar I'd seen before rose to my right, tapered a little smaller. Maybe this was up on the top floor. The room, a little smaller than mine but round instead of long, had a cluster of bright lights dropping from the center, illuminating a raised platform. Sky-blue cushions and pillows made the round platform like a bed or lounge. Along the opposite wall from where I stood was an enormous water feature. A quarter of the room ran with water that slipped over carvings on the wall, all depicting King Lox and his works, like the pillar did. Everything smelled sharp and musky. It made my mouth water. The floors were dark wood and, at the center of the dais, a figure glowed.

My mouth dropped open.

The Sun King.

He was tall, like all the deathless, and incredibly handsome. He wore a thin piece of white fabric pinned at the shoulder with a sunburst. Golden hair curled around his ears, just a shade lighter than mine. A rock jumped into my throat. I had something in common with the god. And I was his favorite. He'd finally called for me.

Beside me, Roshan fell on his face.

My skin zinged uncomfortably. Was I supposed to do the same thing? The guard didn't bow like that. And wasn't it better to stand to be presented to him? Sweat formed at my temple.

"My king," said the guard, tucking the gnarled staff into a

specially made pouch at her side, "this is Jacin." Her tone was flat, but she gestured, open-palmed, at me.

"Jacin." The King caressed the syllables. He walked down the shallow steps toward me. I held my breath, inclining my head.

His pale golden eyes raked over me and he reached out.

When I flinched back, the King chuckled. It was a soothing noise. "No need to fear." His fingertips grazed my jaw.

The contact—my first in so long—buzzed along my blood. My whole body woke up, longing for more.

"Such a pretty one," the King crooned, swiping a thumb along my bottom lip as he observed me. "And eager." His gaze dropped to where I'd half-hardened at his touch.

I didn't even have the sense to be embarrassed. Mostly, I felt too overwhelmed.

The King's hand dropped. I missed its warmth on my face. "Very good," he said, clipped.

King Lox returned to the raised platform, lifted his eyes to the lights, inhaled deeply, and said, "Let them in."

The guard moved purposefully around the room, opening a set of two doors. Roshan still hadn't risen from where he bowed at my side.

Through the doors poured six naked, gold-painted young men, all beautiful in different ways. They strode to join the Sun King at the platform, as confident as dancers who had learned a routine.

Whatever was special about me faded. I had no right to feel disappointed. I was still his favorite, right? I just had to learn.

Focusing hard on the lighted platform, I tried to remember every movement, every touch. A muscular male unclipped the fabric from the King's shoulder, reverently folded it, and set it to the side. The god was the most beautiful among them, shining with his own light. He looked like a statue, ancient and young at the same time, his body carved from marble. Hands stroked and embraced him from every side. He pulled one in for a deep kiss while others knelt in front of him.

My stomach flipped. I couldn't believe I was watching this, that it was allowed. My cheeks and neck blazed, but I couldn't, *wouldn't*, look away.

King Lox all but disappeared among the mass of writhing, muscular bodies. One of them grasped a large bottle of oil and thumbed off the top. He soaked his hands with it and passed it along. Each consort rubbed the oil over themselves, each other, the King... They shone like purest gold.

The King moaned, face tipping up. My blood raced as I traced which person had given him that reaction. It was the male on his knees, now pressing the King's cock down his throat.

I bit my lip hard, trying to be a good learner, but growing stiff and painful and feeling every second how ignorant I was.

How was that one pleasing the King so well? When the bodies parted enough for me to see, I squinted at the one on his knees. His lips suctioned around the King's length as he bobbed.

Okay, okay...

Maybe I'd burst into flames.

The King pushed one down on his hands and knees facing me, shoving the man off his cock to make room. Still caressed by hands everywhere, King Lox, dripping with oil, thrust his hard dick into the man's ass. He rocked back and forth. I couldn't keep up with all the movements. The King gritted his teeth, plunging deep, and the man groaned loudly with pleasure. For some reason, the others started sighing and moaning too—even the ones who weren't being touched at all. Maybe their pleasure was connected to the King's.

The sights and sounds and smells all made my cock ache. I wanted to pump myself to ease the tension, but the King had brought me here to learn. Besides, no one else was allowed to touch me, so it was probably a bad idea to touch myself in front of the King.

His eyes met mine.

I couldn't help it. I gave a quiet gasp.

His gaze welcomed me. Did this mean...? Did he want me up there with him?

I stepped forward, awkward from being so turned on. My calf brushed something soft.

Shit! I hadn't looked down before I moved. My leg had touched Roshan.

His face whipped up angrily, eyes blown wide with fear.

Before I could open my mouth to apologize, explain that it was an accident, the guard swung a weapon hard at his head.

"No!"

But my word was cut off. Blinding pain cut through my leg. She moved so fast, I couldn't see what weapon it was, only felt the slice, the crunch reverberating through my body.

I fell next to Roshan, whose face was a mass of crushed flesh and blood. Bile rose in my throat. Before the piercing pain crested, I slitted open my eyes to see King Lox give an orgasmic yell.

Straining in pain, I welcomed the darkness as it took me.

ORDER CANDLE WAX AND SUNLIGHT NOW!

READ MORE BY ZORA FOX

Fae and Shadow duology
  End of the Forest
  Trapped by the Fae

Deathless Love series
  Wings and Blindness
  Flowers and the Far Realm
  Storm and Sanctuary
  Flame and Warpaint
  Full Moons and Vampires
  Temptation and Tridents
  Candle Wax and Sunlight (coming soon!)

Find all of Zora Fox's spicy fantasy romance titles on Amazon.